THE DEVIL IS WHITE

The Devil is White

William Palmer

JONATHAN CAPE
LONDON

Published by Jonathan Cape 2013

2 4 6 8 10 9 7 5 3 1

Copyright © William Palmer 2013

William Palmer has asserted his right under the Copyright, Designs
and Patents Act 1988 to be identified as the author of this work

First published in Great Britain in 2013 by
Jonathan Cape
Random House, 20 Vauxhall Bridge Road,
London SW1V 2SA
www.vintage-books.co.uk

Addresses for companies within The Random House Group Limited
can be found at: www.randomhouse.co.uk/offices.htm

The Random House Group Limited Reg. No. 954009

A CIP catalogue record for this book
is available from the British Library

ISBN 9780224096829

The Random House Group Limited supports The Forest Stewardship
Council (FSC®), the leading international forest certification organisation.
Our books carrying the FSC label are printed on FSC® certified paper.
FSC is the only forest certification scheme endorsed by the leading
environmental organisations, including Greenpeace. Our paper procurement
policy can be found at www.randomhouse.co.uk/environment

Typeset in Adobe Garamond by Palimpsest Book Production Limited,
Falkirk, Stirlingshire
Printed and bound in Great Britain by
MPG Books Group Ltd, Bodmin, Cornwall

We carry within us the wonders we seek without us: there is all Africa and her prodigies in us.

Sir Thomas Browne, *Religio Medici* (1643)

I can't think there is any intrinsic value in one colour more than another, nor that white is better than black, only we think it so because we are so, and are prone to judge favourably in our own case, as well as the blacks, who in odium of the colour, say, the devil is white . . .

Thomas Phillips, *A Journal of a Voyage Made in the* Hannibal (1732)

It is quite customary of a morning to ask 'how many died last night?'

Anna Maria Falconbridge, *Two Voyages to Sierra Leone* (1794)

Part One

Part One

I

Daylight had almost gone. He had to finish now. The first of the new bookcases, to go between the tall windows, was completed. He swept up the shavings around his bench, making a neat heap. The shelves that ran the length of the opposite wall were already filled with books. He knew a few of the English names. Others had incomprehensible script on their spines. Two volumes, leaning on each other for support like drunken men, announced themselves as *Tillotson's Sermons*.

Since his time here yesterday, someone had piled more books on to the long table in the middle of the room. Well, his work was at an end – he picked up a book and carried it to the window to catch the last light.

His lips moved silently as he read.

> *Of Man's first disobedience, and the fruit*
> *Of that forbidden tree, whose mortal taste*
> *Brought death into the World, and all our woe,*
> *With loss of Eden . . .*

He read on: '. . . *darkness visible*' . . . '*with bold words . . .*'

'Ah – I didn't know there was anyone in here.'

He hadn't heard the library door open. A young man, tall and thin, his long pale face topped by a huge bush of curling black hair, advanced down the room.

Hood knew him at once, although they had never been in

3

the same room before. He had known about him at intervals over the past ten years. He had seen him as a small boy mounted on a moorland pony, cantering in the paddock behind the stables. Then the boy had gone away to first one school, and then to another, and then to the university, and then was said to be travelling on the Continent. The young man was Mr Caspar Jeavons and when his grandmother, Lady Jeavons, died he would own the house and land and all the people of its estate, including Hood.

'Please, please – don't allow me to interrupt you.' The young man inspected the new bookcase. 'And you are?' he asked airily, his back turned.

'Hood, sir.'

'Hood, yes. You're making my shelves. How splendid.' His fingertips ran along the freshly planed wood. 'Excellent.' He gestured at the books strewn across the table. 'You can see how much the shelves are needed. And there are so many more books upstairs. But you must have finished now for the day, surely? In this light? Can't possibly work in this light. And it's so very cold in here. We must give you a fire tomorrow . . . If my grandmother will allow it.' He half laughed in a snort. 'You must know she is a most strong-minded woman. She herself doesn't mind this great cold house and thinks that we should all be equally spartan.'

'I keep warm working, sir,' said Hood.

'I suppose you do. What were you reading when I came in?'

'*Paradise Lost*. It is a poem.' Hood, passing the book nervously from hand to hand, went to replace it on the table.

'I know it's a poem.' Caspar gave that odd snorting laugh again. 'No, no – there is nothing worse than a book half started. Feel free to borrow it. And any other. They're there to be read. 'The precious life-blood of a master spirit, embalmed and treasured up on purpose to a life beyond life.' That's Milton. Anyway.' He strode to the shelves and began to search for something. 'Most of these are my late father's books and not so well

4

embalmed, being half turned to dust, as you can see. Ah, here we are. Another Milton for you. No – do take it.'

Hood placed the book very carefully with the other on top of his tools.

'Mr Snape says that you asked for me to do this work, sir.'

'Did I? Well – you're known for your skill.'

There was a light in the corridor, and a figure silhouetted in the doorway. 'Caspar – who are you talking to in here? What are you doing in the dark?'

'Mr Hood and I were discussing literature, Grandmama.'

'Indeed.' She came into the room, leaning on a cane, followed by a boy holding a candlestick on which two short candles flared backwards. 'I don't think I know a Mr Hood.' She peered at him.

'Carpenter, ma'am,' said Hood.

'As was Jesus Christ, I believe,' said Caspar brightly.

'That is both absurd and blasphemous,' said Lady Jeavons. 'The carpenter must have finished by now. He cannot work in darkness. Come along, Caspar. I wish to talk with you.'

Caspar took her arm and they turned, the candle-bearer following. She began to talk about the fences at the back of the park being broken down by the beasts from Churnside's farm, and he was saying that the matter was not urgent and that anyway, Snape could deal with it. 'On my walk there this morning . . .' the old lady said. But they were at the turn of the corridor and their voices receded and then could not be heard.

Hood wrapped his tools and the two books in the sacking he had laid out on the mantelshelf. The tall mirror above gave back a ghost room and Hood's reflected double faded almost to invisibility.

The London coach had stopped to change horses and Caspar sat in the parlour of the inn and continued his letter to his friend Torrington:

Man must be free, must be made to be free, and must be educated to savour freedom, to taste it, to want it, to devour it. All of Man. And it must surely be true that, should a group of men and women and children be taken from their inherited surroundings and placed in full freedom in a fertile and strange land, what else should we see but true equality springing between them? My friends and I are fixed on Africa. Do you remember Charles Coupland who was two years before us at Ratcliffe? Well, he has found an island, where it is possible we may be able to establish a free and equal colony of the sort we have so often talked about. The island is off the west coast of Africa; it is fertile, empty, and waiting for its settlers, amongst whose company I intend to be. I am on my way to London for a meeting with Coupland. I will let you know more when we have met, but I feel sure there is a place waiting for just such a man as you . . .

2

'A copy of *The Constitution of the Government of Muranda*. And *The Proposals to Settlers*,' said Coupland. 'As a principal subscriber you will be entitled to the maximum of four hundred acres of land. This in the name of equity and in the spirit of our enterprise. There will be no great landlords and no enclosures on Muranda. All, subscribers and settlers, will have land eventually, but the fact of subscription is a necessary evil. It was hoped that gifts of land might be made free to both agricultural settlers and worthy servants, but we have been overwhelmed by applications, some from the most extra-ordinary ruffians. So, a minimum of ten pounds has been asked for from each prospective settler and we hope not to be bombarded by those who may be wholly unsuitable.'

Coupland had been two years ahead of Caspar at school. He had left at fifteen and entered the Navy. Now, at twenty-six, he was Captain Coupland. Tall, broad, robustly built; there was nothing of the youth left in him. Indeed there seemed, to Caspar, to be an age between them. Coupland appeared possessed of a latent power, which only had to show a little of itself to command, while preserving a larger hidden reserve. He made Caspar feel like a boy. And – Caspar questioned himself – what had *he* achieved since school and Oxford?

'It will be possible for servants to become landowners on the decision of the Legislative Committee,' Coupland went on in his clipped, quick way. 'What we want, what we shall have, Jeavons, are gentlemen subscribers to fund us, also forty to fifty stalwart families as settlers: the men with some useful trade; the women and children to form the firm base of a growing community. And then honest servants and such freed Africans as will be willing to join us. It will be a brave new world, indeed. And we shall be the creatures in it.'

Caspar sifted through the documents; each set was several pages long, and impressively embossed and sealed with red wax at the foot of every page. 'It is a great deal of land to apportion between all of us. The island is that large?'

'Crabtree, our quartermaster, was there last year, when his ship put into Freetown. He gathered intelligence. He never visited the island but learned that it is large enough for all, fertile and, as far as can be ascertained, entirely uninhabited.'

'It belongs to no one?'

Coupland waved a hand impatiently in the air. 'Who may claim it as their property, we don't know,' he said. 'There is no great demand for deeds and registries in that part of the world. Crabtree tells me that there are local chiefs or, as they call themselves, kings on either side of the Rio Grande who may decide to make a claim for the place if they see it as being desirable to others. But the borders of their realms are invisible and perpetually the object of altercations and petty wars. We can come to an agreement with the most powerful of them. We are not going there to fight, but I mean to see that we are able to defend ourselves. We shall have a stockade and arms and men. There are a number of freed slaves who will want to join us. I know this from my man Jackson. His father absconded from his master. His mother is a white woman. Crabtree says there are quite a few such half-castes about Freetown and along the coasts.'

'From the Portuguese, I suppose,' said Caspar.

'And the British,' said Coupland. 'The English and Scottish traders all take African women.' He shrugged his shoulders. 'What else can you expect? That is the way of life. But, have no fear –' he gazed steadfastly at Caspar. 'Our enterprise will be somewhat nobler than that. It is an experiment, if you will, to see if a disparate but commonly purposed band of men and women from these isles can settle somewhere completely new and fresh and there live in a state of liberty and equality and build a truly free settlement. You will be a part of it, Jeavons? Doesn't it grip you? The prospect excite you?'

'It does. Oh, indeed.'

'Now – as to where we are, and what we have. We have almost our full complement of settlers and families. I have not met them yet.'

'A ship?'

'The *Pharaoh*. Then there are provisions and stores and agricultural tools – ploughs and the like. Crabtree is dealing with that side. Sir George Whitcroft is to be our Governor. I am to command the *Pharaoh* and to be Lieutenant Governor on arrival at Muranda. We have appointed a Dr Joseph Owen as our surgeon. The Reverend Tolchard will marry and baptise us and,

I hope, not bury us too soon. Also, together with Mr Crabtree, he is responsible for selecting suitable potential settlers. If you read the Constitution,' he tapped the papers on Caspar's knee, 'you will see the composition of the Committee. You will be its secretary and my general assistant.'

'If you think me capable.'

'Well, you're a literary chap, aren't you? I need a right-hand man for the voyage out. There will be a first officer, of course, but I need someone I can trust by my side.'

'Certainly, Coupland, but . . .'

'Good. That's settled. So you see – we're making rapid progress. We have a ship, a Constitution and most of our people. By the way – will you need a man?'

'That won't be necessary.'

'How about the estate? There must be men there. You know our need for craftsmen.'

'There's only one I think would suit.'

'He is?'

'A carpenter.'

'Excellent. We shall need a ship's carpenter. He can build our stockade for us.'

3

Hood's cottage was on the edge of the village. It had one room downstairs, with a window looking out on a vegetable garden at the back and another out to the road at the front. Both windows were small and deep and let in little light even on the brightest day. A ladder led to the bedroom. He could hear Susannah moving about up there.

The book Mr Jeavons had said he might borrow lay loose in his hands. It was almost as if he feared to grip the book. It was not his property. Mr Jeavons had gone away to London. If it were to be found in his possession, would not the book-plate with its coat of arms be enough to brand him as a thief? Who would believe a gentleman would lend his carpenter a book? He turned it again. *Areopagitica.* He did not know how such a word was to be pronounced. And the book was difficult, densely written, its arguments hard to follow. It concerned freedom; the freedom of speech and printing. Why should he be lent such a book? Perhaps Mr Jeavons had radical opinions too. Hood had heard that the young man published verses but then, to judge by the numbers of volumes in the bookshop in the town nearby, most young gentlemen did that. Hood knew the risk in holding *opinions.*

Once more, he took the note from between the leaves of the book: a small, soiled flyleaf torn from some other book. He had hidden it here, fearing that Susannah should see it. She couldn't read well, but well enough to pick out the sense. The writing was ragged and uneven: *For King & Country. Your a Trater. Go carefully see you do not fall.* There was a star-shaped stain at the bottom. Beer, most probably, spilled by some lout down at the Tranter's Arms, if one could be found who could write even this much. They must feel that he scorned them. But also, and confusing to their befuddled logic, he was no churchgoer either. Susannah attended church every Sunday and at the festivals of the calendar. They had married there. But at the start of this year, the second of their marriage, he had ceased to accompany her. She had wept. It was an insult to his wife that she must go alone. What would she tell people who asked where he was?

She was to tell them that he was at home and quite content to be so.

How could she say that? She would have to say that he was ill.

He couldn't be ill every Sunday, he had said and laughed.

Why then wouldn't he come? He believed in our Lord, did he not?

With all his heart. But he could not accept the Church, nor its ways and its power and the way it held the people in that power.

What way? What power? This was all the fault of those books he read. Mr Snape's wife had asked her why he read so all the time. She had said that he was never seen without some book or other in his hand. Mrs Snape had said that some books should not be put on paper for common folk to read.

The disagreement bubbled on for weeks. He reminded her of the job he had undertaken last year, to fit pews in the church with high sides and hinged doors. Why had those sides and doors been added? It was for the Jeavons family, he said, and the other gentry of the parish. They were no longer prepared to sit on the same benches as their ancestors had. Nor to rub shoulders with their tenants and the common, dirty folk. Now they wished to be separated and raised up and locked away. Where in the Scriptures was there licence for that? he demanded.

And why shouldn't they do that? she answered. If they had the money and spent it to improve the church, why shouldn't they have a place for themselves? If he were heard to say such things he would lose what little work he had at the moment.

He had given up trying to persuade her. His wife's head seemed impervious to argument of any rational sort. He heard her again upstairs, going round the bed. She had hung the bed linen to dry in front of the fire. He sat in a sort of tent. Like a foreign prince. An Arabian prince in his white tent. He smiled. He thought fondly of Susannah's oval face and mouth and slim waist and wondered again at how much he loved this obstinate pretty young woman. She was right in one respect. He had no work now. He had finished the bookcases at the Hall. Snape had said that he could only pay him when Mr Jeavons had seen and approved the work. And Mr Jeavons was away in London.

Hood had to wait two more weeks until Jeavons returned to the Hall. He tried to think of some pretext to go up there, to ask for his money. Then, quite unexpectedly, a boy came down. Mr Jeavons wished to see him.

He put on his greatcoat against the cold and followed the boy, who ran on ahead.

Caspar was dressed in a loose white shirt. His hair was disordered. Hood was surprised at the soft and slim and girl-like hand that Caspar unexpectedly extended to grasp his own. Caspar stood back and regarded the carpenter. 'There,' he said in a mystifying way. 'You're the fellow for me.' Then, 'Take a seat, Mr Hood. At the table. I have important matters to discuss with you. Most important matters.'

'Your book, sir.' Hood held it out.

'What?'

'You allowed me to borrow it.'

'I did? You should have kept it. I meant you to keep it.' Caspar waved his hand. 'Now, what do you know of Africa, Mr Hood?'

'I know it is a great place far over the sea.'

'And?'

'That it has black men and many strange creatures.'

'Have you ever seen them?'

'I have never seen a black man. Nor the sea come to that.' His confession made him feel rather ashamed and foolish.

'How wonderful – but you do wish to see them, don't you? I see it in your face. You are not a man born for little things, Mr Hood. You are a man after my own heart. See here.'

Caspar unrolled a chart on the table, weighting it at the corners with a silver box, an ink well, the Milton and a rough block of wood so dark as to be almost black.

The chart showed a wide river estuary with an egg-shaped island in its middle.

'The isle is the thing to examine,' said Caspar. 'Muranda. As you can see, set off the west coast of Africa, so washed by warm currents and mild winds. Heavily wooded, from the most majestic of oaks to this –' He picked up the piece of dark wood. 'Called ironwood by the natives. Feel it. Well named, eh? What couldn't a skilled carpenter make with that, Mr Hood?

'All the plants necessary to sustain life: bananas, pumpkins, limes, pineapples, melons – and others you will have never heard of, let alone seen, but equally good. And buffalo and wild pig and monkey – which, I am assured, is most excellent to eat. The sailors make what they call a sea-pie from him. Then there are great beasts; the elephant and see –' He went excitedly across to a shelf and picked out a book, flipping through it as he came back. The pages fell open to show Hood an engraving of a most extraordinarily ugly creature, like a huge pig, covered with what looked like armour plating and with a great spiked horn on its snout.

'The rhinoceros. Fancy meeting that in Lower Brook,' said Caspar, laughing. 'There are cattle besides. And goats. The honey bees deposit so much in their wild hives that it can be gathered by the bucketful. But the great, the sovereign virtue of this paradise, this little Eden, is that there are no other men.'

'No other men, sir?'

'None but ourselves.' Caspar began to stride up and down in evident excitement. 'Some enterprising friends of mine have settled on this island – settled in mind, at least, to go there, where all the necessities for life are in such abundance – to set up a colony, a Utopia, if you will – you know More's *Utopia?* – a body of men determined to make a new place on this earth. A commonwealth, where all shall share in the land and its fruits and live in perfect peace and harmony. You know yourself, Mr Hood – a village such as Camblin cannot

13

support a free spirit. Camblin, the towns hard by, London even – these are small places in the end for men who yearn to be free. The Americans have won themselves half a continent, Mr Hood – not a village. The French have set the whole of our Old World on its ear. And what do we have here in England? Beer and rain and piss-a-bed poetry, an oppressive legislature and a half-dead king. Those are what we have – those are all that we have. You're a young man still, Mr Hood. We need men such as you. Honest craftsmen. You shall have a grant of land. What do you say?'

'Not so young, sir, at thirty-one.'

'Nonsense. Young enough.'

'I have a wife, sir. And my cottage. What's to become of them if I should go away?'

'Those who have them are taking wives and children. Your wife will go with you. Your cottage is rented from me, I believe. Yes? That shall be kept open and the rent forgone for the period of your absence – if you should ever wish to return. But I cannot see you as a man who would return to captivity after having tasted freedom. Don't answer me now. I shall be here for a few days before returning to London. Then you shall not see me again for some time. Take these.' He went across to the desk and gathered up the copies of the Constitution and the prospectus and gave them into Hood's hands. 'Read these and come back and see me on Saturday in the morning. But, Hood, Hood – I think such a place would answer everything that I believe you wish for – some things that you hardly dare wish for – you'll find your answer here – on the island.'

They both looked down at the paper with its thin lines and sketchy details of the land that was their engraved Eden.

4

'Has Master Caspar been before to this island?'

They lay side by side in the narrow bed. There had been snow again during the night that cast a dim light on the white ceiling.

'He is not *Master* Caspar any longer.'

'I remember him as a little boy when I was a girl. We used to see his face at the windows at the back of the Hall watching us play in the brook. You must remember that.'

'He went away to school.'

'He was back in the holidays. We felt sorry for him. And his mama dying when he was young, and his papa away all the time. He has only his grandma.' She was silent for a moment, then asked again, 'Has he been to this island? To Africa?'

'I don't know. I didn't ask. He knows about it. There are all sorts of other gentlemen in the enterprise. He says they need good craftsmen.'

'Well, you are that. Has he paid you for your work?'

'Yes,' he lied. He turned towards her. 'I asked you to think of his suggestion. I've weighed it over and over in my own mind. Truly weighed it – putting one consideration against another.'

She was silent. His hand sought hers under the covers. He felt the rough cotton of her nightgown and then her fingers. She did not withdraw; rather her hand lay inertly in his, as if not decided one way or the other on further intimacy.

'It's in Mr Jeavons's gift to have us as tenants or not. He has said that he will keep our cottage for us if we do go on this venture, and not think the worse of us if we wish to cut short the enterprise and return home. On the other hand, if we do not go we shall be abandoned in a sense.'

She remained silent.

'Perhaps not abandoned. But our one champion, as I see it, is Mr Jeavons. If we stay, he will have gone away on this adventure and there is no telling when we shall see him again. That will leave me depending for work on our good neighbours. You know what they think of me.'

Her hand had become perfectly lifeless.

'If I choose to think and read, rather than become a brute, a sot in the public house – well, then the worse for me, and them. But I cannot guarantee that I can get work any further afield. What life will there be for us here in that worsening case? We shall stay and slowly stew and become poorer and less liked . . .'

'This is my home. There's my mother in the village. There are my friends.'

'I know. I know.'

'And what is there for us in Africa?' Her voice was full of contempt for that unknown place.

'There is a future. There is land. If half of what Mr Jeavons says is true then it is, at least, a demi-paradise. There is work and freedom. We shall live in peace and harmony.'

She lay without a word for a few moments, then said, 'You have set your heart on this, haven't you?'

'I set my heart on you, long ago,' he said. 'It is still set there. You are – and are to be – my guiding star.'

He gently squeezed her hand and this time it curled and gripped his.

'You shall decide,' she said. 'I trust you.'

Then they turned to each other and embraced tenderly.

5

Human beings – *wrote Lady Jeavons to her grandson* – must be kept busy. What else is there for us to do except to work and worship God? I do not see but that these two tasks may not be more advantageously undertaken in Warwickshire than in AFRICA. For what is there in this place, which you describe in such absurdly optimistic terms, but a hardly known land inhabited by brutes and barbarians, only darkly and grossly approximating to ourselves? All I have heard from you is of slaves and slave dealers. I would remind you that this 'dreadful trade', as you so call it, is responsible for the roof over your head, the food put into your mouth, and the expensive and, it seems, redundant education you have received. Your grandfather's plantations in the West Indies were worked by slaves. How else was the land to be subjugated? Our own people had tried and been found lamentably wanting. The persons, people – I do not know what to call them – imported from Africa were admirably suited to the heat and other conditions of the islands. I will be the first to admit that the nature of their confinement and ill treatment in their passage to the colonies could not but affect the stoniest of hearts. But, hardness and suffering are our lot in the world, dear Caspar. I am quite willing to agree that we should not wantonly inflict

unnecessary suffering. Who would beat his dog or horse
without the sense of a just lesson being imparted to
the poor beasts? And when they are trained, do we not
leave off such small cruelties? They are no longer
necessary. So it may be with your slaves. Do they have
the same fine feelings as we do? Are they wholly sensible
to suffering? In the long run, is not a little upset in their
lives a boon, seeing that their conditions in the West
Indian islands are immeasurably better than the barbaric
lives they endured in their unholy continent?

But do consider, Caspar. If you wish to do good for
'God's forgotten mankind' – whomever that curious term
embraces – do it for your own sake. Our estates were lost
years ago and our slaves exchanged over the gaming tables
by your papa. The estate in England has shrunk and is
not in the best of condition. We have tenants and servants
for whom, in the end, we have some responsibility. Surely,
our own should come first?

Well, you have gone now. Your parting words were
harsh and ill-considered. I hope that you are granted
sufficient age and wisdom to regret them. Please write
before you finally embark. Write to me and tell me of
any requirements you have, for money or any other thing
that may assist your comfort. I doubt that my comments
or strictures will impinge on your decision – you are like
your father in being headstrong. But the estate does need
a young man's firm hand if it is to safely weather what I
see as storms ahead. If you wish to exchange these real
but mundane dangers for illusory adventures in unknown
and, I suspect, unknowable places, so be it.

I close by calling God's blessing down on you, with the
hope that you will fare safely and return soon

To your loving
Grandmama

Caspar folded the letter carefully and placed it between the pages of the book he had been reading, Benezet's *A Caution to Great Britain and Her Colonies, In a Short Representation of the Calamitous State of the Enslaved Negroes in the British Dominions*. Grandmother could do with reading such a book. He would take it with him. The choice of books to take to Muranda had proved agonising, but came down in the end to the classics and the greatest of the poets: Virgil, in Dryden's version; Milton; Spenser . . .

'Not too many books. We shall write our new books for our new world,' he had written to Torrington, in a letter that was rather shorter and more terse than usual. Torrington had turned down the invitation to join the new colony. Indeed, his letter in reply had been quite scornful of the whole scheme. 'Why bother with all that nonsense over the seas when there is so much to be done here?' he had asked.

'It is precisely because this country is so moribund and that those of any spirit must look to fresh lands and adventures that we go,' Caspar wrote back.

His chest stood at the end of the bed. He had already put in fresh linen, spare shirts and breeches, boots, a supply of paper, his box of toiletries; soap and brushes and razors, his good high-collared coat – 'for meeting kings and chiefs' as he had said, half joking, to his grandmother. She had looked down the dining table and said, 'Kings? What kings? Savages and cannibals and brutes, those are the only kings you will find in that place.' With his clothes and personal effects already in place, and with only books, his writing box and a few other necessities to be added, the chest was almost full. What else? A brace of pistols? The portrait of his mother that he had propped against the washstand? His painting box?

He was staying at the house of Coupland – or rather that of Rear Admiral Quayle, Coupland's uncle, a vigorous, weathered, aged version of his nephew. He wore no wig, his grey hair was cropped short, his face brown, strong jawed, and his eyes a fierce blue, half screwed up as if from gazing too long into great oceanic distances.

6

The three men sat in the long dining room, overlooked by portraits of pork-faced ancestors that the candlelight did not flatter.

'All ready, young Jeavons?' said the Rear Admiral, cutting and spearing a piece of roast beef. 'Baptism of the sea and all that?'

'I have been on the sea, sir. But never quite as far as we are venturing.'

'Charles', he signalled at Coupland with his fork, 'is practically half fish. He'll see you safe home if any man can. When do you sail?'

'In the third week of April,' said Coupland. 'The charter agent will bring her into Gravesend a week before and we shall see to victualling her as fast as possible and stow our gear. Most of our passengers will go down from London to embark. What we call the public servants – craftsmen, tradesmen and so on – will come after them.'

'And how many on this venture?'

'We have over one hundred colonists and servants.'

'Good God – where are you going to put them all?'

'There's room. We shall only be at sea for four or so weeks.'

'Never sailed with passengers. Difficult enough with people who know what they're doing.'

'The ship is being cleaned and refurbished now. I've sent down my man with a chart to mark out the living areas so there is no confusion or cause for argument about accommodation.'

'Which man?'

'Jackson.'

'The black feller?'

'Yes.'

'Will they take notice of him?'

'He has my letter of authority. He has a way with him.'

The old man began to talk about his days at sea, then asked to see their charts and said he would advise them, not that they didn't know what they were doing but there seemed, to him, to be rather a lot of cooks peppering this particular broth.

So, after dinner they unrolled the charts, and uncle and nephew talked of winds and currents and rocks and storms and good and bad fortune and drew their fingers this way and that, their great shadows dipping and swaying on the walls over the invisible seas, so much that, with the claret and port they had drunk, Caspar began to feel a little sick and the vision of a great ship bucking through rearing waves haunted his dreams that night.

7

The notice in the window read: *The Committee for the Establishment of a Free Colony on the African Island of Muranda, Second Floor back*. The room had been rented from the lawyer who had helped to draft the Constitution and behind a screen at the end of the room sat the Reverend Peter Tolchard.

William Meares mounted the stairs. He had heard about this expedition from Donnelly. The young man had been lodging with him for the past six months and during that time Meares had ably assisted him in dissipating a small inheritance. They had set quite a delightful pace of drink and ladies and it was now at an end. Meares was unable to return to the position he had left in service to the Honourable John Whiston. He had taken his leave voluntarily but had taken also a quantity of silver cutlery and gold sovereigns. With these he had been able to return a little of Donnelly's generosity, but both now found themselves with empty pockets. And Meares knew that if he should be taken in London on the charge of the vindictive Whiston it would be all up with him. Donnelly had brought him the handbill announcing the expedition, or whatever it was, to Africa. That sounded sufficiently far off to be safe. Psalm singers all, no doubt. He and Donnelly had borrowed the passage money from a Jew on the security of some jewels that Donnelly had obtained from his mother's bureau.

Meares arrived at the top of the second flight of stairs. On the door at the end of the landing another notice announced the Committee's office. He went along. The door was slightly ajar. He knocked and entered.

'I am very much afraid we are not at home to receive callers at the moment,' said a high-pitched, cultivated voice from behind the screen in a far corner of the room. Then a bald-headed, youngish gentleman in a clerical stock looked round the screen and said, 'I'm so sorry. The office is closed.'

'Ah, sir, I didn't mean to disturb you,' said Meares in his most ingratiating manner, holding up the broadsheet. 'It was that I wanted to talk to someone about this noble venture. It seems there is little time remaining in which to sign up to your cause.'

'You wish to join us?' The clergyman emerged. 'You must excuse me. I am the Reverend Peter Tolchard. Mr . . .?'

'Meares.'

'Do take a seat, Mr Meares.'

They sat either side of a long bare table.

'I myself, my brother, my young son and a friend, a gentleman, wish to take places as subscribers, as it says here.' Meares leaned forward, eagerness lighting up his face. 'We are thorough supporters of your cause, the call of settling on virgin land, there to do good . . .'

'Indeed. It is a pleasure to hear such enthusiasm. I really should have the agreement of my colleague, Mr Crabtree, but he has departed for the day. As you say, we have little time remaining, but we do have some places open. Perhaps I could take a few moments to explain a little of our purposes.'

And for the next quarter of an hour Meares was hard put not to show the boredom that threatened to consume his features as the Reverend Tolchard excoriated the evils of slavery and enthused about the way in which the Christian religion would loose the native Africans from the fetters and irons of erroneous and primitive beliefs. Their community would be 'a single shining light in a dark world'.

Mr Meares's intent expression convinced the Reverend Tolchard of the man's goodwill. The amount of subscription was agreed, money paid, the clergyman made out receipts and handed over copies of the prospectus for the new and welcome members. Now, if Mr Meares could just give an address, a letter containing instructions as to when the ship would sail could be forwarded within the month.

It could be sent care of Mr Donnelly at the Golden Star, Eastcheap, said Meares.

The two men shook hands and when Meares had clattered back down the stairs the Reverend Tolchard sat down and added the names of his party to the almost full register of settlers.

8

Caspar had been kept very busy by Coupland for the past few weeks. He wrote home to apologise to his grandmother for his prolonged absence. But, he wrote, great things were afoot. All the murk of the capital had been swept away by the vision of Africa. That shining continent would be his spiritual destiny – and his fortune.

His finances were surely in need of repair. He had raised money for this expedition on the promise of his inheritance. The Hall was already mortgaged. But debt was to be the stepping stone to fortune. And what would his inheritance in England amount to? Three thousand acres of agricultural land in Warwickshire, divided between tenant farmers whose rents taken all together were an income hardly sufficient to keep the Hall in order. Debts had piled up to see him from school to Oxford and now to London. London was dirty, cold, smoky and foggy at this time of early spring, but a few thousand miles away lay an island with emerald forests and golden sand, surrounded by a glittering azure sea. He would have land of his own, out of the reach of mortgage brokers and money-lenders. He would have position in a shared kingdom.

Muranda, he turned the name over in his mind. He saw it in huge letters on the bill printed to appeal for subscribers. *Muranda*. In such a place all that was best and noblest in man would rise to the surface; all the hopes of the American and French Revolutions would be put into practice, uncorrupted by any remnants of the old order. Their children would receive an education in a benign and natural world. The division of land and labour would be equitable. He, as a poet, might require help with his land. Well, that was only fair, as his songs and odes would be made for all of the community and would be his chief labour. He had read the Constitution and other documents several times. The triumvirate of governors might look authoritarian on the face of it, but the Legislative Committee, composed of those elected by the settlers, would surely take precedence in all but the direst emergency? He imagined their grave deliberations in the stockade that Hood and others would build for them. A bonfire illuminated their faces. After their proceedings were finished and the women and children came up to the fire, then the musicians and poets and storytellers would reign supreme. And the freed black men and women – how they would be raised up and educated in their heads and hearts until they too deserved land and places at the fireside.

> *Muranda mine – what kindest wind*
> *Will blow our bark unto your shore*
> *– The breath of Freedom! Ay, there . . .*

Ay, there was the start of it. He rushed to his desk in the window and got the three lines down in a hurry while he could still remember them. An hour later he had added another twenty lines to his first ode to Muranda. It was a little irregular metrically, but that could be amended later.

His poem placed him by the fire, with the Committee members and the subscribers and the women and children gathered around. Behind them, partly in shadow, partly in flickering firelight, stood the servants and labourers. And furthest back, almost lost in the night, the Africans looked on.

9

The Committee met at the beginning of April.

'So – these are the final numbers,' said Sir George, scribbling figures on the paper Mr Crabtree had handed to him. 'We have a total of a hundred and one men, of whom thirty-eight are subscribers or public servants, the remainder common servants. Of women and children, there are ten wives accompanying subscribers, together with five children; the public servants have ten wives and fifteen children. Additionally, there are seven women, servants to the subscribers.' He paused to add up his figures. 'This makes in total a hundred and one males, twenty-seven females, and twenty children: a grand total of one hundred and forty-eight souls.'

'I don't think I have ever heard my wife described as a female,' said Dr Owen. 'Though that she indubitably is. No – no offence taken, dear sir.' He waved his hand as Sir George leaned forward to stare down the table. 'Mode of classification. Quite necessary.'

Mr Crabtree had said, on first hearing of the existence of a Mrs Owen, that he had thought the doctor was married only to the bottle. Owen's face today was a burning red, with broken wormy veins in the cheeks and a nose that was purple rather than its normal blue. That, two weeks before, he should have produced at the general subscribers' meeting such a pretty woman, a good ten years younger than he, with frizzy blonde hair and a winning smile, had taken them all by surprise.

'That is about the number we envisaged at our first Committee, I think,' said Crabtree. 'Yet I hardly think that the number of actual subscribers and the money they have put up will meet the expenses of the ship and equipment and provisions until we reach the island and become productive.'

'Some additional subscriptions have been taken out by what we might call absentee subscribers; those who have purchased land but do not intend to travel with us,' said Sir George.

'Who is to farm the land of these absentees?' asked Dr Owen.

There was silence for a moment.

'The farming of the absentee holders' lands does not constitute a problem,' said Sir George. 'They are simply acquiring land as an investment. For a future date. I must say that I regard these investments as essential if our endeavour is to be successful.'

'I hope there is no intention on their part to settle – in the future – tenant farmers on these lands,' said Owen. 'There is no provision for that in our Constitution.'

'I would hope that the gentlemen – or their genuine heirs or assignees – may be persuaded to join us in person at some time in the future,' said Sir George.

'I thought the purpose of this expedition was for us – all of us – to form a colony of equals,' said Caspar. 'Equal in our work and hope and . . .'

'I think we are aware of our purpose, young man,' said Sir George sharply.

'I think I can assure everyone', Sir George went on, 'that with the additional investments that I have obtained we can place our expedition on a sounder footing than we originally thought. There are sufficient funds to charter the ship for six months and to purchase a smaller cutter for our needs when the ship has to return to England.'

'Why so long for the ship?' Owen asked.

'We shall need somewhere to live, Doctor,' said Coupland. 'Before our colony is established and we have suitable living quarters we shall have to use the ship as a floating town until we can build our own.'

'I was told, when I was at Sierra Leone,' said Crabtree, 'that there are substantial buildings and a harbour on the eastern side of the island, facing the mainland. An abandoned Portuguese trading post. We should be able to adapt those for our use in quite a short time.'

'One would hope so,' said Coupland. 'The less time we have to spend on board a moored ship the better.'

'And all our stores?' said Owen. 'And one hundred and whatever the number was of people. Quite a crowd.'

'We have room for all the necessary stores and provisions for our journey,' said Coupland. 'Much that is not needed until we land can be stored on the cutter and follow us. Mr Crabtree will tell you, better than I, what personal stores can be carried on board the *Pharaoh*.'

Crabtree turned over the papers in front of him. 'The rules are not set firmly at this moment but we feel safe in allowing each subscriber one half-ton of supplies, with another half-ton for those with wives and children. Personal baggage should include all of such articles as clothing, household accessories, tools of trade and such salted or preserved foodstuffs as may be safe. The provision of these by passengers will reduce our own outlay.'

'Thank you, Mr Crabtree. Some wine, I think,' said Sir George. 'Captain Coupland – you wanted to say something about the ship?'

'Yes. The ship we have, the *Pharaoh*, was a warship. The guns have been removed, but I would go to the expense – with the committee's consent – of obtaining ten cannon, some of which can be placed in the gun ports and be readily removable to the island for our defence, if need be. The remaining empty gun positions and the rest of the lower deck will serve as accommodation for the subscribers and some of their servants. The great cabin will be divided between premier subscribers and their families. Officers and warrant officers will have to double up in the small cabins. It will be a tight squeeze, gentlemen, but this is no passenger clipper. The crew has to be housed. There are also the animals.'

'Animals?' said the Reverend Tolchard.

'Chickens, for eggs and flesh. Two cows for milk.'

'How long do you envisage the voyage will take?' asked Sir George.

'With no complications, and depending on the weather, between four and six weeks. The shorter the better, obviously, but we shall have supplies sufficient for over a month at sea. We can restock water and food at Teneriffe, if necessary.'

'When do we start?'

'We have to arrange, to save any undue expense, for our own supplies and the crew to be on board at the most two days before all the prospective settlers have put their affairs in order and brought down their baggage to Gravesend, all together as near as possible, so that we may load in the shortest possible time. The date I have set is April the fifteenth. That is only two weeks from now – but I would ask, Sir George, that the Committee, which has done such a sterling job in selecting our party, must now bear down hard on the subscribers and public servants and ensure that they know our timetable. We cannot and shall not wait for stragglers on sailing.'

'You know my objections to your proposed sailing date?' said Crabtree.

'That our arrival will coincide with the start of the rainy season? Yes, but we are almost ready now, and to delay for another six months would place our sailing date near November and winter conditions in the north.'

Crabtree looked around the table. 'I would like my

apprehensions recorded. It is not a good time to arrive, but I am willing to go along with the majority of the Committee.'

'Well.' Sir George slapped both hands smartly on the table. 'Then are we agreed, gentlemen, upon the date proposed by Captain Coupland, and that our efforts should now be bent fully to achieving a smooth embarkation? A show of hands, if you please.'

All raised their right hands, except for Caspar. He was busy writing the minutes, and it had been made clear to him that, as secretary, he could play no part in the reaching of decisions.

10

The great oak travelling chest, made fifty years ago by Hood's father for a gentleman who never came to collect it, stood in the centre of the room. The chest contained Hood's best coat, and Susannah's wedding dress and Sunday dress, shoes and boots. Their few pieces of silver and crockery were placed with care between soft clothing. A parcel of books for Hood and a box of needles and threads and patches for Susannah. *Paradise Lost* went into Hood's greatcoat pocket for reading on the voyage. All else was wrapped in blankets and tied into bundles. From six in the morning they waited for Snape. Outside, the drizzling spring rain became a steady, heavier downpour.

'Here's someone now,' Susannah said excitedly, gazing out of the window. 'Oh, it's only an old hay cart going past.'

But the old cart, a hay wagon with fenced-in sides that made it look like a tiny paddock on wheels, did not go past. It stopped in front of their gate. The driver turned his head and Susannah saw Snape's face glower under his hood. Seeing her at the window, he beckoned in a savage way.

'It's Snape,' she said. 'Snape's brought an old hay cart.'

Hood opened the front door.

'Are you not ready?' Snape called out.

'You're taking us to London in this?' said Hood, coming up to the cart.

'What did you expect? Come on. We must go.'

'Have you no sheeting?' said Hood. When there was no answer, he went on, 'I'll get the canvas from the shed. That will cover some of our goods at least.'

'Then get it. We must be away.'

So Susannah and Hood manhandled their chest and chattels out to the wagon and loaded them on, with little help from Snape who merely picked up one or two of the smallest and lightest things and with a 'Are you sure you really want this?' or a 'Is this to go?' disdainfully pitched them into the wagon.

At last the canvas was stretched over and tied. Hood sat on the board beside Snape, his coat collar turned up, and his hat pulled down. Susannah sat behind, just under the dripping edge of the canvas, her shawl pulled round her. Snape flicked his whip once, then again, swore, and with a jolt they were on their way.

II

A boy dipped in honey. That was good. Jackson liked that. At his age. 'Your skin's like a boy's dipped in honey,' was what Becky had said. Then, as they lay in the dark, 'Were you a slave, Charlie?'

'I'm no slave. I'm a free man,' he had said.

And he repeated it again to himself, 'I am a free man,' as he breathed in the early, animal air of the street. He was walking briskly to the river. A man, thirty-five years old with a few grey filaments in his hair, but a woman could still say that about him – a boy in honey. His back was straight, his step rolled and sprang. A free man. A servant, but a free man. And wasn't everyone in the world someone's servant? All served the King and the Queen served the King and the King served God. That was the way of it.

His father had been a house slave in Montserrat. And his father had been a real black man. There he had been a man of some importance. A man dressed in a black coat – butler to the household. It was when the family came to England that he couldn't be that any more. All the servants in the English house were white and his father told him that all at once he was regarded as lower than the lowliest kitchen boy. And none of the family said a word for him or to him again and he had all the dirtiest jobs reserved especially for him. My God, this grey sky and cold, grey people in a grey countryside in winter. But then the family had taken him to London. His head had reeled. The city was intoxicating. It stank of freedom. He served them there, but when they said they were going back to the North Country he had slipped away early one morning into the mist and unfathomable chaos of the capital. To seek his fortune.

That fortune turned out to take the form of an old clothes shop in the Borough, and of the pretty, small, fair-haired widow who kept the shop. They had met at chapel, married at chapel and in 1756, his son was born and given the names Charles Wesley, after, said his father, the writer of his favourite hymn: 'Love Divine, All Loves Excelling'. He would then begin singing it. He said that he had only the one name given to him in Montserrat: Jackson. No Christian name – just his master's name. They shortened it to Jack, or Jacko, if they felt especially fond of him. At least, he said, the house servants didn't get beaten like the men in the field. Montserrat had been a fine and beautiful island, but beauty was nothing without freedom. His son was to keep that in mind.

And now Charles Wesley Jackson had in mind the smell of that shop, where he had been born and brought up. There was a foretaste of death in the odours of long abandoned and unworn clothes. The sour, damp smell of old dried sweat – a fugitive, sour-sweet reek, of old attracted or gathered dirt, and dirt turned to dust, and dust itself that rose like sullen smoke, visible through the light of the back window on fine days as the clothes were turned over by this customer or that. The family tried to keep those smells out of the living rooms above the shop, but they seeped up the stairs and clamoured at you when you opened the door to go down.

In the upstairs room his father told him tales of Africa; told him of the terrible day when he and his fellows had been rounded up and chained about the neck and ankle and marched to the coast. After three days of sitting in a compound that became a stinking midden, they were loaded on to the ship. Not *a* ship, but *the* ship. The ship that would stand above all and before all forever in his mind. His father wouldn't tell him of the journey from Africa to the New World. He said that no one who had not shared in that hellish voyage would be able to believe the horrors of it. How any survived, he did not know. He told of work in the fields and how he had been chosen, while still a boy, because of his good bearing and handsome features to be a servant in the plantation house. He had soon picked up their English. He was only a boy. Boys learned quickly how to please. His master, Mr Jackson, liked little Jack to play with his own son, a couple of years younger. He used to say that they were like so, and entwine his two little fingers. Like night and day, inseparable. Meaning well, I suppose. Meaning well.

His father's face clouded and he said, 'Though I think that was a joke on me, you see. I was night: the boy was day. But then – did I never tell you of the time young James Jackson and I went fishing and went into the forest and caught one of the white men at that with one of our girls. We hid in the bushes and watched . . .'

'Don't tell the boy that,' said his mother sharply from the other side of the room.

But in that room, as time went on, and he began to grow up, so did his father grow outwards, lazy and fat. His father stayed fat for several years, and then suddenly became thin and grey and seemingly half his size all over a summer. When he went down the stairs he stepped slowly and gingerly. He complained of pains in his stomach and asked just for fish – no meat, no vegetables, no bread as he could not digest them – just white fish, fried. He took to his bed and after a while could not get out unaided, and then not at all, and the room began to stink of his unavoidable incapacity and then a rank odour came from him that was like the burning of something terrible inside and that was worse, far worse, than any dead smell from the clothes downstairs.

A doctor came and said he could do nothing for him. The

doctor whispered on the landing, his voice impatient – his fee had been twopence short – that the old man would die within a month. He died that very night and Jackson's mother was inconsolable. He had just turned his face to the wall, she said.

Jackson jogged easily across the street between two carriages. That death had been more than twenty years ago and he had not seen his mother for at least two years now. She eked out a living from the shop, but he did not care to go near it. He had worked since his father's death as an ostler's boy, an ostler, a servant, a dancer at the Theatre Royal, acting once as a savage, amongst a crowd of young Englishmen with their faces blacked, who danced around and were slaughtered one by one by a party of gallant English redcoats in some artificial battle or other. Then he had gone as body servant to Captain Coupland on a couple of voyages – and been envied by the crews, because he enjoyed so much more leisure and liberty than any of those poor damned tars. He had intended to visit his mother before this voyage, but now there would be no time to get back from Gravesend to London.

One more narrow street and the first masts became visible over the foreshore buildings. How odd and frightening his father would find it to think about his son going back to Africa, perhaps to the very place from which he had been ripped all those years back.

But what sort of a name of a place was this to start out from – Gravesend?

He rowed himself out to the ship.

He clambered up the side rigging and swung over the rail. A few crewmen sat on a hatch, smoking and playing cards. They ignored him and he made his way down on to the gun deck where he was to mark out the accommodations.

Tomorrow the ship would be alive with the coming of the whole crew and the settlers, but today all was quiet. Her crew was not fully mustered and were probably breakfasting ashore.

He was alone on the long gun deck. Captain Coupland had given him lists of the settlers' names. He spread the papers on a shelf at the most forward gun port. From his coat pockets he took a folding three-foot rule and a lump of chalk and began to measure and mark spaces; three feet by six for a single man; four feet by six for a married couple, an extra foot and a half for children. He chalked the whole length of the deck, two deep on each side. It was long, slow work. When he had finished he sat on a wheel of one of the guns and lit a pipe. It was nearly noon. He heard a boat scrape alongside and then voices above. One was Captain Coupland's. Footsteps passed over the deck: they descended the steps. Two men came down: a young one he hadn't seen before and the Captain.

'They look like the dispositions of coffins,' said the young man, as he walked across the gun deck.

'A short voyage,' said Coupland. 'Six weeks at the most. A little hardship will weather them for what is to come. We're supposed to be intrepid colonists, not a tea party. Morning, Jackson. You've got on, I see.'

'All getting shipshape, Captain.' Jackson gestured at his work.

'This is Mr Jeavons. He is one of our party,' said Coupland. 'My man, Jackson.'

Caspar had seen black men on the streets of London but had never been introduced to one. This was a man, of the type, of the race, to whose liberty and future their expedition was bound.

'When I'm not about you will obey Mr Jeavons,' said Coupland. 'No one else. Refer them to me if they do not, or pretend they do not, understand you. There is a crew coming aboard tomorrow, and stores. The next day the colonists and their servants will arrive. It's going to be a deal of work. Personal baggage and effects are to be piled here in the centre of the gun deck. Other stores in the holds. You'll have to show Mr

Jeavons. He is a novice in these matters. At least she looks clean, eh? Have you attended to the great cabin yet?'

'Marked up, Captain. But the carpenter will have to put up the shelters.'

'Well enough – he should be here tomorrow.'

Caspar was fascinated by Jackson. He was light skinned, slimly built and well balanced, his forehead high, his tightly curling hair had a strange sandy tinge, his eyes a bewildering green-grey. In his thirties, Caspar guessed. Physically the man combined grace and strength in a way that made him feel oddly inferior.

Coupland took a sheaf of papers from his satchel. 'Jackson, I want you to take these to the Blue Anchor. Mr Crabtree is staying there. You know him? These are the supplies he should have put in hand. They are due aboard tomorrow. Stay with him while he marks those that are arranged, and any he may have had difficulties in obtaining. After that you must go to the yard of the King's Arms and arrange a carter to bring aboard the livestock you will find there. You have money from yesterday sufficient for your expenses?'

'Everything taken care of, Captain.' Jackson took the papers, tipped a finger to his forehead and swung away from them and up the steps.

'Now', said Coupland, 'we must look to the subscribers' and our own quarters. Come along.'

'You put a great deal of trust in your man,' Caspar said as he hurried after Coupland.

'There are very few men I trust,' said Coupland. 'Jackson is very good. Very able. He has attached himself to me, and I have become attached to him. But he has not been tested. I don't trust any man until he has remained faithful under test.'

'What is this test?' asked Caspar lightly.

'You'll see. Well, perhaps you won't. Let's hope not.'

12

Hood dreamed that night of a great forest of oak and elm and beech. Now he saw its green dark mass, now a city reared up and hid all but the tops of the tallest trees. He came once more in view of the forest and stood beside a wide slowly rolling brown river. On its banks felled trees were being sawn into planks and carved and curved until they fitted together and the floor of the forest and the river became wooden walls and decks. The decks grew mossy and grassed over. Masts began to shoot and buds appeared and unfurled as tiny green and blood-red flags. The dream disappeared into sleep.

When he woke the light was grey at the window, but it felt late. From the street below came a rumbling and thudding and harsh voices echoed upwards into their room. He pushed back the blanket and leaned on his elbow. Ships' masts above the grey and blue-grey slated roofs showed him the reality of his dream.

'Wake up, Susannah. Wake up. This is a fine start. We've overslept.'

He jumped out of bed.

As if in instant confirmation of his fears there was a loud knocking on the door and it was opened by Snape.

He stared stone-faced at the naked Hood.

'You knew you had to be out of here by eight. It's gone well past that.'

'I am sorry for your trouble,' said Hood, covering himself with his shirt. 'We shall be out now.'

Susannah said, 'How can I rise decently with you standing there and the door open to the world?'

'Ten minutes,' Snape said and banged the door shut.

'Why do you always give in so weakly to people like that?' she scolded him as they dressed hurriedly. 'You let everyone rule you.'

'He's my master's man, in the end. If we upset him we upset his master. We have no choice. We'll be rid of him in a little while.'

They found Snape sitting in the breakfast room. He was eating a chop and had a half-drunk pint pot beside him.

'I've ordered nothing for you,' he said. 'There's no time. If I'm to be a carter I would like the occupation to last as short a time as possible.'

'We're ready if you are, sir,' said Susannah.

Snape ignored her and spoke to Hood. 'Have you found your ship?'

'No.'

'First find your ship. I'll eat my chop the meanwhile.'

Hood hurried down this street and that, following the smells of wood and tar and river, to the ships. The *Pharaoh*. She was pointed out, lying in mid-channel. If he wanted to get out he must get a boat, or wait until someone came ashore from her. How, Hood asked, could he do either of these things? The man gave slow instructions as if to an idiot. He must be at Alderman's Wharf and get permission to board and then wait to be allowed to take a boat out.

But to whom could he apply about that?

The man could not help him there. He would have to wait and see if he could catch somebody from the ship.

13

Jackson worked for most of the afternoon, supervising the loading of the lighter that plied back and forth to the ship. Mr Crabtree hurried about on the quayside identifying each box or chest or bale or crate, chalking it H for hold or S for stores. There were bales of canvas and casks of biscuit and salt pork and beef, and barrels of fresh water and beer and casks of wine, lengths of timber, paint and varnish, salt and apples, ploughs and spades and shears, candles and oil and hammocks, palliasses and rough blankets, a crate of chickens and another holding a goat, and another that held another goat, one for milk, and one, as Jackson said, 'for making little goats'. Lieutenant Fortescue, the First Officer, bellowed instructions and orders when the lighter pulled alongside and his crew winched up the goods and lowered them down through the main hatch into the hold, where the waisters stacked and swore and dodged the crates and casks and bundles swaying above them, darkening the sky. 'This will go on all bloody night,' said one. 'Well, at least we won't be able to see the Captain's darky then,' said another.

For Jackson, as the Captain's servant, did not have to work in the hold. He stood jauntily on top of the loads in the lighter and called out, 'Awake up there. Here's some more, boys,' as they winched him up to the ship, and he jumped down on to the deck, calling out where this and that was to go.

When Jackson got back from his fourth trip, a hay cart was

turning on to the wharf. A tall, black-suited man led the horse by the bridle. The cart was loaded with bundles and on the board sat a man of perhaps thirty with a red, country face. Beside him, a young woman looked out at the river. Crabtree called across to Jackson. 'This man has brought our carpenter – get him and his goods aboard. He is needed. Take him straightway to the Captain.'

Hood and Susannah went out on the lighter.

'I'm afraid we shall have to climb, my love,' he said as they bumped up against the ship and stared at the wooden wall curving above them.

'Don't you worry, Mr Hood. Your lady will go up in style. See here.' Jackson fixed a hook into the sling around the bundle of their linen and clothes. 'You just step aboard this, lady. Place your foot here. And that one there and hold tight and you'll be right up there in a moment.'

So Susannah came on board, swinging in and stepping down, breathless, on to the solid deck.

On the quay, with dusk settling on the river, Snape turned the empty cart away. 'May you all drown,' he said under his breath.

14

The next morning colonists began to come on board. Sir George, as befitted his future as Governor, was to share Coupland's cabin. Dr Owen and his delicious Phoebe were to sleep in the small sickbay. Crabtree and his wife, and no less than five other husbands and wives and their assorted children were to sleep in the great cabin, behind the screens that Hood had been put to making. The work was not yet finished.

'We must all sleep in here?' said Mrs Scott.

'There will be compartments, ma'am,' said Captain Coupland. 'They will be taken down by day and erected after dinner each night.'

'And what about the children?' said Mrs Rowell. 'They are surely not to come here in with us to these, these . . .'

'Hutches. Hutches is the word you are searching for, my dear,' said another of the wives.

'There will be room for all, ma'am. I am sure of that,' said Coupland.

'We are lucky there are no babies,' said Mrs Ashworth. 'It would be quite intolerable.'

'And how are the sexes to be segregated?' asked Mrs Scott.

'I beg your pardon?' said Coupland.

'Some of the children are too old to be mixed together pell-mell.'

'I see.' He turned to Caspar and said, 'You deal with that matter, Mr Jeavons, if you would. Now ladies,' and he led the women away, one of them asking, 'Where is the kitchen?' and his voice, deep and calm, saying, 'We call it the galley, ma'am. Allow me.'

Caspar was left with Hood.

'Am I to continue, sir?' Hood asked.

'Oh – yes, by all means. Yes. Have you help? It seems an awful lot to do in such a short space of time. Where have they lodged you?'

'Mrs Hood and I have the carpenter's stores.'

Caspar looked around the great cabin.

'Is there room in here?' he whispered. 'For all the chief subscribers and their families? For all of them? What about this?' He gestured at the long dining table.

'It is to be turned over at night to make a bed.'

Caspar laughed.

But Hood went on in a serious tone, 'It is all for the venture, sir. Isn't that right? We must make the best of everything for the good of all.'

'Ah, yes.' Caspar composed his face into a serious mask. 'Yes – you're quite right.'

Hood and Jackson and the sailmaker worked through two days and much of the night, making the screens for the cabin and gun deck. Coupland sent them to bed at four in the morning.

At first light, a clear bright morning infiltrated the gun deck through open gun ports and overhead gratings and showed white compartments, partitioned up to shoulder height in canvas and wood.

And from eight o'clock more of the settlers began to arrive. All morning long, the new colonists and their wives and children and servants processed down to the wharf and through piles of baggage and tools. They were taken off in the lighter and winched up in baskets and slings and the chief subscribers were shown to the stern cabin, where their palliasses and partitions were stacked ready for the night. The lesser settlers milled on the gun deck and were taken aback by the smallness of their allotted quarters. Last of all came the lighter with the public servants and the common servants and finally everyone was aboard.

The *Pharaoh* and the cutter, the *Sprite*, were readied to sail with the turn of the tide.

15

Hood and Susannah dined with the sailmaker and bosun and cook in the bosun's quarters.

The dinner was roast fowl and boiled potatoes and parsnips and Hood devoured his with great relish. But they had got out into the channel and the ship had begun to pitch and yaw, and Susannah sat white-faced, picking over her food. The ship creaked and groaned. The cabin lamp swung and the dark satellites of their shadows went this way and that on the walls.

'We dine later than usual,' said the bosun, explaining the hours and watches of the ship. 'You'll have to get used to our ways. I'm afraid it's a long and hard day on board.'

'Indeed it is,' said the cook. 'I hope you don't mind being roused at five thirty in the morning. A bit hard for those off the land to become used to perhaps; I've always observed it to be so.'

'A carpenter of course may rest a little longer, eh?' Here the bosun gave the cook a nod and a sly glance that passed over Susannah and ended with a wink and another nod to the sailmaker. The bosun lowered his square, very brown face back to his plate and took another mouthful off his fork. He began to speak again through the motions of eating.

'I think you have never taken ship before, Mr Hood?' he said.

'No, sir. Never. But I cannot think the hours you describe

44

are so much different from the land. We rise early in the morning in the summer and go to bed late at night, well wearied.'

'Ah, but a ship is not a land, Mr Hood. We keep the same hours winter or summer. We don't sail only by the sun, but equally by stars and moon. Our day is fixed. No lying abed of a winter's morn. Eh, lads?'

'Ngah,' said the cook, chewing stolidly.

He was as fat as a cook should be, with protuberant red cheeks, a mouth of redder blubber and long, scant, yellow hairs laid across his head. His ham-like hands almost hid his fork and spoon.

The sailmaker said nothing but stitched small quantities of food between his fingers and his thin lips, ceasing only now and then to take a sip of beer.

'And this is an odd sort of voyage, eh, Mr Hood?' said the bosun. 'We have little more than a skeleton crew.'

'Hasenquist,' said the cook and laughed boisterously and nudged the air between him and the bosun.

'My friend Mr Canterbury, our cook, refers to our other friend Mr Hasenquist, the sailmaker here. Who – as you can see for yourselves – resembles nothing so much as the human skeleton in a fair.'

Hasenquist sniffed. 'As you wish, Mr Arkwright,' he said. 'By all means let us get these jokes and other nonsenses out of the way before we are two days out.'

'There, you see, Mr Hood,' said the bosun. 'Our humour is rather unappreciated by Mr Hasenquist.'

'Perhaps he's got the needle. Stuck in his own finger,' the cook bellowed.

Susannah rose suddenly. 'Youmusexcuse . . .' She rushed from them, holding on to the table's edge then, brushing round the back of Hasenquist and fumbling with the latch of the door with one hand, the other clasped to her mouth, she ran out.

45

But even as Susannah hurried up the ladder to the upper deck, raced to the rail, clung to a rope, and vomited copiously over the side of the ship, in the great cabin at the stern, the gentlemen were discussing higher matters: matters of state and moment.

16

The dining table had been moved over to one side to allow a sail to divide the cabin. Behind this makeshift curtain, the women had retired to prepare the children for the night.

The five members of the Grand Committee sat around the table: Sir George Whitcroft, Captain Coupland, Crabtree, the Reverend Tolchard, Dr Owen, and their secretary, Caspar Jeavons. A Mr Knox, a merchant, was their guest.

Coupland had confided to Caspar that Knox was a necessary evil. He had paid a great sum for his passage; a sum Sir George had pitched so exorbitantly high that he thought no man would take up the offer. But the merchant had not baulked. And Sir George had informed the Committee that they simply could not let such money pass out of the enterprise. Anyway, Knox would be leaving them when they could put him ashore on the mainland across from their island settlement. So he was not one of their party, of their enterprise, and Caspar could not help disliking at sight the man's narrow yellow face. It was one of those faces that always look too old for their possessors, as if nature had fashioned a mask for them.

Sir George proposed a toast to their voyage, more particularly to Muranda, that their endeavours might be crowned with success. They rose, but the merchant, Knox, raised his glass a little laggardly after the others, a queer lopsided smile on his face. Caspar saw that his mouth remained closed for the toast.

'Muranda.'

When they retook their seats Knox spoke for the first time.

'I am grateful for your company, gentlemen, on this voyage.'

'And yours, too, Mr Knox,' said Sir George. 'You are an old hand on the coast, I believe. Of our company, only Crabtree here has visited the place. Perhaps I could ask you to favour us with your own observations.'

'I can't say that I know Muranda at all closely. It is a large island. Not, at the moment, inhabited. But claimed, I think, by kings on both sides of the river.'

'Maybe why it's deserted,' said Dr Owen. 'Can't make their minds up. Fought themselves to a standstill.'

'That may be so,' said Mr Knox. 'Or they may not consider it worth their trouble.'

'It is fertile. A prize, I should say,' said Crabtree, bridling a little.

'No doubt – to you. But the continent is vast. Perhaps they can afford to throw such a place away,' said Knox. 'The blacks are very idle in those parts.'

'I think my man Jackson would argue that point with you,' said Coupland, leaning back and staring hard at Knox. 'I think I would too on his behalf.'

'There are exceptions to every rule, Captain,' said Knox. 'And I would opine from my brief acquaintance with him that your good servant is not a pure-bred black. Been some watering of the ink pot there. But, as you said, Sir George, I know the region. They are most lazy men there.'

'Some make a deal of profit from trading in the labour of these lazy people,' said Caspar.

Knox turned a little to face him. 'I did not say they are lazy when put to work – in another place, and under supervision

47

– only that left to their own devices they will gain a bare sufficiency to live for the day and then choose to remain idle. They have not the gift of *application*.'

'I have no doubt that is your genuine opinion, Mr Knox,' said the Reverend Tolchard. 'It is one that is commonly advanced to justify the kidnapping and transmission of these poor wretches into slavery. It is one with which I profoundly disagree.'

'Ah, I had realised from reading the articles of your association – which I have done, most carefully – that you are anti-slavers. It is a view that will not bring much applause from those you'll meet on the coast, white or black. And you will need all of their goodwill in case of difficulties. I do warn you, there *will* be difficulties. Of many sorts.'

'Now, now,' said Sir George with smooth emollience. 'We have no intention of sailing under that flag. I think that I speak for the rest of the Committee when I say that although we are all united in favour of the abolition of the slave trade, that is not the purpose of our particular mission. Our colony will of course need help. Reverend Tolchard, you wish to say something more?'

The Adam's apple in Tolchard's throat worked up and down energetically as he spoke. 'No, not as abolitionists immediately, but we do intend – and this is in our articles – to accept the labour of the free natives, our fellow human beings –'

Knox smiled.

Tolchard went on: 'In a way that may perhaps atone for that system of theft and violence that is the slave trade and to impart to the native population the advantages of civilisation, the comforts of a secure and moral life, and the inestimable blessings of the Christian religion.' Tolchard sat back, red in the face.

'So, your mission is a philanthropic one. I applaud you. I wish your endeavours well,' said Knox. 'But the trade is a very large part of our economy on the coast. Unless you can suggest

48

an alternative to the English planters in the West Indies, I think it will continue unabated. And unless you can provide a viable alternative, it will deserve to.'

'I cannot go with you there, sir . . .' Caspar burst out hotly.

'There is another way, though,' Knox went on, 'that I can see how the trade might be supplanted. That is by natural growth in the slave population in the islands of the West Indies so that it may become self-sustaining and need no further importation, and so put an end to what anyone must see as an unfortunate trade.'

'Vile and murderous,' said the Reverend Tolchard.

'Not pleasant, I agree,' said Knox. 'But consider, gentlemen, our own interests for a moment. Is it not possible, that by sweeping away one evil, you may create a still greater evil?'

'What do you mean?' said Caspar.

'The trade is at the moment lawful. You agree?'

'I must *agree* only with the Reverend Tolchard,' said Caspar. 'And how can a trade be lawful if it can only be carried on with the aid of violence, rapine, torture and imprisonment.'

'But yet it *is* lawful,' said Knox, giving again that infuriatingly twisted smile. 'It must be lawful. If you look to abolish something that is at present carried out under English law, then it must be at present, as it has been in the past, lawful.'

'Everyone knows the trade will be abolished. Sooner or later. And the sooner the better in my view,' said Coupland.

'Very well.' Knox took a sip from his glass and laid it carefully on the table. 'But take the great port of Liverpool. The city was once a fishing village. It has risen in prosperity in direct relation to the growth of our trade in the West Indies. The merchants of that city have proceeded according to law for the past several centuries, and to date they continue to trade according to law. What is to become of them, the owners, the mariners, the port workers and their dependants? Are they to be recompensed for their loss of livelihood? Even now, this endless chatter in and out of Parliament about abolition is dangerous, in that it lessens the security of their future prosperity by casting doubt on its continuance. What compensation may they expect?'

'They are to be paid blood money for resiling from the act of murder? Is that what you mean?' said Caspar.

'I think, gentlemen,' Sir George intoned, 'that common courtesy demands that we grant our guest his voice without casting doubts upon his motives or sincerity.'

Knox smiled across at the Governor. 'I thank you, Sir George, but I am more than capable of taking care of myself with the young man.' He turned again to the general company. 'If you do succeed in abolishing the trade for us English, what guarantee do you have that some others will not carry it on, either openly or covertly, or piratically? And the other countries – where are they in this? France, for all her Revolution, has not ceased the trade. The new United States of America, for all the prating of equality in their fine Declaration, continues with the trade. What of Spain and Portugal? They will simply step in to fill any breach we may leave. Indeed, seeing the advantages the trade has brought to our own country, I think one could argue that if we were beginning from a fresh start, might it not be seen to be advisable to start such a trade, rather than abolish it? I admire this gentleman' – he indicated Caspar with a wave of his hand – 'for his sense of moral purpose, if not his practicality. But, I ask, in all sincerity, if he has no interests in the West Indies himself?'

'No. I have not,' said Caspar. 'My family has not. Not now. Our present wealth, such as it is, results from honest labour in the fields of England and the selling of what may be produced from the land.'

'"Not now,"' said Mr Knox. 'Bravo. An honest man, gentlemen. But I bet that your house was built on sugar money. And I hardly think that as a gentleman, and a poet, I believe of some renown, that in England you yourself pull parsnips or weave hedges? We all use the labour of others.'

'Before Mr Jeavons explodes, perhaps I may say a word?' Dr Owen sat forward, his huge red face grinning beneath the swaying lamp. 'I speak as a Welshman. That is, I suppose, somewhere between an Englishman and an African in the common view. And from that viewpoint, I would only like to remark that it seems more than a little strange to me that the arguments in favour of this trade are founded on such a lopsided view of our human race. In none of Mr Knox's arguments do I perceive any glimmering of a view that the slaves, who are the subjects of this trade, are in any way members of the human race. On the contrary, the slavers imply – no, say – that these poor creatures labour in their native lands under a burden of degraded mental and physical characteristics, such that only shackling, shipping and beating can release their true natures – that is to labour unceasingly and uncomplainingly and with no prospect of freedom as our slaves. I only say that it seems a strange argument. What do you say, Mr Knox?'

'I say that you are quite right in certain respects. I do not deny that shackling and beating are sometimes carried to extremes. The rapine and murder alluded to earlier by our young friend are, I would suggest, exaggerations for the purpose of debate. A horse may indeed work better if well fed and happy. But he must be broken first.'

'Some men', said the Reverend Tolchard, 'do not perceive their fellow men as beasts to be broken and made to labour for others' gain. One of the purposes of this expedition, this essay, is to prove the contrary. That all men are born free and –'

'Ah, our friends the Americans again and their wonderful Constitution,' said Knox. 'Yet, for all their talk about freedom and equality, I have noticed that they do not extend these choice rights to their black brethren. We do not have slaves in England any longer, yet they have them still in that land of freedom.'

'I thought that all men of goodwill could not help but agree that this atrocious trade is an evil and should be extirpated, not in a year, or ten years' time, but now.' Caspar leaned back after delivering himself of this. His hands were shaking.

'That may well be. Twenty, ten – who knows? But, let me tell you, Mr Jeavons, that in one year alone the trade brings six million sterling of revenue into Britain. It may be bad for Africans; it is highly beneficial to our fellow countrymen.'

'I am also a merchant,' said Crabtree in a firm slow voice, gazing intently across the table at Knox. 'I have some small lands in the West Indies. And what you say is true – about the breaking of slaves. The way in which they are broken in order to perform their labour is, and necessarily is, a system of stripes and lashings of calculated cruelty. The system would not work otherwise.'

'My dear sir . . .' said the Reverend Tolchard violently.

'No, hear me. I say it is necessary. I do not say it is right. The trade is unjust and inhuman; it is no defence of it to say that we must act unjustly and inhumanely because if we did not others would do so. No known morality or system of ethics allows that the iniquity of others is a justification for our own misdeeds. It is to our disgrace that we continue this trade and, as other gentlemen have said, part of our purpose in founding a colony in Africa is to create a society based on the knowledge that men are fundamentally created equal, whatever their present apparent unequal degrees of civilisation, and that, given the correct circumstances, all may lead free, productive lives under God's good guidance.'

A resounding round of approbations, expressed in 'Bravo' and 'Indeed' and 'Hear, hear', greeted Crabtree's speech.

A woman's voice was heard from behind the white sail-curtain.

'Gentlemen. Would it possible for you to speak a little lower? The children cannot sleep when you cheer so.'

They looked at one another. Then Sir George laughed. 'We are indeed sorry, madam,' he said in a loud stage whisper.

'We shall retire. Thank you, Mr Knox, for instigating such a lively discussion.'

'I think you'll find it livelier at your destination, Sir George,' said Knox.

17

The ship, riding easily, sailed between the coasts of England and France. Forward, Hood and his wife Susannah lay on their own mattress in the carpenter's store. He held her in his arms and they both pretended to be asleep. Hood inhaled the odours of spruce and pine and oak, the urinous smell of rust from iron pins and nails, the reeks of tar and paint. She tried not to shiver in the after-cold of her nausea.

In the stern cabin, the gentlemen extinguished the lamp and settled themselves on to their mattresses and fell asleep soundly for the most part, though Caspar gazed for some time and with some hatred at the white wig which Mr Knox had hung on the wall, where it glowed in the night's residual light like a misshapen moon.

Part Two

I

Caspar wrote for the first time after leaving England to his old school friend, Torrington. He began:

Friday, April 20th

I write this journal as if it were a letter to you, my dear Torrington. God knows if you will ever see this script, but it makes the writing easier when I can keep you in my mind's eye as, I hope, an eager reader. So, here, the ship, myself and all the rest of our strange company.

First, the ship. The routines of life on board are at the same time logical and strange. Time itself does not follow the pattern on land. If the sun or stars are obscured for too long a time, you might as well try to take the hour from a broken pocket watch, one to be taken out and shaken and tapped and held, silent, to the ear; or from a square, solid, grey church tower with its brass-handed clock stopped for the past five years; or from a sundial in a moonlit garden. For time, in this ever-changing world of wind and sea, must be exactly known, and is measured by the nearest we have to stability, the recorded changes of the heavens.

The whole of creation is out of kilter here. The solid, settled land is here replaced by an endlessly moving, incalculably powerful fluid mass. If we should take a tiny part of its constituency and pen it in a glass, or put just a little into a deep well, it will remain perfectly calm, unmoved except if I tilt my hand, or a child drop a pebble into the well to gauge its depth. Otherwise, the water will remain quite still; transparent, guileless, powerless. But here, at sea, its depth is unfathomable. It is protean, both male and female. When calm it wears a woman's flowing gown of blue and green silk, with furbelows of white stitched with threads of gold and silver; but let the weather get up and it becomes male and throws on cloaks of grey and darkest green and purple and black and hurls itself about like a giant ruffian. It does not surround us, so much as suffer us. In the midst of the great sea our little vessel ticks and groans and whispers and creaks as it is pressed and harried by the waters. But, just now, it is calm, and so I am able to write.

I write this on Coupland's small desk in Coupland's small cabin . . .

2

Up on the quarterdeck, Captain Coupland, straight-backed, legs a-straddle to ride with the roll of the ship, set their course. At last they were bearing forward on his command, in his elements of sea and sky.

The crew were his servants, the colonists the flock in his care. No doubt great difficulties lay ahead; they would be overcome. Morality armoured the Captain in a second, impenetrable skin. They were bound for a new land, to form a free colony, to farm and harvest, to introduce the love of God to the needful inhabitants and, by their example, to assist in the eradication of the curse of African slavery.

It would be done. It would be. But his fellow members of the Committee – they were really a poor lot, a poor crew. Sir George a pontificating buffoon. The surgeon, Owen, a drunk. Crabtree, a dried-up ship's chandler. And little Jeavons? Well, he might make a man of him. As a young midshipman, Coupland had seen men die without complaint and seen others, whose bodies were whole, fail miserably. Time would tell.

It was not vanity that made Coupland revel in his command. He thought, quite genuinely, that he was not cursed with self-regard. It was the law that made him captain of this ship.

And an island was, after all, no more than a large ship. If these others should prove wanting, well, then he would have to bear that load too.

3

Caspar wrote on:

> Coupland was not joking with me when he said that there is no authority greater on board a ship than the master. There is the King, but he is absent in his palace; on the sea, the captain is his viceroy. Above the King there is only God, and he is about on a multitude of

other business; the captain is his representative on earth – or, at least, water.

And below him? The First Lieutenant, Fortescue, who barely speaks to me, perceiving me as the Captain's favourite. There are two Lieutenants junior to him, who are as satellite moons, rising one in the morning, one in the evening, attendant upon him, or taking his place when he rests. A boatswain, whose chief duty is to shout at the sailors. Another warrant officer assists him in this.

The men are divided into three classes, theologically arranged. The first and highest, youngest and fittest angels, foretopmen, flit amongst the highest rigging, furling and unfurling sails as if they were wings. Below these are the fo'c's'le men, who inhabit the upper deck and haul yards and ropes and spit on their hands. And below deck, are the poorest creatures such as those old sailors who are suitable only for mending sails and swabbing the decks. So you see that a sailor, given sufficient length of service, will descend in a sort of natural and increasingly melancholy progress from aerial glory to close darkness under the decks: heaven to earth to the underworld. Captains generally retire to the country.

Under the watch system men are on duty four hours on and eight off, and so again. Those not on a watch work all the day and when not at work they sleep, eat, or are at leisure. I think they eat better than the poorer people ever do on land. Here, again, the peculiarity of sea-time enters our life.

The subscribers do not want to keep ship's custom by taking their supper at six in the evening, so we dine at eight, and can still see lights in the fo'c's'le where the sailors are drinking and singing. Similar noises come from the forward end of the gun deck, where some of our prospective colonists carouse. It seems that not all of them are quite the moralists we expected. Some, I suspect, have been driven into this expedition by other desires than the wish for a better and more equitable society. I know that Coupland is worried by what he sees as grumbling and sometimes insolence from some of our party. But it is to be hoped that we all settle down as soon as we near our destination. I feel nothing but the greatest excitement. It is a great pity you cannot be of our party, my dear Torrington. I shall continue this tomorrow. Captain Coupland has sent his man, Jackson, to fetch me to the cabin.

4

'We have been a fortnight at sea and already the ship is coming to resemble chaos. I don't know what is going on forward, Jeavons. Do you know that, after the little rough weather we had yesterday, a deputation come to see me to complain of conditions.'

'They're not accustomed to the life. The servants in particular . . .'

'These were subscribers. Men I had taken to be at least honest and courageous, if not all gentlemen. There were six of them. They were accompanied by Dr Owen, no less. He said that they had represented their concerns to him and he felt it incumbent upon himself to bring them to see me.'

Coupland glared at Caspar, and went on.

'A man named Reeves began it. Not a full subscriber. A bookseller – those fellows are always lawyers under the skin.

Reeves has no fewer than four children on board. Why on earth Crabtree and Tolchard allowed these absurdities, I do not know. I think we must have been desperate to have accepted some of these people. Reeves complained that this was not what they had expected. Living conditions unbearably cramped. Children and women being sick in their bedding, which they then cannot wash for lack of a copper and if they do manage to wash their linen and clothes there is no possibility of drying them. He complained further that the food is always salt beef and pork, with little variance. That they have smelled roast fowl coming from the galley and that such dishes have been borne through the gun deck and into the stern cabin by my man Jackson and the cook's assistant. The correct title is cook's mate, I told him, but Reeves only rattled on full tilt. He said that there have been other delicacies, brought aboard by the chief subscribers; coffee and chocolate had been sniffed, almonds and cucumbers had been sighted. A few such delicacies shared amongst the rest of the expedition, he said, might make their lives a little more comfortable. They and the public and common servants, who have no rations at all except those doled out on ship, look askance at such fripperies going to a favoured few.

'What was I to say, Jeavons, to such nonsense? That the prudent and forward-looking subscribers should be robbed of their small luxuries to placate the servants? To provide them for those who have spent much of our journey so far in drunkenness and idleness and gaming? Then young Mr Donnelly, late of Oxford University, I believe, spoke up. He had no complaint himself, he said, about living conditions. Anyone who had been away at school had known far worse, but he found himself constrained to complain on behalf of others. The women, particularly the younger ones, were in despair at the lack of privacy, and at the saucy looks given to them by the sailors and by some of the servants. The children were running amok and mouthing oaths they picked up from the crew.'

'Mr Donnelly is a fairly priggish young man, I'm afraid,' said Caspar.

'Then a man called Meares said that the gun deck was nothing but a seaborne midden and that we should take the pox or something worse unless something was done.'

Coupland paused and stared down at the chart on the table, moving a finger on it as if trying to locate his troubles.

'So, I turned to the good doctor and asked his opinion. I might as well tell you that it was my opinion that he was already half drunk at that time of day – a little after noon. Owen told me that conditions on the lower deck were indeed cramped and dirty. Two of the children he had seen seemed to be carrying a mild fever and if that were to prove to be contagious and spread then the situation would be more than uncomfortable. I asked him what should be our course of action.'

'What did he say?'

'He said that the passengers should be required to exercise at least part of the day on the upper deck. They would benefit from the sun and air. Their servants must gather together all clothes and bedding, wash them and hang them over the side and that the mattresses should be brought up and thoroughly aired also. The decks to be washed down with vinegar. Any children who are sick must be put into some space on their own so that their illness not be spread.

'I must say that my opinion of him was a little improved by this sensible and wholly practical speech. I called Fortescue and in front of them all gave the necessary orders for the gun deck to be cleared and cleaned forthwith.

'When Fortescue had gone, I thanked all of the petitioners for their kind interest, but reminded them that this is not some sort of superior inn, but a ship, and that all had embarked willingly and seemed happy at the prospect of a bright future in Africa. There was, I reminded them, a certain price to be paid and a small amount of discomfort had, unfortunately, to be suffered now for the greater good in the future. It is very difficult dealing with men who are not members of the crew. I had to remind them also that, on board a ship, the captain is their king, no less.'

'I had no idea of these complaints,' said Caspar. 'I must admit I've kept myself pretty much here in the stern. The gun deck does not, to be frank, smell all that savoury.'

'That's as may be. They will be helped even if they cannot help themselves. You can do something for me, Jeavons.'

'Anything. My duties aren't particularly onerous at present.'

'I want you to find a sleeping space on the gun deck. To observe what is going ahead down there and to keep me informed.'

'I'm to spy?'

'Not *spying*. Of course not. But I cannot be everywhere on this vessel. I can't be expected to change babies' clothes, or nurse the sick or taste the subscribers' dinners. I want to know what is being said – and by whom – and I want to know in good time so that I can put right any legitimate grievances. You are our scribe, Jeavons. I simply want you to relate honestly how things are amongst our people.'

'Won't they think it strange that I come from what they see as our luxury into their squalor?'

'Say that the stern cabin is overcrowded and too close in this warmer weather. That there is actually more air and light on the gun deck. That will put you in good standing at once.'

'I hope so,' said Caspar doubtfully.

'You may have my man Jackson to assist you.'

5

I know it is not the convention to start such a confidential
and formal document as this with a personal statement. I
must say that I feel uncomfortable with the duty you have
placed upon me, but I have here tried to faithfully report
what I have seen and heard.

There was a great deal of banter when I first went
down on the gun deck. They chaffed me on being
expelled from the great cabin because of some grave
misdemeanour, or perhaps simply that I had taken a
fancy to one of the young wives. But in amongst all this,
a few hard questions were shot at me. One asked where I
was to sleep, all the good berths having been taken?
Another: why should a young gentleman wish to sleep
with the servants? This was said with a voice of great
insolence behind my back, but when I turned I could not
see amongst the men's faces which of them had spoken.
Your man Jackson made me comfortable beside one of
the cannons; behind it, rather, so that I might lie and
appear to sleep while I listened and observed.

The prospective settlers fall into two groups: those who
are decent, these are the better type of settler, and those
who can only be called half decent. The problem is that
the men have no occupation on board. Hardly one of

them is used to shipboard life, and they play no useful part in it. They are seen as a nuisance by the ship's crew. They idle on the deck in the day and encumber the working of the ship and often obstruct the hands as they go about their duties. They drink a deal from an early hour, starting at breakfast and going through the day with beer, then with fiercer spirits at night. They sing and dance until a late hour, disturbing the sleeping seamen in the fo'c's'le, and their own women and children. The common servants are already – some of them – inflamed by what they see as the inequity of the public servants being given grants of land and themselves having no rights in this matter. I have some sympathy with this view. One of the servants said to me bitterly that he had thought they were going to the land of milk and honey, a new world where all would be free. 'A servant', he said, 'is not a slave, but may as well be. He is free to change his master, true, but it seems he will always *have* a master.' This is still a rare attitude amongst the servants, but I fear that it may spread to others. At present, most are still for King and Country and those they regard as their superiors. They are not inspired by the ideals of the American Revolution, still less by the French; for many, their reasons for undertaking this expedition seem to revolve around thoughts of personal gain that, for one reason or another, they could not attain in England. Indeed, I had hoped for more spirit from them.

The subscribers and most of the settlers and public servants make up a better lot, but not all of them are – what shall I say? – of equal value to our expedition. The best of them is Hood, the carpenter from my estates, an intelligent and shrewd man. After him comes Reeves, the bookseller, who is a little delicate for the rough life on board ship; I fear his health may suffer during the journey and have asked Jackson to keep an eye out for him. I am afraid that I must differ with the sentiments with which you expressed your opinion of Reeves. I believe he is thoroughly imbued with a fervent spirit and desire for this endeavour to succeed. His only fault seems to be a whimsical and drifting nature. The Reverend Tolchard informs me that the man is a bankrupt and that this is a common thing amongst booksellers, who sometimes become so enamoured of their stock that they are loath to sell their books. As for some of the other public servants I must express surprise at another of our Committee's choices. The man Meares has, I know, already complained to you about conditions on the ship. I do not think his concern is for others, but solely for himself. The whole Meares lot, the brother, Donnelly and a half-grown boy, seem to be bent only on idleness and vice. The drinking is bad enough and is undertaken by all, including the boy. But worse, and far more deleterious to the morale of the gun deck as a whole, is that they are leaders in organising games of chance. This is not a matter of whiling away the tedious hours. The stakes are not a few pence or even shillings, but it has come to this, that the bets are backed by promissory notes *giving over parcels of land.* So that the Meares family – for whom the element of chance appears to be largely missing from these games – have amassed promises of land from certain of the public servants, and even from one or two of the gentlemen subscribers, who have joined in the play. With the assistance of playing cards and bone dice we are creating poverty amongst many otherwise honest settlers and making estate owners of a few worthless others. I fear that these half-drunken gambling games, undertaken in a presumably light-hearted spirit, can lead only to the most serious dissension and trouble when we reach our destination. Already, I see the grave realisation of their own folly on the faces of some; the knowledge that the payment of a premium and their own hard work and sacrifice have resulted in the prospect of them landing in a new world where they will own nothing but the clothes they stand up in. For, in a fruitless attempt to recoup their losses, some poor wretches have even pledged their spare linen. It has become a mania for some, so gripping them that they play all day, lose, and then take to borrowing from the winners against their own futures. It is the case too, with some, that they are gambling away land that is yet to be granted to them. The two or three subscribers who have foolishly joined in these games are likely to set foot on land as paupers.

As you can see from this, the gun deck appears to be divided between those who are respectable and intend to remain so, and those who may have appeared to the Reverend Tolchard as respectable, but who are far from being so. The Meares family is the worst. But there are others, mainly the single men, who seem prepared to join in any of these idle sports. The deck has divided physically as well as spiritually. The men with families have retired to the stern, and the raffish and single element occupies the forward quarters. There is gaming, drinking, fiddle-playing and dancing. One cannot object to the latter activities as they promote a general feeling of well-being and are healthy exercise in themselves. That is, unless they are also accompanied by drunkenness and loud talk and singing well into the night, disturbing the women and children and those sailors at rest. I have kept silent at such times, not wishing to prejudice my standpoint as a seemingly neutral observer, and your man Jackson has been quite invaluable as a go-between betwixt myself and what I can call the two 'communities'. Not that he has always, or most often, operated on my instructions. One would have thought his skin and the way that his colour is regarded by some would have militated against his having any influence, but it is really extraordinary the way that he can soothe opposing parties. He will move amongst the stern passengers, quieting the children, flattering their mothers, conversing gravely with the men, carrying requests to yourself if requested, then he will come down to the Meareses' end of the deck, and dance and play upon some sort of pan pipes he calls a syrinx, and drink man for man without ever appearing drunk and so win the approval of the drunken assembly. By gradual means, he will somehow magically quieten them and then sit and tell outrageous stories of women and men, who seem to be almost black, mythical gods come down from some warm Olympus in these tales of endurance and adventure, ribaldry and bawdy. The women especially look upon him kindly and, remarkably, the men do not appear to be jealous.

There remains one other large and growing problem. Of the common servants of the subscribers, who join gladly in the worst activities, being mostly young or younger men and women, what is one to say? They are servants who may have been gainfully employed in a large house, but in our small wooden world they are under used. For what is their role to be? Whether their expectations are founded in any promise, real or illusory, and any preconception they, rightly or wrongly, may have gained by reading our advertisements and Constitution, it seems there is high expectation amongst them that they shall be in some way provided for on the island. And, to speak frankly, what need should we have of ladies' maids and footmen where we are bound? It seems to me that we are in danger in carrying *in parvo* the whole structure of that society we have left behind; that is to say: a hierarchy of gentlemen, a few craftsmen and other useful free men, and a quantity of disaffected and generally useless servants. Useless, that is, unless they are to be set free and given some role in our new democracy.

I apologise if I have wandered from the point of this report, but I feel impelled to write down what cannot perhaps be heard in open Committee. I hope that you will not be offended if I write to you in a frank and open manner.

In confidence,
Caspar Jeavons

6

'I hadn't imagined you quite such a puritan, dear Jeavons,' said Coupland. 'You're not too uncomfortable out there, are you? You are doing such a sterling job that I'm loath to remove you.'

'I am spying on these people.'

'Nonsense. You are our secretary. You must keep a true record of whatever we do. There is my log, but that is a dry document. There is the weather diary. None of these can record what happens between the people on this vessel. I cannot write a journal of impressions and of the movements of life and thought in the community – that's your task. I am determined to hold us together. We have much to do and I need all the help I can get to accomplish the task ahead.'

'They will lose trust in me. If they have any now.'

'Play a part, Jeavons. For just a while. You are a poet. Poets write plays sometimes. Think of it as a play. Write your part. It will be only a few more weeks until we reach port. You have already confirmed what I half knew.' He tapped Caspar's report, which lay on his desk. 'This gaming is a scourge. If it is not dealt with it will cause a serious disturbance.'

'But how can you stop them? These people are not under any real authority.'

'The ship has a captain.' Coupland's face hardened.

'With all due respect, they will say that they have little enough pleasure as it is.'

'Well, perhaps I cannot stop them gaming,' said Coupland. 'But I can ensure that no one benefits. Let us compose a letter to Mr Meares and his friends.'

'A matter of some urgency and delicacy,' Caspar had said to each Committee member when presenting the Captain's request for a meeting.

They met that evening, before dinner. Sir George Whitcroft asked for the names of the gentlemen who had been seen gaming. Coupland refused politely but steadfastly to give the names, or any indication of how he had come to have knowledge of them. When the order was issued, in the name of the Committee, and backed by his legal authority as master of the ship, then there would be an end to the matter.

That evening, a notice was posted at the main mast. Jackson had been provided with a marine's side drum, which he wore jauntily on his hip, suspended by a red sash from his shoulder. He beat a steady two-beat with his sticks, while a seaman nailed the parchment to the mast.

By Order of the Master of the Pharaoh, *and with the authority of the Executive Committee of the New Colony of Muranda, the following order is promulgated with immediate effect.*
It is with great concern that the Committee has observed the growth of the pernicious practice of gaming and the wagering of large amounts of money and other possessions.

*The Committee, to whom all must look for protection
and the confident knowledge that all must be kept in good
order, cannot allow this danger to industry and frugality and
good morals, the practice of which are essential if an infant
colony is to thrive.*

*We therefore order that no gaming debts or wagers, of monies
or other collateral, shall be recoverable whether on board
ship, at any port at which we may put in, or at our final
settlement: on the contrary, we extend full amnesty to all
who have lost and have given promissory notes of money or
land for the future and advise those who have lost any such
to withhold payment.*

*Any who continue to gamble will be subject to the law of the
sea and will face whatever penalties the Captain deems fit
and just.*

(signed)

Sir George Whitcroft (Lieutenant Governor)

Charles Coupland (Master of the Pharaoh*)*

That night Caspar found his bedding, left neatly in the morning, in tumbled disorder. His small case of books had been tipped over and books lay face down, or open on their backs, the pages of one faintly stirring back and forth in the draught through the open gun port. On the other side of the cannon, the Meares family and a couple of subscribers' servants had formed a circle and sat, cards in their hands, playing with gravely serious faces, one every now and then placing a card down, one leaning forward to put what looked like a coin on a small pile on the deck. Up at the stern, most had gone to bed already; the partitioning sheets moved in the light from the one lamp at that end. The figure of Jackson, in white shirt and white trousers, came rolling like a jaunty wraith along the deck. He nodded cheerfully at the card players and came up to Caspar. His eyes took in the disorder behind the cannon.

'I seem to be in a mess here, Jackson.'

'You do, sir.'

The man moved forward and bent and began to rearrange Caspar's tumbled possessions. Caspar heard a muffled laugh from the card players and he determined to make a move.

He stood above them. His body, obscuring the lamp, cast a huge shadow over them. He spoke in a soft, confident voice.

'I see, Mr Meares, that you are determined to flout your captain's instructions and continue with this gaming. Well, we shall see.'

He turned to Jackson.

'I wish you to bear witness that Mr Meares and several others gathered here are continuing to gamble despite the notice posted by the Captain today. Will you ask if the Captain might step this way?'

'Hold on there, Black-as-Night, Night-be-My-Witness,' said Meares, rising up into the lamplight. 'Before you do that, please tell me, young sir, what precisely is it that we are supposed to be doing here as such guilty partners?'

'I say you are gaming. In direct contradiction of the Captain's orders.'

'I say we are not. What after all are we supposed to be gambling with, or for? See here.' Meares pointed down at the pile of coins in the centre of the circle. He bent and picked up a handful. He stirred them round in the palm of his left hand with the forefinger of his right. They slithered and rustled. 'Just bone and wood,' said Meares, smiling at Caspar. 'There's no gold or silver here. Merely tokens. Bone and wood counters as you have for children's games. We are playing just for the pleasure, Mr Jeavons. There's no gaming here. It is just a child's game.'

The others began to titter and look up and one began to laugh outright and then the others could not help but fall in, until all them were rocking and hooting with laughter.

'Just a child's game,' spluttered Meares, turning his hand so that the counters fell to the deck and rolled and twisted there until they lay flat. 'A child's game.'

7

No one knew where Jackson slept, or even when or if he slept at all. He was about all day and vanished into the night and appeared early the next morning, refreshed and lively as ever. On this night, the gun deck was lit at the stern end only by one dim lantern. The curtains of the last stern partition were lifted and Jackson emerged and padded softly up to where Caspar lay. He shook him gently.

'What?' Caspar mumbled from half-sleep.

'Some trouble, Mr Jeavons,' Jackson whispered.

He pushed off his blanket and followed Jackson back along the deck to the end partition. This was, he knew, the space allotted to Mr and Mrs Ford and their three daughters. Jackson held the curtain up so that Caspar could enter. A candle was lit inside. Mrs Ford was tending to one of the children, while the other two small girls huddled together against the wall of the ship. Mr Ford, on the edge of the couple's cot, turned as Caspar came in.

'It's our Mary,' he said.

Mary's face was flushed and perspiration beaded her forehead and glistened on her upper lip. Mr Ford said that they had been woken by the groaning of Mary. As he spoke, the child's body became rigid as her mother tried to comfort her; her eyes opened and she moaned for water. Then her arms and legs began to convulse in a fit. 'Why don't Mary stop?' said one of the other girls. And Mary did stop, but a few moments later her convulsions began again, in greater, unrelenting measure, as if her body was trying to tear itself from the bed.

'I'll fetch the surgeon,' said Caspar.

Dr Owen was in a deep sleep, involved in a dream concerning himself and Mrs Crabtree, the wife of the quartermaster of this expedition. He (the doctor) was slowly and ceremoniously disrobing Mrs Crabtree, though in the dream items of clothing would suddenly and unwelcomely return on to Mrs Crabtree's body, or disappear much too quickly to satisfy his lingering erotic delight. 'Ah, madam,' he said aloud from sleep, and there followed a jumble of muttered words as he achieved his desire. His wife Phoebe, oblivious, slept jammed tight beside him in one of the two beds in the sickbay. She and Owen had made love to the roll of the ship earlier; this had not prevented Owen's dream, nor his somniloquent celebrations of imagined adultery. But now in his dream somebody began to beat upon the bedroom door and Mrs Crabtree dissolved beneath him and Dr Owen sat up and someone was hammering on the cabin door.

Dr Owen dressed as he listened to Caspar's description of the child's symptoms.

'Calm yourself, sir,' he said. 'Children often seem worse than they are. We shall take a look.'

The doctor moved quickly through the corridors and down the ladders to the gun deck. When he arrived, Mrs Ford was vainly trying to rouse the child who had now ceased to move at all, lying like a doll in her arms. Owen felt her pulse. The child's face was pale and still. Owen turned her on to her front and worked her arms up and down. He ceased, bent forward and listened intently. He began to work her arms again, and bent forward again, his red ear at her thin glistening back. He turned her slowly so that she lay on her back and listened to her heart. He stood up awkwardly in that cramped space.

'I am very much afraid, ma'am, that your child is dead.' He pulled the sheet over the child's face. The mother drew her other two daughters to her. They all stared at the surgeon.

'The fit, whatever it was, is the cause of her death.' He looked from the mother to the two children and then up at Mr Ford. 'Join me outside a moment, dear sir, if you will,' he said.

Outside the curtained partition he asked Ford when this sickness had begun. A day or two ago Mary had complained of a headache and had grown very thirsty, said Ford. This evening, she had said she was hot and when her mother had undressed her for the night she had seen a red rash about Mary's lower body. She had woken them in the small hours.

Owen thought for a moment. Then he spoke in a gentle tone. What the family must do now was remain where they were, in this compartment. They might wrap their poor child in a suitable clean sheet or something of the sort. He would return very quickly. His profound regrets for their sorrow.

The doctor made his report to the Captain at six that morning.

'Before her death the child complained of a violent headache. She had a great thirst and she was obviously running a high fever. I examined her after death and found a diffused reddening of the skin on the lower abdomen and a rash of small points of extravasation.'

'What?'

'Pimples exuding blood. The one disease I know of that exhibits this combination of symptoms is smallpox.'

Coupland fixed Owen with his stare. 'Is the ship possessed by it? How did it start?'

'It is my opinion that the child brought the infection aboard with her. There is sometimes a gap of some weeks between infection and the first show of illness. By chance the family is one of the more respectable and virtuous and they have kept themselves to themselves largely. We may have avoided a general contagion. It may also be a less virulent form. We can only hope so. Some things need to be done immediately.'

'I am at your command in this matter, Dr Owen.'

'It is essential that the cause of the child's death be attributed to her fit. Any suspicion of an outbreak of the pox would make matters very much worse. The Ford family must be placed in quarantine – have we any spare room away from the general quarters?'

Coupland thought for a moment. 'There's a small cabin below decks used by marines at one time. It's a store now.'

'If it is suitable they should be isolated there. All of their clothes and bedding will have to be destroyed. I'll need an able assistant. Can I have your man Jackson? And in the morning the whole of the two decks must be thoroughly cleaned with vinegar and a general laundering ordered of all bedding. Then we shall see.'

So Jackson was called and, a few minutes later, he and the doctor escorted the Fords along the gun deck; Mr Ford in the vanguard with Jackson holding a close-lantern, the two shivering girls in white nightdresses clinging to Mrs Ford, and the doctor looming up behind. They went down the steep steps to the hold. And then, twisting and turning, they made their way through a close-walled maze of bales and chests, to the room selected for their isolation. The Fords had been told that they must make no noise and they would be made as comfortable as possible and that Owen would visit them regularly.

They left the Fords to settle as well as they could in the cabin where space had been made by piling boxes and chests against the walls. Back on the gun deck they tiptoed between the sleeping passengers, and only one man saw them.

William Meares was a man who slept little. He was not given to drink, it was not conducive to the keenness of eye and brain required of the gambling man. He had seen the party, the tall adult figures and the two small girls in dim white, creeping past; the florid face of Dr Owen caught in the lantern's light at the top of the hold steps. Now he watched the doctor and Jackson return. He continued to watch as, in a little while, Jackson walked back the length of the deck carrying a small wrapped bundle across his arms.

After a brief and pathetic service by the Reverend Tolchard, the body of the child was committed to the sea. Caspar stood on the steps leading to the wheel deck. He was indecisive. He did not want to go below. Neither did he want to go and look over the side rails, to derive his usual great pleasure from the cutting of the ship through the water, the wake and the wallows and the many subtle movements and colours of the sea. These pleasurable thoughts were spoiled by the over-riding image of a short white bundle that slid from the end of a tilted plank, fell to the water, bobbed for a moment or so on the surface and then was swallowed by the indifferent ocean. He became aware that Knox, the merchant, was at his shoulder.

'The deaths of little ones are most affecting,' Mr Knox said, tamping down the tobacco in his pipe. 'All we can see is the promise of life unfulfilled. A child of good parents, I believe. They are often more susceptible than those of the poor.'

Caspar felt a violent desire to get away, or, failing that, to deliver some robust answer to him. But what would that be? The man sounded sincere enough.

'Death,' Knox went on. 'I can see you are not accustomed to it, Mr Jeavons. You must get to terms with it, I'm afraid. There is a lot more of *that* where we are going. Africa is not like any other place, you see. Look out for themselves as much as people might, the ill-humours of that place search out even the healthiest and wealthiest and those most circumspect as to their health and fells them without a thought. But then, why should he have a thought – Death? No.' Knox, at last having got a light from his box, sucked at his pipe and screwed up his eyes, looking out at the sea. 'It is an insensate thing. But they are very liberal in their measures of this commodity in Africa. Very liberal.'

8

Thursday, May 10th

My dear Torrington, I must tell you of the fear that has come upon us with the discovery of an infectious disease on board, and the consequent death of a young child. Two days on from that tragedy, we committed to the sea the body of the second daughter of Mr and Mrs Ford. Mrs Ford is now herself ill of the smallpox; her husband, having taken the disease as a child, is, Dr Owen assures us, immune from further attack. The third, and eldest, daughter appears to be so far free from infection. The family remain in isolation in their makeshift lazaretto. Coupland has ordered that the gun deck be washed down with vinegar daily and yesterday all clothing and bedding were boiled. The colonists and their servants were instructed to wear only clothing that was fresh, that is, that had not been exposed or worn before. So, we had the oddest spectacle of the women servants walking about in their Sunday best, if they had such spare clothes, or draped in white sheets, like classical statues by day, and like shrouded ghosts at dusk on the upper deck or in the dim lantern-light of the gun deck. Some of the children, having no other clothing, ran about naked for the day while their clothes dried on the side rigging. The less wealthy of the men, finding themselves in the same case, covered their loins in rough towelling or oddments of sailcloth from the sailmaker's store, complaining greatly of the roughness and abrasive effect on their vital parts.

The chief subscribers were in great finery. Sir George made his entrance on the poop, dressed in a royal blue coat and white satin breeches. (It was told to me by one of our sailors that in a sea battle officers always wear their best silk stockings as wool or worsted clings to wounded or burned flesh, but silk slides off.) The ladies of the subscribers emerged in great splendour, in their finest dresses, so that the upper deck resembled the Vauxhall Gardens on a Sunday afternoon. Those who did not appear the whole day hid, I think, half naked behind their canvas screens.

While this carnival was going on, the doctor supervised the smoking of all the sleeping quarters. We are to put into Teneriffe for water and supplies and to unload our sick – there are a few others suffering from injuries, particularly amongst the sailors, and Dr Owen says that one of the younger children needs to rest on land. Indeed, we had all been looking forward to a landfall after almost four weeks on this wretched vessel, but the current and the wind blowing north-easterly have plagued us for the past few days and we cannot progress. It is most frustrating, because we can see the Canaries in the not so far distance, but can get no nearer to them. Of the coast of the African continent there is as yet no sighting possible. However, the First Officer assures me that the wind is changing to blow from that direction and that we should be able to make Teneriffe by mid-morning tomorrow. There is to be a meeting of the Committtee tonight, after dinner. Mr Knox has been asked to attend. He has made some representation to the Captain as to possible objections to our landing being raised by the Spanish authorities. He says that he knows these islands and that they do not have a great love for the British. I do not think that any nation would entertain much of a favourable opinion of Mr Knox. We shall see tonight.

9

'Our position, gentlemen, as it presents itself to me – and you have placed me in control of the vessel – is that we have made poor progress. I promised you a swift voyage of four weeks, six at most. We are still a long way from our eventual destination. Prevailing winds have not been favourable. We have not had a full enough or experienced enough crew to take advantage of the few good breaks in weather. I know also that some on board have been disturbed by the bout of disease we have suffered – the doctor will make us a full report.'

Dr Owen sipped at his glass, placed it down, laid his hands across his stomach and began: 'I haven't much to say that you don't know already. Mrs Ford is likely to die within a day or so; it is inevitable. It pains me to say this, but there is only so much that can be done in the case of smallpox. It is chance or luck if the patient survives. But, I think that, generally speaking, the worst may have been avoided. The incubation period is well past and we have no new cases. The timely precautions we took, in the matters of the washing of clothes, swabbing of decks, smoking and so on, have, I hope, rooted out the last traces of any threat to the rest of the ship's company.'

'Give thanks to God,' said the Reverend Tolchard.

'I'm obliged to you,' said Dr Owen.

They were quiet for a moment: from behind the curtain of sailcloth they could hear some of the women and children whispering. Their whispering stopped when they realised that the gentlemen had also stopped their talk. Coupland spoke again, now lowering his voice.

'Mr Knox – you wished to bring to our attention some points of relevance to our Teneriffe landing?'

'Yes, Captain, and may I thank you – all of you, but particularly you, Sir George – for allowing me to join your meeting. I agree with the reverend gentleman that thanks are due to the good God for our deliverance. All I say is that the Spanish on those islands –' he waved a hand to the great cabin's windows, 'may take a slightly different line.'

'I know that we do not always see eye to eye with the Spanish,' said Sir George, 'but we are a British ship, by God.'

'That is a powerful argument,' said Knox in his dry way, 'but they may still refuse us permission to land.'

'We have no choice in the matter,' said Coupland with some irritation. 'Our fresh water is nearly out, we are living on salt provisions and are still far from Muranda. In short, we have no choice but to put in and restock our supplies.'

'What can the Spanish do?' said Sir George to Knox.

'What they will do', said Knox, 'is send out a party to inspect your ship. To ascertain if our intentions are gentle. And also to see if your ship is carrying any contagious disease. If they find any signs you will be refused permission to land and quite possibly be fired upon to persuade you to leave. If all is well, they will let you land. They will like the thought of the money an incoming vessel may bring.'

'But we do have disease here,' said Dr Owen. 'In the shape, none too pretty, of poor Mrs Ford.'

'Can you hear her?' asked Knox.

'Hear her? What do you mean, hear her?' said Owen.

'Is she silent?'

'She is dying. She is as silent as can be expected under the circumstances.' Dr Owen's face had gone very red.

'I ask for a very good reason, Doctor,' said Knox. 'Your only way out of this, gentlemen, is a little deception.'

'What deception?' said the doctor.

'I don't like the word,' said Coupland.

Sir George waved his plump, chairmanly right hand gently in the air and said, 'Well, we are in a pickle, we might as well hear what the gentleman has to say.'

'Where do you have Mrs Ford?' asked Knox of the doctor.

'She is below the gun deck in the old marines' quarters.'

'Out of the way then?'

'That was the object,' said the doctor.

'Quite so. Do you think it could be concealed?'

'Mrs Ford?'

'No – the room in which she is quartered. It's pretty out of the way? If the Spanish did go down there, and they probably will, could the door be concealed?'

'I don't quite understand where you are going,' said Coupland.

'A trader I know had an outbreak of fever on board his ship. He put those still alive into the powder room, and had the door concealed by a length of false panelling. Then he walked the port inspectors straight past it.'

'You mean to wall the poor woman up?' said Dr Owen in an appalled tone.

'Now, Doctor,' said Sir George. 'If I understand Mr Knox correctly, this will be only an interim expedient.'

'Merely for an hour or so, if we are lucky. For the duration of the ship's inspection.'

'Well, Captain,' Owen said trenchantly, turning to Coupland, 'I wish it to be known and plainly understood that I refuse absolutely to have anything to do with this. That it is done without my approval and, as de facto ship's surgeon, I would have hoped my word might have carried some weight. Unless you are all determined to go ahead with this chicanery.'

'Rather a strong word, Dr Owen,' said Sir George, 'for a harmless deception which will speed us on our way.'

'The alternative is quarantine at Teneriffe for heaven knows how long,' said Knox.

'I insist that I be absolved of any responsibility for this charade – a softer word,' said Owen. 'And I further ask you, Captain, to make an entry in the ship's log recording my protest.'

'Very well,' said Coupland. 'But now, can we move on? If the wind holds good from the west tonight we should make the port of Santa Cruz some time in the morning. This whatever you may call it had best be prepared overnight. Jeavons, would you mind asking Jackson to fetch the carpenter and would you then take the matter in hand? Are we all agreed? Except for the good doctor, of course.'

Hood and Caspar followed Jackson's lantern along the narrow passage. The door of the cabin was opened a moment or so after Jeavons knocked. Haggard-faced, Ford blinked out at them.

'I thought it was Dr Owen,' he said.

'How is Mrs Ford?' Caspar asked.

Ford blinked again, then looked at Caspar as if he were not quite sure who or what the young man was.

'Might I ask you to step into the passageway for a moment, sir?' said Caspar.

'She is not dead,' said Ford.

'No, of course not,' said Caspar. His voice, he realised, sounded horribly jovial. 'Please.'

He stood back and the other man stepped out. In the instant he did, Caspar caught a glimpse of Mrs Ford's face by the light of the bedside candle.

He had been wondering how on earth he was to explain Knox's plan to the dying woman's husband. He must be direct, that was the way. That would be Coupland's way. He explained what had to be done.

'But this is not right. I cannot leave her,' said Ford.

'You may stay with her, of course. It will be only for a matter of few minutes. My men here will place the false panel over the door when the inspection is due, and remove it immediately after the Spanish authorities have gone. We would not ask you to do this if it were not essential. We mean no disrespect. It is in all of our interests that we put into land as soon as possible.'

Ford shook himself, as if waking.

'How is my daughter?' he asked.

Caspar hesitated.

'Mr Curwood and his wife have her safe, sir,' Jackson's voice came from behind Caspar.

'You say we dock in the morning? My daughter and I shall go ashore then, if . . . if Betty is gone. We shall not rejoin the ship. I wish you well with your expedition, but, you must see, I have lost the heart for it.'

'You must do as you see fit, Mr Ford,' Caspar said gently.

Ford turned to go back into the cabin.

'Do we have your permission?' said Caspar.

The man, re-entering the cabin, did not look back but only said thickly, 'Do as you see fit.' The door shut on them.

'Make your measurements, Mr Hood. Prepare a false screen.'

IO

My dear Torrington, we have now reached Teneriffe.
We sailed in the shadow of a great black cliff. Birds
circling at the very topmost height of the cliff seemed
to float forth from their hidden nests in the clefts of
the rock, soaring and dipping and swooping to see
some small prey. Though so far up, they were visible as
large birds and so must have been falcons or eagles.
They are fit inhabitants of the cliff, whose rocks are so
frighteningly and fabulously malformed in their strata
that it seems a giant has seized and twisted and buckled
them. The rocks are black or ochre or burnt sienna and
look as if they have been roasted in a hellish fire. We
rounded into the bay at last and caught our first
glimpse of Santa Cruz.

On the lower hills, red and yellow houses are set in a
tumbling fringe. Above the small, sprawling city the
mountains rise up, with only their lower slopes washed
as it were with a light coat of green vegetation, and
where they mount even this gives way to barren hillsides
and grim peaks. It is not a hospitable sight, but, as we
gradually swung about and sailed closer to the mole that
juts into the sea from the harbourside, we saw – I stood
with Coupland on the poop deck – the tiny figures of

two soldiers turn out of a short squat tower. They began to wave their arms at us. In not too friendly a fashion, by my reckoning, but Coupland pooh-poohed what he called my 'excessive timidity'. He was preoccupied just then in giving orders for the anchoring of the ship and I was judged, quite rightly, to be somewhat superfluous to his immediate tasks. Officers and men jostled me aside in their business, urgently running back and forth. I have seldom felt less of sailor, or, come to that, a man. Because even the least of the men, the common sailors, who have the capacity to know these beasts of ships and the arts of the sea, are superior beings *on the wave*, however contemptuous we are of them when they wallow drunkenly on shore. Coupland shouted to me to fetch Mr Knox up to him. I looked for Jackson, to lay off this order, but he was nowhere to be seen. Cursing to myself, I went down the ladder. I had to look all over the ship for Knox. The passengers by now were all thoroughly agog, crowding the rails on the port side, eager at the near sight of land. I passed their backs unseen. I found Knox in the stern cabin. He was seated at the table with Sir George. The two had a couple of bottles between them and I surmised from their respective demeanours that Sir George had taken considerably more of the liquor than had Knox. The baronet had put on his best surcoat of blue silk, and wore a sash and star aslant his peach waistcoat. I must break off now . . .

'Jeavons,' he bellowed. 'Join us. We are celebrating landfall.'

Caspar said he had breakfasted, that they were about to drop anchor and that the Captain wished to see Mr Knox.

'Good,' said Sir George, without waiting for Knox's reply. 'Action at last, eh, Jeavons? You will join our party. Mr Knox is to act as our agent and translator.'

Knox here turned back to Sir George and whispered something.

'Ah yes,' said Sir George. 'The business with the carpenter and Mrs, ahem, Mrs Whatever – the poor woman who is . . .?' He cocked an interrogative eye at Knox, then at Caspar, and meeting with no answer, continued, 'Who is, presumably, still extremely unwell? That business – the concealment – is most distasteful, but necessary; has that gone ahead, Jeavons?'

'I don't know, sir. It is rather, I think, within the Captain's discretion.'

'I think you may take it – excuse me, Sir George –' said Knox, 'that the Captain will require it to be done as soon as ever a boat sets out from the mole and the Spanish wish to board us. I would suggest it is done now and remains in place until we leave the port. What if we are all ashore and the Spanish steal a march on us by boarding then? Who would be here to order the necessary concealment?'

'Mr Knox is perfectly right,' said Sir George. 'The thing must be done at once. We cannot afford failure in this matter.

Please convey my wishes to Captain Coupland, Mr Jeavons. It must be fixed firmly. Fixed firmly.'

Mr Knox returned to conference with Sir George, a sort of satisfaction residing in the set of his shoulders and back, which Caspar found most presumptuous. But what was he to do?

The soldiers had gone from the end of the mole. On the harbourside a few figures had gathered to watch the ship come in. Coupland turned to Caspar and said, 'It looks as if they are not particularly interested in us. We'll go to them.' He gave an order for the longboat to be lowered, and then led the way down to Sir George and Mr Knox in the cabin.

'We shall go ashore, gentlemen,' said Coupland. 'There appears to be no one of authority to greet us, therefore I think we should initiate events rather than follow them.'

'You're right, sir.' Sir George smacked the table in front of him and got up.

'We shall need money, Sir George.'

'You shall have it, Captain.'

'Here's the tally of what we need and my estimate of what we should have to pay.' He took the paper from his pocket and passed it to Sir George, who reared back his head and thrust it at arm's length to read it. He hummed and hemmed and snorted his way down the list.

'Mr Knox – you'll forgive me, Captain, if I ask Mr Knox's advice? He is familiar with this place. We have talked about it a good deal this morning. I think it fair that he should see this and give his opinion. He is to act as our interpreter and it is right that he should know from what base we start.'

Knox took the list and read.

'You know your business of course, Captain. But I think you may have overestimated the amount you need to spend on your provisions. This is a far poorer place than England.'

'Good. Good,' said Sir George. 'Need all we can save for the colony ahead.'

'If I may say, Sir George,' said Knox with a slight apologetic cough, 'you will save on provisions, no doubt of that. But you would be advised to hold a little gold in reserve as – shall we say? – presents for our hosts. Things are done here in perhaps a more, ah, open way than at home. In short, sir, the Captain-General will need to be taken care of in a pecuniary sense.'

'Bribe, eh?' said Coupland.

'Let us call it "coming to an understanding",' Knox said, and smiled.

As they clambered into the longboat and pulled away from the ship, they saw that the two soldiers had returned to the end of the mole and were staring across to them and waving madly. Then one broke away and ran back to the squat fort. Soon a whole platoon of soldiers stood along the edge of the mole. As their boat neared, the soldiers began to shout words they could not understand.

'Tell them we are unarmed and friendly. We wish to trade, that is all,' said Coupland to Knox.

They bumped against the side steps. The iron muzzles of a dozen muskets pointed down at them.

'Ask them where their damn officer is,' said Coupland.

'They say their officer is at Mass.'

'Their commander – this Captain-General or whatever he is called?'

'At Mass too.'

'Tell them we are coming ashore. That I bear a warrant and charter from His Britannic Majesty King George the Third of England to their master the Captain-General. We have important business with their superiors. They are to put up their weapons. They can see that we are unarmed.'

Knox began to speak in Spanish, in a surprisingly commanding voice. The sentries on the mole glared down, but when

Knox had finished one of them gestured roughly with his musket that they might mount the steps.

'We have permission to go ashore. They will accompany us to the Captain-General's house.'

They walked down the mole, one soldier leading them, a second following, his face fierce, his musket prodding the air before him. Off the mole, a high stone arch opened into a wide cobbled plaza. A dog trotted purposefully down the wide gutter. On the four sides of the square the buildings were three-storeyed dwelling houses, their fronts painted white and ochre and yellow and blue, the window frames in green. Shops and cafes broke the lines of houses. Above the roofs the men could see bald brown hills. There were sentries at each corner of the square, slouched over their grounded muskets.

'Place looks deserted,' said Sir George.

'They are all in church, no doubt,' said Knox. 'The town will be astir by noon. Then go to sleep again this afternoon.'

Their footsteps sounded loudly as they crossed the empty square.

'Difficult to walk on dry land, eh, after being at sea,' said Sir George, weaving slightly. 'Far to go, Mr Knox?'

'A few dozen yards only, Sir George,' said Knox. 'The Captain-General's house is at the corner.'

They halted outside a double-fronted stone house four storeys high; stone steps led up to its massive double doors. The foremost soldier ran up the steps and rapped the brass knocker twice. They waited. Sir George wiped his face with a handkerchief. Sweat trickled from under his white wig.

One of the doors opened a little way and an elderly maid, her skin creased and darkened by sun, leaned out. The leading soldier shouted angrily at her. She opened the door wider, left it open, her face expressionless, and shuffled away into the dimness of the house. The soldier beckoned them up the steps.

*　*　*

The reception room to which they were taken was long, cool and empty. The Reverend Tolchard looked up with distaste at a huge, dramatically and darkly toned painting of the Crucifixion at one end of the room; Sir George regarded a massive carved oak throne mounted on a dais at the other. Their heads were reflected in the mirror above the fireplace. The glass was slightly rippled and had a green tinge to it so that the Englishmen appeared as if underwater.

Soldiers stood on each side of the open doors. Their looks of fierce hostility had given way to bored scowls. They waited. Coupland began to check again the list of provisions with Crabtree. Knox had crossed to the window and was staring out into a garden. Sir George looked at the pictures, at the mirror – who was that large sweating green man in a blue-green coat in its depths? He was unpleasantly surprised to recognise himself. There came the ringing of several pairs of boots in the hallway and a small square-shouldered man in a scarlet uniform coat trimmed with much gold braid and a canary yellow, watered silk sash across his chest propelled himself into the room.

'Mr Knox. Mr Knox. They did not tell me it was you. Not at all. You must forgive me. Your friends? I am Captain-General Marquez.' Like a smouldering cannonball that had arrived spinning at their feet, the Captain-General swivelled this way and that, bowing repeatedly, saying over and over, in his excellent but heavily Spanish-accented English: 'Yes. Yes. Yes. Delighted. Delighted. Delighted,' as Knox introduced each of the English party.

'I have come from Mass, gentlemen. You have not, no? That is a most sad occurrence.'

'We have a padre on board the ship,' said Mr Knox.

'Our services went ahead this morning, sir,' said Captain Coupland.

'Your *English* services. *Protestante.*' The Captain-General smiled. Then, in rapid and irritable-sounding Spanish he gave orders to the soldiers. They hurried to bring chairs for his guests. He himself marched forward and sat down abruptly in the raised throne.

Knox began to address the Captain-General in Spanish.

'No. English would be best,' said the Captain-General. 'I have been conversing with your friend Mr Fullerton, Mr Knox. I have taught him my own tongue and he has taught me his. That is correct?'

Knox bowed his head and said, 'It seems I am redundant as an interpreter, your Excellency.'

'No, I think not. No one else here has my command of your language. You will be needed.'

The Captain-General leaned back and slowly and with seeming benevolence looked at them as they seated themselves.

'You, I am very sorry to say, you gentlemen of England, glad as I must be to greet you, should not be here.' He stopped and smiled at them again. 'I am afraid, no. We have very, what do you say, strong, regulations about the coming ashore of sailors. I can see that you are gentlemen, but even gentlemen can carry . . . *peste* . . .'

He looked towards Knox.

'Illness,' said Knox.

'Stronger, Señor Knox. A stronger word is needed. I must ask your Captain to swear to me that you bring no "illness" before I allow you to remain in my harbour.'

'Captain Coupland?' said Knox.

'I know my place, Mr Knox, thank you,' said Captain Coupland, rising from his chair. 'I can assure you, sir, that our ship is free from any disease.'

'Very good,' said the Captain-General.

'We have put into harbour,' said Sir George, 'to re-provision our ship. We require mutton and beef, chickens, water and the like . . .'

'Yes,' said the Captain-General. He beckoned one of the

soldiers forward and spoke to him. The soldier saluted and hurried from the room.

'We can, naturally, my dear sir, pay for all stores in gold.' Sir George tapped the wooden box that sat on his lap.

'I know of no other currency,' said the Captain-General genially.

More footsteps were heard from the hall. A soldier presented himself at the door and shouted something. Another small figure, this one in a fusty brown suit of long coat and breeches hurried in.

'My surgeon, my health-what, Mr Knox?'

'Health inspector?'

'Exactly. Gentlemen, Dr Simeon. Dr Simeon will look at your ship.'

The Englishmen stood and bowed to the doctor.

'You have your own surgeon on your ship?' asked the Captain-General.

'Our Dr Owen,' said Coupland.

'Good. Before we are able to carry out any further business, these two must meet on your ship. I regret that I cannot, in the English way, shake hands with you. You understand. My men will accompany you back to your ship. The inspection will take place. It will be well. We hope it will be well. Then I shall be pleased to have you and your officers to dine with me. Your business will be transacted. We shall all be most happy. Your talents will be needed, Mr Knox: Dr Simeon speaks very little English. If all is well, we shall meet this evening. I hope, indeed, we shall.'

They marched back across the square, accompanied by the ragged squad of soldiers and Dr Simeon. The longboat drew off slowly and sluggishly with its full load. Dr Simeon sat on the centreboard, flanked by two soldiers. They were only moderately sized men, yet they made the doctor seem very small. Indeed, with his face as wrinkled and furrowed as a dried-up nut, and his scanty black hair drawn tightly back and fixed into a pigtail, he resembled nothing so much as a small ape done up in a costume. 'Simian' was more the word, thought Caspar. He must have smiled involuntarily, because the doctor, seeing him, glared back. The doctor rasped out some question to Knox, and Knox too looked at Caspar and shook his head very slightly as if to warn him. Then he said something to the doctor, who laughed in an unpleasant sort of way.

The ship loomed above. A ladder was let down. As Caspar stood ready to climb up, Coupland took his arm and said in a low voice, 'See that Hood has done what is necessary.'

It seemed that most of the colonists and their children and servants were on the main deck, crowding against the rail to gaze at the town. Dr Simeon, gaining the deck, appraised them with quick darting suspicious looks. Jackson was despatched to find Dr Owen. Caspar hurried below deck.

Dr Simeon said something to Knox. Knox turned to the Captain, 'The good doctor is insisting on inspecting the whole ship at once, in particular the sickbay.'

'Please,' Sir George boomed, 'let us repair to the great cabin and let the doctor sample our hospitality. We cannot really talk here, not in this arena.' Sir George led the way, through the throng of passengers. And to the cabin, a few moments later, came Dr Owen.

The two doctors, the one large-boned and red-faced, the other small and monkeyish, were introduced to each other by Knox.

'Dr Simeon would like your assurance that we have not suffered from, nor do we harbour, any infectious diseases.'

'To the best of my knowledge, sir, as at this present moment, I can give such an assurance.'

'He wishes to know, further, what other illnesses have been suffered during our voyage.'

'The usual accidents inherent in sea-going life have affected a few of the sailors. They are recovered.' All of this Knox translated to Dr Simeon, who in turn relayed his questions.

'No deaths?'

'Two.'

The eyes of Dr Simeon brightened.

'He requires the details,' said Knox.

'Two of the children were lost overboard in a storm. They had somehow got out on to the upper deck. You know how things are in storms. They were not missed in the uproar and chaos. By the time the father and mother raised the alarm, the storm had abated and the ship was many miles from where they must have been swept away.'

The Spanish doctor appeared disappointed, but muttered some words of what sounded like sympathy.

'He would now like to inspect the whole ship. With you, Captain Coupland, to accompany us if you would. And Dr Owen to show us first the sickbay.'

The lower deck was now clean and fresh smelling, and empty – except for William Meares who lay on his bedding under a small greying cloud of pipe smoke.

As they approached him, Dr Simeon spoke to Knox.

'He wishes to know if this man is sick.'

'I shall ask him,' said Coupland. He sounded irritated by the whole affair.

Meares did not stir as the party halted at the foot of his mattress.

'This gentleman here – a doctor, a Spanish doctor from the port authority – wishes to know if you are unwell, Mr Meares?'

Meares puffed out a little more smoke, then took the pipe from his lips and raised his head an inch or so from the bolster. 'You may tell the gentleman that I am infernally well, Captain. A bit of rest is all I sought – from that gabbling lot above. But it seems I am not to be granted even that.' He closed his eyes and lay back with a soft, vexed sigh.

Steps pattered behind them along the gun deck. The

Reverend Tolchard hurried to catch up with them. He was wearing his cassock and bands, and carried the Book of Common Prayer.

'Captain – if I might have a word.'

'Yes?' Coupland said testily.

'At what time shall I be able to take the second of my morning services? It has been put off twice in all this excitement. With you and Sir George ashore, I had no authority . . .'

'As soon as these Spanish gentleman are away, then we shall be pleased to come to service.'

'The doctor wishes to know why the priest has been summoned?' said Knox. 'Is the man dying?'

'Sometimes, Mr Knox, I suspect you have a rather malicious sense of humour,' said Coupland. 'Tell him no in Spanish, damn it. Let us get on with this.'

It took more than this to satisfy Dr Simeon. Intensely suspicious, he insisted that, if the man was well, he should rise.

'Mr Meares – if you would not mind . . .' said Coupland.

Grumbling below his breath, Meares suffered himself to be poked and prodded, to have his tongue and eyes examined by Dr Simeon. At last the doctor was satisfied.

The sickbay was clean and well stocked. At last they made their way along the corridor to where the old marine quarters were situated.

'These, as you can see, are disused as living areas, and are used to house extra stores,' said Coupland. They passed the panelled-over door and into the room ahead where a light shone. Here Caspar, Hood and Jackson made an innocent tableau: Caspar leaning on a stick; Hood holding a piece of paper and a silver pencil, seeming about to mark off a piece of timber; and Jackson gazing intently down into the mouth of a sack held between his two hands.

When Dr Simeon had finished his peevish and fruitless inspection, he was put back into his boat and waved away.

'Well done. Well done, lads,' said Captain Coupland. 'Now

I think we should go to service, to shrive our souls of this deception.'

'The panelling is removed?' said Caspar to Hood.

'Yes, sir.'

'And how is Mrs Ford, Doctor?'

'Dead, sir.'

12

Monday, May 14th

We slipped poor Mrs Ford's body over the side in the dead of night. Dr Owen had said that she must be dealt with as soon as possible, owing to the warmth of the climate. We tried to keep her committal a secret. Mr Ford could take no part. Coupland has forbidden him to go ashore as he wished. The Captain is afraid he will let slip some word about the smallpox. The poor man did not protest. He sat feebly in the corner of that horrible, small cabin when we came for his wife's body. Two of the women had to work round him, washing and preparing the body, dressing it in a black shroud – Mr Knox's suggestion – as less visible in the dark. Mr Ford sat with his head between his hands. When the Reverend Tolchard said gently to him, 'We are ready for you, sir,' the man simply nodded and said nothing and did not move.

'I loathe this awful, secretive way of going about God's business,' Tolchard said to me softly as Jackson and Hood brought the shrouded body up the narrow way. We emerged into an obscured night. On the poop deck we could see the wheelman bent over the binnacle lantern and the shadowy forms of Captain Coupland and his first officer. They paid no attention to our miserable little party, and went about their nautical business of watching the seashore, where now one lantern burned at the end of the mole and a few windows glowed dimly in the town. Jackson attached iron weights to the dead woman's feet, twining a chain round and round most expertly with hardly a link chiming against another. We placed her body on a polished beam and Jackson and Hood rested it on the side rail. The parson whispered his words, we breathed amen, Hood and Jackson heaved gently and Mrs Ford slipped away and fell into the sea with what seemed an almost discreet splash. There was a slight delay as the tip of her shroud bobbed out of the water, then she went down and only a few bubbles broke the surface, then nothing and the sea lapped against the side of the ship as before.

And today the ship is a teeming anthill. The Captain-General has sent word that the Civil Governor has given consent for the passengers and crew to come ashore if they wish, and for the ship to purchase whatever provisions it needs. So, the ship is being re-watered and restocked with chickens in cages and barrels of freshly salted meat and new biscuit, and the passengers have set foot on land for the first time in a month. The ladies are visiting the shops and stalls of the plaza; the gentlemen who are single are no doubt seeking out the drinking places and a brothel.

I was cumbered with the presence of the Reverend Tolchard. He wished to look around the town's architectural delights and so we stood before the edifice of the cathedral of Santa Cruz. A woman passed us. Her skin was a creamy coffee colour; her eyes frankly engaged mine, then her gaze flicked away. I watched her swaying body walk along the side of the square. Tolchard – who I begin to think is rather a fool – was talking to me. 'It is hideous,' he said. 'Quite hideous. Don't you think so, Jeavons? I cannot go in. I really cannot. There is something about this – this overwrought architecture that depresses and stultifies one. It is papist of course, and so alien to my own beliefs. But really, I do find it altogether too . . .'

But I slipped away, to go up the side street into which the woman had disappeared.

13

She was waiting in a doorway at the top of a steeply stepped alley. When she saw Caspar, she smiled and disappeared into the house. When he arrived at the door it was open, but nobody was to be seen. He looked up the staircase. All at once a man turned the corner of the stairs, tucking his shirt into his breeches as he came. He gave Caspar a hideous grin, exposing yellow and browned teeth. Caspar was about to step back into the street when the woman came to the crook in the stairs, said something in Spanish and beckoned him up.

His heart beating, he mounted the stairs, their bare wood echoing his steps. At a landing she had gone ahead of him. She stopped in front of a half-open door and made a grand gesture as if to waft him inside, all the while smiling and saying, 'Ingles – here. Lady here.'

So, she was the madam. She backed away a couple of steps as he came up to the door, directing him in, like a horse into its stall.

The wall above a rumpled bed was whitewashed and tolerably clean. The midday sun was reflected off the white wall of the house opposite through a tenuously thin lace curtain over the window. By the window frame hung a bronze tortured Christ on a dark wood cross. Over the back of a straight chair were strewn unidentifiable but decidedly feminine garments. A screen showed a Chinese dragon writhing and twisting, and from behind the screen a young girl stepped. She was dressed in a loose gown, her brown face washed clean, her hair drawn tightly back from her forehead.

She pointed to the bed and smiled.

'What?' said Caspar.

As if to encourage him, she crossed to the bed and sat down. She patted the covers beside her and smiled at him again. From the room next door came a loud laugh. Then, through what must have been flimsy partitioning rather than a wall, came a loud English voice, that of Sir George Whitcroft.

'Sorry. Damn thing. Just a moment if you please, madam.' Then silence.

What was he supposed to do?

He sat down beside her. He could smell her perfume, a fleshy, orchidaceous odour. She took his hands in hers and placed the palms on her breasts. She looked into his eyes and smiled. Could it be that she was only a plain simple girl who was new to this game, who wanted only kindness? She slipped his right hand dextrously inside her gown and he felt her warm breast.

'Ah.' His breath escaped in a sigh.

Then there was all the business that was almost new to him, the moves that seemed to come all at once, awkwardly and urgently. He must get to lie beside her on the bed, to kiss her mouth, to open her gown, to regard with wonder this new four-legged animal that had arranged itself, legs and arms flung out, in the shape of a star. Now he was deaf to any other sound in the brothel. His right hand was guided down to that warm, moist, enthralling, alien region, while she stroked his face. She was opening his breeches, and there were more awkwardnesses and hurried fumblings in this delightful play while his coat was eased away. Ah, and then she was guiding him, as he raised himself above her, and then he felt something, then nothing, then some softness and before he knew it a quick, unsatisfactory release into her body and a sadness at losing himself so soon, at the loss of pleasure. But he had done something, been somewhere and he felt immense gratitude to her. He bent his head. He tried to introduce his tongue into her mouth but she twisted away.

'You won't speak?' he said softly. 'How can I say it: that you are such a sweet girl to me?' Her face turned slowly back on the pillow. Its expression was solemn and the eyes stared as if seeing straight through him. She freed her hands from his shoulders. She opened her mouth and pointed. To show him that she had no tongue.

Part Three

Part Three

I

'What would you call this, Jeavons? Not evening. Not evening in our sense, our English sense. How remarkable.'

The ship was at anchor. The sun, a huge glowing hemisphere, hung on the lip of the horizon. As they watched, it was swallowed whole and darkness began to rise.

The ship stood on the western seaward side of the island, it being thought better by Coupland that they negotiate the strait between island and mainland in the day. But the settlers, lining the rail, had seen enough as they had sailed nearer, in the thick dark-green forests that covered the hills and came down to overhang the sea or were drawn back to reveal a series of sandy bays, to show them a new world, fertile and beautiful.

'You see, Jeavons,' said Coupland, turning his back on the last of the dying furnace of the sunset to face Muranda. 'Now they are full of joy. I have brought them to their destination. And you? Are you not overjoyed?'

Caspar said nothing. Truly, he could think of nothing to say. Except for the most ordinary feelings, those he shared with the meanest of the colonists at the rail; how he, like them, was escaped from England, and soon would be released from the sway and smell and noise of the ship and sea. And a first terror at how far they had come, and how far they seemed from any world they knew.

'It is magnificent,' he said lamely.

'Wait until you go ashore to see if it is magnificent,' said Coupland.

A scraping fiddle sprang up on the main deck and some of the seamen began to sing lustily.

'I suppose that the drunkards will be getting drunk again,' said Coupland. 'Where did this rabble come from? Greater care should have been taken with our choice in London, I think.'

Later, the company dining with Sir George in the stern cabin heard the revels still proceeding on deck.

'They had better be sober in the morning. Work to be done,' said Sir George, wine glass in hand.

'With your permission, Sir George,' said Coupland, 'I would like to post a notice on the main mast, detailing the tasks for the next few days. Also, before we make our way into the channel between the mainland and Muranda, we need to reconnoitre fully from this seaward side.'

Caspar sat down at the table, beside Mr Knox. 'From what I can see, Mr Jeavons,' said the merchant quietly in his ear, as Caspar tried to follow the conversation, 'you have picked a merry bunch of rascals to found your colony. Or they've picked you more like.'

'What do you mean?'

Knox's long nose jutted out under the lantern like a piece of planed and varnished wood.

'Simply', he murmured, 'that your whole enterprise seems to have been chosen on a rather overly charitable basis.'

'. . . I rather thought the party for tomorrow might consist of myself, you Coupland, the Reverend Tolchard, Mr Jeavons, Mr Crabtree and Mr Knox – Mr Knox?'

The nose turned under the light.

Sir George said that he understood that Knox spoke some of the language of these parts.

'It is a sort of bastard Portuguese, Sir George, together with bits of the native tongues. There are several.'

Sir George nodded, satisfied, and directed his attention to Captain Coupland once more.

Mr Knox whispered. 'As I was saying – you should take care, Mr Jeavons. Some of them seem decent enough, but some would appear to have hoodwinked your more gullible Committee members. The most honest are men who have failed in some way and hope to make their fortunes with you; others, I think, are little more than common thieves and ne'er-do-wells who regard this as a route of escape . . .'

Caspar could scarcely bear to hear Knox's rancid opinions on the settlers. Perhaps some were coarse and unruly and a few others sly and, he suspected, work-shy, but there were many good men and women amongst them. And he reasoned that a long sea voyage is not a venture likely to place even the best of us in a good light.

The Committee had agreed their business for the next day and began to settle down for the night. The racket up on deck carried on after they had extinguished their lights, but after a while Coupland got up and went out of the cabin and they heard his voice sternly commanding the revellers to be quiet, that they must rest. There was much to be done tomorrow. From the gun deck a few of the more respectable, or at least sober, passengers added their voices in agreement, saying they could not sleep for the noise. There were a few drunken shouts, but they were soon stilled. A small child began to cry. At last, there was silence, except for the constant low groaning and creaking of the ship as she rode at anchor and rain began to drum on the deck above.

2

The rain had cleared by dawn. Hood and others busied themselves on deck, erecting awnings to give shelter from both sun and rain.

The longboat was lowered and Sir George's party, together with half a dozen of the crew, well-armed, rowed towards the island. The sea was calm and, further out, a school of dolphins leapt and flung their rainbow spray into the early sunlight. A few minutes later they grounded on the beach and got from the boat. Caspar felt a mixture of fear and exultation that he had finally achieved his destination.

The nearest trees were magnificent palms, high and straight as ships' masts, and further in were smaller trees and thick bushes aglow with fruit and flowers. As they walked amongst the trees, the most brilliantly coloured birds flapped and flew off, disturbed by these strangers, or remained, steadfast and high, giving out what struck the visitors as most comical whistles, hoots and low honks. As they pressed deeper into the woods, the sun struggled to follow them through the canopy of leaves. The smell was heavy and sweet where the trees grew more closely together, but the air lightened and grew fresh as they came to a clearing. Every now and then a startled deer skittered away, swinging its hind quarters through the trees. After what must have been about half a mile through woods, they came out on to a series of meadows of perhaps two or three acres, divided almost as the largest English fields by lines of smaller trees. Across the other side of this flat area, between the far trees where the forest resumed, a faint milky mist rose where the sun had only now begun to reach and more deer, too far for them to startle, stood as if carved. The sun shone on the grass and on where the grass appeared to have been burned off and the earth roughly hoed and turned.

Caspar was so moved by the beauty and tranquillity spread before them that he turned to the Reverend Tolchard and said, 'Why, this is heaven. A paradise.'

'Mr Jeavons.' He appeared disturbed. 'Never say it. There is no such place on earth.'

'Perhaps not,' said Coupland, staring about proudly. 'But a rare prospect nonetheless, Mr Tolchard? Jeavons – we can make something of such a place, can we not? If not a heaven, then the Hesperides.'

'Indeed, I think we might.'

'One could almost be in your park at home, eh?' he said. 'And – good God – there is your elephant.'

The beast, huge and with great dignity, walked out of the engraving from Caspar's library and stood between two trees.

'Enough meat there for fifty,' said Sir George, rubbing his hands together.

'Indeed,' said Mr Knox. 'The proboscis is especially good roasted.'

Almost as in demonstration the beast extended its enormous trunk and lifted it to gently twist and pluck fruit from a bough.

Sir George regarded it with appetite, but turned away and pushed at the exposed earth with the toe of his boot. 'How does it come about, Mr Knox,' he said, 'that an attempt appears to have been made here at cultivation? I thought we had the island to ourselves.'

'You do. But some of the mainlanders may cross to use the better land to grow rice from time to time. For some reason they do not settle here but travel across to gather whatever they can. It is a very hit and miss business – a matter of harvesting rather than constant cultivation. They will leave this field for perhaps another two or three years before trying it again. Or they may fear slavers coming from this sea side. The Portuguese also settled for a short while. And did not prosper. The remainder gave up and retreated to the towns up river. The only visitors now come to trap game. You'll have no bother if you cause no bother.'

'It all sounds very irregular, Captain Coupland. We have heard nothing of these incursions,' said Sir George.

'You'll find that boundaries and rights are a little loose here,' said Knox.

'Perhaps. Perhaps. I prefer to do things the English way, firmly within the law.'

'I regret to say that English law does not run in these parts, Sir George.'

'Well, that may be so, but we must come to firm and binding agreements with those of our neighbours who reckon they have some claims on us.' Sir George's face took on that earnest heavy look it assumed when he felt the weight of affairs upon him. 'If they imagine, if this *king* of theirs somehow imagines that this land', his cane swept the meadows, the far trees and hills, 'comes under his sway then we must disabuse him of that notion and regularise matters.'

'He *is* a king. He has a kingdom, and a people.'

'Is he? Surely not a *king*?'

'Not as our King George is perhaps. More like a king of Scotland. Wales, perhaps,' said Mr Knox. 'He has a lot of land. Perhaps half of Wales in area.'

'A half a king of Wales does not sound too imposing.' Sir George laughed loudly, looking round at his companions. 'Eh? Eh? Not as large as our Prinny even. Ha.'

'He rules,' said Mr Knox drily.

'Well then, as I say, we must come to some accommodation with him. Pro tem – until we are established here. Don't want our men bumping into their men, do we? Agreement.

Everything settled. I have the King's warrant. That is in our charter. I act, however humbly, in the King's part.'

Coupland turned to Mr Knox. 'We were thinking, sir, that you might be of assistance in contacting this king. What was his name?'

'Tabellun.'

'Tar-belly?' said Sir George.

Coupland ignored him. 'If we can arrange a meeting, perhaps, as Sir George has indicated, we can come to some amicable but binding agreement that the island is to be in our lawful occupation.'

'They may come to terms,' said Knox. 'They usually do. They're a pragmatic people. It all hangs on what you can offer them. It's long been my experience that commercial agreements are far longer lasting than treaties.'

'You must advise us then, Mr Knox,' said Sir George. 'For a consideration, eh?'

'Out of the goodness of my heart, Sir George. And for any unavoidable expenses I may incur.'

The two men laughed in that complicit merriment that binds men of the world together.

Coupland looked about him. 'I think we have seen enough for today, gentlemen. Yes? This side of the island is excellent for cultivation, but the natural place for our settlement is the bay in the strait where we shall have shelter and access to and sight of the mainland.'

'There will be great rejoicing on board. This should put fresh heart into them?' Sir George was expansive and jovial. 'After a long hard voyage – land at last. They will be glad to be ashore. As shall we all.'

'I'm afraid they'll have to contain themselves,' Coupland said. 'There can be no landing willy-nilly. We have no lawful right to the island as yet. And when we have, we still need to explore thoroughly and then to build our settlement.'

'I do think, Sir George,' said Knox, 'that the Captain is

correct. You are safer on board ship at the moment. At least you have shelter there. The rains can be a great terror.' Knox spoke in that equable way he had of imparting bad news. 'And you can't build here, in the open, with no stream near. The water will run off the hills there, on the other side.'

Coupland agreed. 'We'll settle where the Portuguese did. At least they had some sense. From the chart the strait is perfectly negotiable and we can draw quite close in. There's a jetty and some of the buildings the Portuguese put up.'

'Our friends on the mainland will see us tomorrow then,' said Sir George.

'They'll know you are here already, I can assure you of that,' said Knox.

'For what reason did the Portuguese leave?' the Reverend Tolchard enquired timidly.

'Who knows,' said Knox. 'The usual. Fever. Perhaps they upset the natives – not an advisable thing to do. Anyway, those who survived left.'

'Well, at least we can use their abandoned buildings as a start and have some temporary accommodation,' said Crabtree.

'But – to stay on board,' said Sir George. 'Please remember that the vessel has to return to England in September. I'd hoped this wretched shipboard life was coming to an end.'

'I am afraid that the ship is our only sure solid habitation at the moment.'

'From the look of the cloud it will be soon raining again,' said Knox. 'I suggest we hurry our pace, gentlemen.'

3

By the time they returned to the ship the sky had darkened almost as if it were night. Over the sea, sheet lightning shone dimly and intermittently behind the curtain of dark cloud. Settlers lined the rail as the boat drew near and the explorers began to come up on deck. Their cries were 'Is it good?', 'Is it fair?', 'Can we go ashore?'

Sir George levered his portly frame over the rail, saluted them and raised his hand. 'It is indeed good. It is fair. Soon. Soon.'

Rain began even as he spoke, pitting the deck in great isolated splotches, to be followed by a sudden enormous downpour so that in only a few moments all had fled below.

In the stern cabin the Committee celebrated. In addition to the members who had gone ashore others were now present: Jackson, Hood and Dr Owen.

Coupland began to summarise their progress thus far. He explained how delays in their programme might occur if the rains continued with this ferocity. Mr Knox broke in to say that this was still only the start of the rainy season and that this present downpour was far from being the most severe they could expect; indeed it was light in comparison to what would surely come later. Coupland agreed and said that was why the ship must serve for a time as their principal dwelling.

He turned to Hood and said that the carpenter must erect, with as much speed as he could muster, a house of wood and canvas above the main deck, to afford shelter from the storms and extra room in which to move about. It must be waterproof and yet admit fresh air. The doctor would explain further the benefits of this plan.

Dr Owen turned from the window.

'A necessary evil, gentlemen. I am concerned about the general crowding and lack of cleanliness on the ship. What will effectively be provided as another deck will enable us to keep the ship clean – and all of our linen and clothing. With general humidity and the air from the land carrying to us heaven knows what in the form of contagious agents it is essential we make every effort to reduce risk on board.'

'Mr Knox knows these parts and something of their medical hazards,' said Coupland.

Mr Knox smiled pleasantly. 'There is no doubt that the land is well enough equipped with hazards of every sort. It is a melancholy fact that a good half of all European newcomers to these parts succumb to some fever or poisoning or malignant disease within the first twelve months of their sojourn.'

'I do not intend that to happen,' said Coupland decisively.

'No? Well, you may be lucky.' Mr Knox smiled again.

'But is not the local population generally robust?' Sir George asked. 'I've heard so.'

'Enough of them die young, so that one supposes that those who survive must be pretty robust,' said Knox.

'Well, well – so shall we be,' said Coupland. 'Now – it can be done, Hood? Expeditiously?'

'If you give me instructions I shall see they are carried out,' said Hood.

'A house. A house, man.' Coupland smacked his hand on the paper on the table. 'Plan. Drawn. Wooden struts. Roof. I leave the details to you. Oil cloth to cover the top. Canvas the sides, to roll down as blinds. You see my meaning? Good. Start to gather your materials now. Begin work at dawn.' He turned to Caspar. 'The wind that brought the rain is to our advantage.

Give my compliments to Lieutenant Fortescue and tell him that we sail to anchor in the strait at first light tomorrow.'

The next day found the *Pharaoh* anchored in the broad strait. On its near side, not more than a few hundred yards away, were the beach, the deserted sheds and storehouses of the Portuguese and a dark cleft of trees widening up between the twin pointed hills. And, looking the other way, about a mile off, the coast of the great continent. A few huts of some crude kind were set high up on the silver foreshore, and the figures of men and women moved amongst them.

'Our neighbours,' said Coupland, raising his telescope to view them. 'We shall have to pay a call.'

4

Saturday, May 26th

My dear Torrington, I write this now that it is quiet on board in the dead hours of night.

Mr Meares has appointed himself spokesman for all our malcontents. I fail to understand how we cannot all be fired with the greatest enthusiasm for our venture, but it pains me to note that Mr Knox may have been right in imputing baser motives to some of those who joined ship in London.

This morning Jackson fixed on the main mast the Committee's declaration – largely dictated by Coupland. This said that though building would begin at once on the island, for the next few weeks the settlers must be content to confine themselves to the ship. Mr Meares came up to me and asked forthrightly for a meeting with the 'Captain'. I didn't like the rather leering and insolent way he said this last and told him so. I was not to worry about that, he said, but I was the Captain's puppy dog and should simply take his message.

Coupland said that he had no objection to meeting the man. Fifteen minutes he could give him. He had a meeting this evening with Hood to review progress. Meares could come in after that. My notes of their conversation are as follows.

Captain Coupland greeted Mr Meares, who was accompanied by those he called his colleagues, Mr Dodds and Mr Abercrombie.

—Coupland: I can give you fifteen minutes, sir. You know how very busy we are.

—Meares: That is what we wanted to speak about, Captain Coupland. This here – and here he brandished a copy of the prospectus – promises us land and accommodation. So far, we have neither. You and the Committee are the only ones to have set foot on the island and now you seem to be preparing the ship as some sort of prison for us. When are we to land there?

—Coupland: Wrong side, Mr Meares. You are pointing to the mainland. The other, the port side, is our island.

—Meares: Being a seafaring man, you would know that, sir. I am a mere tradesman. But I signed up to this venture with expectations of its promises being fulfilled. Forty acres of land. Opportunity for more. Nothing was said about living aboard a floating coffin for as long as may be decided.

—Mr Dodds: By others.

—Meares: You, it seems, are the final arbiter of all our

lives. A free commonwealth. That is what it says here. We have seen an island. And we have seen this piece of paper. But we haven't seen our land. Our houses. Our places. We cannot even go ashore.

—Coupland: I would draw your attention, Mr Meares, to article twelve of the piece of paper you hold. No – I know it by heart. 'It is expected every person, on landing, must assist to clear the ground on which the town is intended to be built.'

—Meares: But nothing is said about building. Town or otherwise. And how are farmers to live in the town? Aren't there men suitable for building work?

—Coupland: We are the only men here, Mr Meares. I hope we are men enough for any job.

—Meares: Very droll, Captain. It remains the fact that we have no accommodations except the ship and now discover that we have to make our own on land. Is there nothing we can acquire?

—Coupland: The island is uninhabited. But it is well wooded and there is everything present to house and sustain us.

—Meares: Are there no native workers? No blacks to be had?

At this, Coupland grew angry and terminated the interview. He said to Meares that surely he had expected to make some effort. That this was an expedition, and an experiment in establishing a new society. And he reminded him forcibly that while he remained on board the rules of naval authority bound him and everyone else.

5

When they assembled for the Committee meeting, Sir George had cut out some pieces of paper and labelled them as STOCKADE and BLOCKHOUSE and HOSPITAL and CHURCH and STORES and so on, and was moving them about on the tabletop with increasing excitement, saying, 'You see, the hospital here, gentlemen, eh? Capital. And the food stores here. Eh, Crabtree? And we must have a school for the children. Give me some more paper, Jeavons.'

As he bent over his imaginary city one of the seamen knocked on the open door and stood, cap in hand.

Sir George turned impatiently. 'Well, what the devil do you want?' he demanded.

'Begging your pardon, gentlemen, Captain Coupland, sir. There are two gentlemen on deck.'

'Gentlemen?' said Sir George.

'Black gentlemen, sir,' said the seaman.

'Visitors?' Coupland laughed. 'Where do they come from?'

'Pardon, sir. I don't know what they are. As I say, they are black men and don't appear to speak our tongue.'

'How did they get on board? Don't we keep lookouts any more?'

'Don't know, sir. They have a longboat alongside. There are a great many others in the boat.'

'I'll come up. Rude to keep visitors waiting. Sir George?'

But Sir George had turned back to planning his Georgeville.

He waved a hand airily. 'You deal with it Coupland, will you? Now, Crabtree, we'll want . . .'

'Mr Knox, you speak their language?'

Mr Knox got up.

'Not you, Jeavons,' said Sir George as Caspar rose to accompany Coupland and Knox on deck. 'I need you to minute our plans.'

Sir George proceeded to plan his town and Caspar made a poor pretence of noting down his wishes, which changed every few moments or so, while waiting impatiently for Coupland to return.

He and Knox came back after about twenty minutes, by which time Sir George had subsided into his chair and lit a pipe.

'Anything of importance?' he asked.

'An embassy. From the King across the water.'

'A rather unfortunately Jacobite remark, if I may say so,' said Sir George.

'Not intended, I assure you, Sir George.'

'Forgiven, forgiven. Well, who were our ambassadors?'

'Two of the King's sons. Fine chaps. They had seen our ship anchor and us go ashore on the island. The King would like to remind us that he is pleased to welcome any friendly visitors, but would like to know the purpose of our visit.'

'What did you tell them?'

'That we hope to settle here – peaceably and after due discussion with any who have a true claim to the island.'

'Um.'

'Knox – perhaps you should tell the rest – you spoke directly to them.'

'The gist of the matter is this – their father, the King, had instructed them that, if that were the case, and he has dealt before with the Portuguese in this way, then he invites us to discuss the whole matter at his palace along the coast. He wishes us friendship and hopes we shall respect his sovereignty until such time as we come to some agreement regarding the island. As a sign of his friendship he would like our king – which, I suppose, is you, Sir George – to accept this cane.'

'What a handsome thing,' said Sir George, taking the cane by its ornately carved handle. 'Looks like one of ours.'

'Portuguese, I would think,' said Knox.

'And when does His Majesty want to see us?'

'He would like you to visit him within the next few days. I strongly advise that you establish contact as soon as possible. The purpose of his sons' visit was also to ascertain our strength. They can see we're not a slaver but we at least look like a warship so they are unlikely to attack us. He will prefer to trade.'

'Attack us, be damned,' said Sir George. 'We'll see him tomorrow.'

'I think we should wait until the cutter arrives. That must be only a matter of days,' said Coupland. 'We shall need the ship here. We'll use the cutter to go to the King.'

6

'Fellow members of the Committee, subscribers, settlers and all our servants.' Sir George addressed them, a great red bull in his red coat and its white facings. 'I know that this has been a long wait and a sore one. But, now, I and Captain Coupland go to secure our position on this island. We go to treat with King Tabellun over there. 'He gestured grandly towards the forested coastline behind him. 'We have every confidence that we shall be able to purchase this land of ours, this island that the good Lord has marked out for us. We go with all your interests at heart. We shall be away for two days, perhaps more. Mr Knox informs me that we must show our goodwill by accepting hospitality and that there is no danger to us in this. He assures me the laws of hospitality here are as strong as they are at home. Lieutenant Fortescue will be in charge while we are gone. He will see to the usual watches and to the safety of the ship. I stress again that no harm in any shape or form shall come to you while you remain on board. The island is not yet ours in terms of legal possession. I must ask you to remain patiently aboard until we return. Plans have been drawn to enable us all to make secure shelter on the island as soon as we have legal title. In the meantime, until we return with our charter, I would ask you to be of good cheer. And so, for God, King George, and all our souls, I bid you farewell for a brief while.'

And so saying, Sir George mounted the deck rail as if awkwardly mounting a horse, straddled it, swore, found his footing on the other side, swung his ungainly bulk and other leg over, twisted a moment in the rope ladder, righted himself and his cocked hat, bellowed out 'Wish us bon voyage,' and began to descend heavily, swinging from side to side, until the feather in his hat disappeared from view.

7

The cutter had a crew of ten seamen, and the company of Sir George, Coupland, the Reverend Tolchard, Mr Knox, Caspar and Jackson. There were two cannon on each side and swivel guns fitted fore and aft and each man had a pistol and sword, although Mr Knox breezily informed them that none would be of any avail if their hosts should take a dislike to them.

'Well,' said Coupland, 'we shall give a good account of ourselves.'

Knox replied that it would likely be their closing account. Let him handle matters at the outset, he said. He had met Tabellun before, and it was well known that kings never forget a face. They had so little to do that it was their chief occupation: knowledge and charm, knowledge and charm, gentlemen. And there came a great harrumphing cough from Sir George.

But the day was fair. Tabellun had his capital some twenty miles up the coast and the wind was blowing from the south. It rained the first hour and then quickly dried out in scorching sun. They had set out at ten in the morning and made good time, spotting at about one in the afternoon the old Portuguese fort that dominated Tabellun's town. The anchor was dropped, and Coupland ordered the longboat to be loaded with a selection of the goods they had brought to trade. That done they rowed in towards the shore. As the boat beached a small group of Africans came from between the trees and stood silently watching the new arrivals.

Two men were told off to guard the boat and goods. 'We must leave our weapons,' said Knox. 'We cannot enter the King's presence carrying them. We are only a small number amongst hundreds of well-armed men. You might put up a fight but would be swiftly cut down.'

So, Sir George decided that he and Coupland, Caspar, and Knox as interpreter, should march up the beach and confront the waiting Africans. As they came near, Caspar examined their new hosts. They were dressed in a motley array of clothes: trousers or baggy breeches and either shirts or bright woven sleeveless cloths draped round the upper body. They were tall handsome men, very dark, much darker than Jackson, at whom they stared particularly. Each of them carried a long musket and had a sword at his side. Sir George pushed forward and held out a hand to the man who looked to be their leader. There was no move to take his hand. Sir George looked round at his companions in some bewilderment.

'Mr Knox,' said Coupland, 'perhaps you could introduce us.'

Mr Knox spoke to them in a wheedling sort of way, moving his hands a great deal, and twisting his upper body almost like an eel to ingratiate himself. To his long sentences the Africans responded with short sharp remarks or silences. It was almost as if the white men were invisible to them and that only as Knox continued to speak did they begin to take form. All at once, their leader was decisive. He said something abruptly to Knox and gestured to the line of trees above the beach. On the hill, the old fort was silent and empty and a huge bird sailed from the top parapet and flapped away across the land.

Knox said, 'Everything is well, Sir George. We are to follow them.'

Once off the beach, the path twisted through woods that at times became so thick that only occasional dapples of light like small intensely bright lanterns lit the way. Then the path opened and followed a narrow reeded channel of water. As they went, Mr Knox gave instruction to Sir George and Coupland. None of them were to attempt to shake hands with the King or indeed to make any physical contact with the native population. If some were repelled by the appearance of these black folk, he said, they must remember that the native Africans had a repugnance for white people. They associated them with contagion and plague.

'Their devil is white,' he added in a throwaway manner.

'What a monstrous thought,' said the Reverend Tolchard. 'Do they know nothing of our faith?'

'They may have gleaned something from the behaviour of our people,' said Knox. 'We are quite near, I think,' he said.

And indeed they could hear the cries of children playing. One of the Africans at the front shouted out and a greeting came back from some woman's voice. The woods gave out into a clearing. The river here was a creek, with several canoes tied up amongst rushes. Children played, splashing in and out of the stream, and higher up women were bent over, washing clothes.

A tall fence of bamboo surrounded their town, which Coupland estimated at about half a mile in diameter. He calculated the defensive utility of such a barrier and reckoned it to be more a means of demarcation; the true defence against attack was the tortuous approach through thick woods.

As they drew near, a crowd of children who had come gleaming and naked from the water ran on ahead and around them and again ahead, announcing their coming.

Once inside the gate, what did they see? In the nature of any group of individuals each saw something different. Sir George's eyes awaited grand buildings, seats of authority amongst the many small round huts that looked to be constructed of yellow-brown earth or clay of some sort, with conical thatched roofs supported by wooden posts so that the effect was rudely classical in nature – like a straw hat on a Greek temple. The Reverend Tolchard searched for spires and found not one. Caspar saw with excitement his first alien town, or, rather, a giant village. He supposed those dwellings were inside as rude as those tumbledown hovels in his villages at home in England where the poorest lived. But not with that air of poverty. Jackson, following, observed his masters and hoped they now had what they wanted. To him it looked a poor sort of place. Knox saw what he was used to seeing. The people of the town stared from their mat-covered doorways as the strangers were led in a roundabout fashion between the huts to a central plaza.

'Ahead is the King's house,' Knox announced. It looked no palace, but rather a conglomeration of several huts of rather larger size drawn together. 'Before we can enter', he continued, 'we must remove our hats as a mark of respect.'

The leading African halted and drew aside the rush covering that served as a door. Sir George bent low and went into the hut. When the last one had come in, the mat door fell shut and left them in darkness. Then they were led through another mat door, via a brief intermission of light, into the next hut, and again thrown into almost complete darkness. The smell was of warm straw, not at all unpleasant, mixed with the smell of meat cooking somewhere. Sir George stumbled. 'Soon there,' said Mr Knox. Another dark passageway, but with light ahead at a turning, and then out into a bright courtyard.

A group of some six old men sat on the ground at one side of a high-backed ornately carved chair raised on a dais. On either side of the chair were tall dark wooden statues that were, to Tolchard at least, frighteningly savage in their aspects.

And the King himself? This must be him, the man who had entered and, without looking at his guests, had proceeded to the carved chair. Sir George looked on the King and then back at his companions and rolled his eyes in amusement.

Coupland found nothing amusing about Tabellun. To his eyes, the King cut an impressive figure. Tall and broad, about sixty years of age perhaps, his head nobly proportioned and with a cap of white tightly curled hair, he was dressed in a long blue European coat with gold epaulettes and braided cuffs. This was the man who, Mr Knox had told them earlier, was the most famous warrior and hunter of those parts. He had lived for ever, his people said, and would live for ever. Certainly he looked to be fit and strong. His eyes regarded them with an interested, somewhat amused gaze. Then he smiled broadly and sat down, beckoning to them to do likewise.

'We must sit on the floor,' hissed Mr Knox.

They disposed themselves awkwardly. Behind the King's chair women and children were seated along a bench. Caspar presumed they were of his family. The children were little more than infants and one stared at Caspar, then by and by lost interest as all children do when faced with the uninteresting behaviour of adults.

Now they were all settled. Sir George quite clearly resented his inferior position to the King and sat cross-legged with a sour expression about his mouth, as if he wanted to say something unpleasant but had, at least for the moment, sufficient wit not to.

An attendant passed a cup to the King. He tossed off the draught in two gulps, returned the cup and motioned to other servants to come forward and serve his guests with excellent rum.

It was then that Tabellun saw Jackson, who was standing in the hut doorway in front of two seamen. The King despatched one of his men to draw Jackson forward to stand before his throne. Tabellun spoke and Knox rose, bowed, and answered in the King's own tongue.

'Who is this man?' the King asked through Knox. Was this a slave? He had never seen a black man pale like that, and he beckoned him forward and put out his hand and touched the skin of Jackson's right arm. White man? Black man? he asked.

When Jackson heard the question conveyed through Knox's mouth his face flushed with blood.

'No, certainly not a slave,' said Coupland. 'A member of our company. Tell him that.'

Then why did he not sit with them? the King asked.

'He is a servant.'

Ah, a slave, and the King nodded and Jackson was dismissed with a wave of the King's hand to stand behind them once more.

Mr Knox, as the only one qualified to do so, conducted all of the proceedings on their behalf, prompted by Sir George on occasion, but mostly provided by Coupland with questions and comments for the King.

At Sir George's behest, Knox stood and delivered his greetings to the King from King George, the English people, and their representatives here – and gave their names. They were here for purely peaceful ends to settle and cultivate such lands as they could legitimately possess.

The King held up his hand and said, Mr Knox reported, that by 'possess' he presumed that they meant the word 'purchase'?

'Of course. Of course,' said Sir George. 'We are eager to come to terms as soon as possible. We have brought goods . . .'

And gold? the King asked.

Perhaps they might show their goods?

Sir George beckoned to one of the seamen, who put down a roll of embroidered cloth and on the top laid a ceremonial sword in a silver and gold chased sheath. These, Sir George explained grandiosely, were of course only representative samples of their wares. He proposed that a sufficient quantity of goods be exchanged for occupation of and title to Muranda together with fifty gold crowns and for that they should have full sovereignty over the uninhabited island.

And guns? The King interrupted him via Mr Knox. What of guns?

So it was bargained that some of the cloths should be replaced by a dozen muskets. They at last came to terms. The total purchase price for the island was to be:

12 muskets
30 flasks of powder
 1 eighteen-gallon cask of brandy
20 flasks of rum
30 pounds of tobacco
15 knives of assorted sizes
50 gold crowns

Sir George produced the deed of cession the Committee had prepared in London and Mr Knox read this aloud in the King's tongue. The terms of barter were added.

The King had only one request that was out of the ordinary: that the settlers should not in any way harm the elephants of the island. They were not native to Muranda, he explained, but swam across the narrowest point between the mainland and the north-east of the island, and then returned. They were a valuable source of meat and ivory; fair game in his territories, but never hunted on Muranda except by the King. This had been the custom of his ancestors and he could not consent to any agreement that did not respect his ancient rights.

This was cordially agreed and a clause was written in to protect the beasts and the King's right to slaughter them. The King made his cross upon it and Coupland and Sir George signed on behalf of the colonists and all was done.

8

It was time to feast. White cocks had been sacrificed before their eyes, the blood staining the dirt floor, and were now roasted and served with rice and fish and yams compressed into a sort of dough. All ate with their hands as the gourds passed around and they cleaned their fingers with bowls of water that the serving men held. They drank the King's palm wine and he drank the French wine Sir George had brought. And under the influence of drink, Sir George waxed, his red face broadening, his disdain breaking down into an appreciative chuckle as the King regaled him through Mr Knox with stories of past glories in military combats along the coast. It became clear that this man did command the country around, and all of the land up to the delta of the river that flowed into the strait of Muranda. Over that river was another tribe, the Manchugas. Tabellun told Sir George solemnly that these men coveted the island but did not dare contest its domination by his people. He hoped Sir George would join him when his court came across to hunt. 'A Royal Hunt,' bellowed Sir George. That would indeed be a capital thing. He would join in with that.

The King then became interested in the Reverend Tolchard's clerical garb of black cassock and white stock. Upon learning he was their priest, Tabellun became excited and asked about their gods. Tolchard reddened and grew a little confused when Knox translated. He looked at Sir George who nodded to him to continue.

'We have only the one God,' Tolchard began. 'There is only one God, though in three incarnations: God the Father, God the Son, and God the Holy Ghost.'

The King listened and then explained amiably that there were many gods and ghosts here: in the forests, on the river and in the earth. These were the spirits of the dead who must not be insulted. The gods and their spirits must be placated and honoured. He would give his new friends gris-gris to ward off evil. Clapping his hands he roared out at one of the old men, who scurried to the corner of the yard, where stood what looked like a large clay oven. The old man reached inside and came back, holding reverently in his hands a number of small cloth pouches with strings attached to them.

These were the gris-gris, Mr Knox explained. Each pouch contained a charm on a piece of paper. Sometimes a verse from the holy Qur'an; sometimes, more likely, simply a squiggle of nonsensical lines copied from some long-forgotten original.

The King motioned with his hand, and the old man proceeded to distribute the charms.

'Do you mean to say that these people are Mohammedans?' Tolchard whispered.

'Well, I suppose you might call them Mohammedans as much as anything,' said Knox. 'The Arabs have been trading up and down these coasts for centuries and reckon, no doubt, that the people of these parts are converts to the Prophet. As much as the priests at Sierra Leone reckon that the natives there are good Christians. The people believe what they want to. As it is we must wear their gris-gris around our wrists or throats. It will please the King.'

The Reverend Tolchard tied his, not to his wrist but around the sleeve of his cassock, not caring to have it next to his skin.

The King said that he was no stranger to the white man; the Portuguese had been on this coast for many years, as had

French and Spanish and English traders. But he perceived that they were quite different. Farmers, not slavers – was that not true? Men who came in peace? Which was just as well, he said, as no one had ever succeeded in subjugating his people. He had no interest in anything but peaceful relations with those who might become his neighbours. Tabellun said that he supposed they would be in need of slaves to work in their new domain. He could procure these easily, but it would obviously have to be a fresh transaction. The price would depend on what they selected from what he had to offer. He was most surprised when Captain Coupland said, no, they did not agree with the use of slaves, but would be glad to employ native labourers and to pay them a wage. Here the King muttered something to his counsellors and one old man smiled toothlessly up at him.

9

The feast went on a very long time and when the King said he hoped that they would stay as his guests that evening and then rest and sleep, the night was almost upon them. As Mr Knox said that it was not possible in the circumstances to refuse, Sir George accepted the invitation gracefully.

The King began to pay a deal of attention to the person of Tolchard. His position as a priest interested him greatly. He too had his priests, he informed Tolchard. He had seen the churches built to their god in the townships where the Portuguese lived. Tolchard hoped that the King would enable him to expand further on the message of Christianity. He asked if they had a church or chapel in the town here? There had been a church many years ago, said the King. It had fallen into disuse when the Portuguese settlers departed. They were not sturdy people, he said. Most died. The others went up the coast. He did not know what happened to them after that. Their own 'church' was, as Mr Knox put it, 'what they call a juju house'.

'Jew?' Tolchard questioned him with a startled expression. 'Surely not?'

'No, no,' said Knox. 'You shall see it in our perambulation about the town. The King has promised us some entertainment this evening.'

Soon the King rose from his chair and their extended feast was at an official end. The royal retinue processed to see the King's entertainments.

As they went again between the narrowly crowded houses, the people stood in their doorways and examined them. And were examined in their turn.

'Fine-looking specimens of humanity,' said Coupland. 'See, Jeavons, not one of them is stunted or deformed or half starved as are some of our people in English towns.'

Sir George nodded genially as he went on his way as if he were a visiting king. The people answered him affably enough with smiles that showed off their white teeth, or with a right hand placed across the breast and Sir George began to ape this salute and drew laughter and more approval as they went on their way. All of the men they saw were armed, and Coupland had to admit to a twinge of unease at his party's unarmed state. Might it be that Tabellun, instead of leading them to some entertainment, was in fact luring them to their deaths?

Death, in a way, was, indeed, what came next to their eyes. Or rather, the dead. Mr Knox, who had been striding forth, almost at Tabellun's side, lagging just a little behind in respect, halted suddenly with the King. 'Mr Tolchard,' he said. 'The

King considers that you will find this of interest in showing the ways of his people in their religious practices.'

Tabellun had stopped in front of a large hut. It had the only substantial door yet seen. One of the King's ministers took what looked like a piece of chalk from a pouch and made a white cross on his forehead. He approached the door and opened it. The King invited his guests to enter after him.

The doorway let in enough light to see the interior. The floor appeared to be surfaced with large cobbles. In the centre of the hut a pole rose up through the thatch. From this pole hung human heads. But only the skulls, re-provided with eyes of white stones placed behind the sockets and painted with black pupils. These, Mr Knox said in a hushed voice, were the remains of the King's enemies, the chiefs of tribes unwise enough to challenge him, and the generals of their armies, taken as prisoner in battle and ceremonially slaughtered to provide these decorations. The floor cobbles were the skulls of the commoner sort.

'Unspeakable. Unspeakable,' the Reverend Tolchard breathed.

The King beamed at Mr Knox's translation of the priest's words. ('I told him, "Most remarkable. Most remarkable,"' Mr Knox explained later.)

Almost equally remarkable were the other furnishings of the hut. A huge allegorical painting, French or Spanish, its classical myth hidden behind dirt and gloom, in an elaborately moulded and gilded frame, leaned against one wall. An ornate sideboard, somewhat mildewed and holed by woodworm, supported an array of empty and dusty bottles and vials. Propped in each corner were spears and guns and shields – no doubt the property of their late owners displayed on the central pole.

When they emerged from the juju house, the sun was westering down and the town was cast into shadow. The Reverend Tolchard was silent and a little shaken, Caspar thought. Coupland asked if he was unwell, but Tolchard said no, and shook himself and smiled wanly. And as if released from a spell as they left the silent house of the dead, they heard the welling sound of drums. The King's procession led on until they came to an open area. There was a large crowd already there that parted as the King approached.

A dance was in progress.

Several trios of women were on the floor of the square. The trios circled about one another, closed, bumped hips, let out soft cries of joy, circled again, went in and out to one another, twisted, bumped hips again. The music for them was given by three male drummers on the far side, one with a set of small drums hung from his shoulder in front of him, the middle drummer with a large single drum, played at one end with both hands, the last with a sort of military kettle drum that he beat with a padded mallet. As Caspar listened, these three kept a shifting rhythm, now rising to a climax, then subsiding to an amiable tempo. And when the drumming grew to its greatest intensity the dancers cried out in ecstasy, and when it subsided they went into a gabbling good-natured gossiping song. The King had asked for his chair to be brought up and now sat and clapped and called to the women, and they answered with responses met with laughter by King and crowd.

There seemed no logical end to the dance. The drummers dropped their hands and the women simply stopped in their curving and curling ways and walked off gracefully into the crowd. Chairs in a multiplicity of sizes and shapes from simple kitchen chairs to armchairs of mahogany and velvet, all more or less distressed by time, appeared for the King's guests.

As did more drink. The French wine they had brought as a gift had disappeared long ago at the feast and now they drank palm wine. It was sufficiently strong.

Caspar had often thought, in long bleak dark English winters, of how men and women could possibly amuse themselves without good books to read, good food and drink, and the warmth of a fire. Certainly a great many of his fellow creatures in England had few such comforts but lived as the beasts do, searching for whatever warmth and food they could find, and if they could not find enough of either, then perishing in want and misery. But here was a people who seemed to exist without labour, in a state of easy merriment; to be sure they were not immune to disease and the end of all, but while they existed their bodies and movements seemed to say that all that would do for tomorrow: *carpe diem*. Caspar tried to imagine the grave ladies of his own society exchanging bumps of their buttocks in a good-humoured dance. But perhaps they did so in their extraordinary private world, and their revels were barred to him as a member of the male sex. Perhaps women in every country and every society possessed and enjoyed this suppressed, hidden vitality they showed only rarely to men. In love. In whatever that was. He thought of the girl in Santa Cruz.

He found himself seated once more next to Mr Knox. Knox said, 'I am afraid that you will have to suffer more of these rude amusements.' The sun went down. Fires lit the dance ground.

But Caspar had no difficulty in watching these 'rude amusements'. He reasoned that when we consider the plays of the Greeks with their masked choruses, their strange and alien morals, their grotesque humours coupled with austere and terrible revenges, how could we put our domestic entertainments in the balance? So it was that he watched the succession of dances that were performed that night with a sense of wonder – perhaps an intoxicated wonder, but nonetheless, wonder. Savage, yes. Unlettered – none, as far as he knew, of these people could read, nor was there any written literature but the scraps of Mohammedan law in their gris-gris. There was only the dance.

And here came a line of twenty or so men, emerging from one side, jogging up and down in concerted strides. Their bodies were painted and oiled so that their muscles and sinews shone in the firelight. Long loincloths of cerise and pink and indigo blue flapped on their thighs. Their elbows and knees and ankles were wrapped round with ruffs of bleached grass. In each hand a rattle was held and these were shaken in time to the drums as the men ducked and weaved around one another, forming again into a line, whereupon one of their fellows would detach himself from the middle of the line and place himself facing the others. Then they would shuffle slowly up and down no more than a foot or two, raising their knees in a slow, dreamlike march backwards and forward, forwards and back as the man in front went down on one knee and blew into a conch. It was as if he phrased and threw a question at them, because after each hortatory phrase on the conch, they answered him with a low rumbling chant. To which he seemed to pose another question, and they to answer it. And so it went on, with the constantly changing rhythm of the drums and call and answer of the dancers. Then, with a sudden declamatory shout from the dancers and a repeated thud-thud of the drums, the dance – the performance, the play – came to an abrupt end.

Now it was dark. The last light in the sky, which had left a few high tiny pink clouds, closed away and the only illumination was thrown by the fires about the square.

The sandy space was clear. The faces of the crowd, etched on the night, looked on, waiting for someone or something.

A tall figure enters, his face painted white except for exaggerated black eye sockets, his body painted with white bones on his black skin to show it as a fantastic articulated skeleton that moves in the firelight. After him, there comes a line of men, prancing and chanting monotonously. The first dancer is the principal: the chorus stand swaying and stretching out their arms as he dances before them, taunting them with urgent movements. But how fearsomely graceful he is, as he paces as a lion or capers as a monkey in front of them. It becomes clear that they are attempting to trap him. They form a semicircle, extending their hands towards him – from which he escapes, arms and legs whirling. They attempt to hold him again, and again he breaks free. But gradually they encircle him and he cannot now escape and they close in on him so that all that can be seen are his last frantic motions to be free and then he is somehow subsumed amongst them and disappears. They arch over him; they shuffle off together in a great many-backed beast, carrying their hidden brother away.

So it struck Caspar. And it struck him afterwards, in solitude, thinking about this night, that although these people might have no written literature – their songs seemed to be ritualistically delivered choruses, not individual constructions – their extended dances were dramas of which he could only crudely ascertain the meaning. That they were dramatic stories, of however symbolic and primitive an order, must be true.

It was also true that their party was by now pretty merry with the wine they had drunk. If Tabellun had so desired, now would have been the time to slit their throats. But the code of hospitality was strong here. The drink became stronger. The King had ordered his servant to bring more rum and large draughts were served. The dancing went on, now the women, now the men, never the two together; it was not a social mating occasion à la Vauxhall Gardens or my Lady Whittington's Ball, this dance. And Caspar thought how it would have been a very odd and glorious sight to have seen the consternation if these drummers had supplanted the fiddlers at one of their English functions. An interesting effect to see if his people, reclothed in loose flowing garb or stripped half naked, would look anything like as naturally elegant as these natives.

But the music so affected one of them that he rose up and began to sway about. This was Sir George, who made up in wallowing motions and energy what he lacked in grace. The King was most amused, turning in his chair to call to him and clap him on. He signalled for Sir George's tumbler, held in his swaying fist, to be refilled and Sir George held it out as steadily as he could while capering about on the spot. He then lifted the almost full tumbler of rum to his mouth, drank it off in one draught, stood stock still, looked about him in stupefaction and fell like a short fat oak backwards to the ground.

'I think', said Coupland, 'that it may be time for us to retire. Mr Knox, how's it to be done without offending the King? For how long do these things go on?'

'Sometimes half the night,' said Knox. 'We may not retire until the King does.'

So they sat on, while Sir George slept on the ground. Later the Reverend Tolchard wondered if it would have been better if they had danced, but the general opinion was that they would have obtruded and made themselves ridiculous in their heavy clothes and with their English bodies.

More wood had been piled on to the biggest fire in the square and a thousand sparks whirled into the night, but almost immediately it began to rain, and the moon was extinguished by cloud above the hills. It was raining in those large pendulous drops that stir up and pit the dust and sand as they fall. 'Thank the Lord,' the Reverend Tolchard breathed and then looked rather ashamed. The King rose abruptly and it was made plain that they were expected to do the same. They would be shown to their beds and the King wished them a pleasant night. He would be pleased to receive them in the morning. So, with a wave of his hand he walked off under palm leaves wielded as umbrellas, leading the way back to his great house. The rain came faster and thicker and sheet lightning lit the sky behind the hilltops.

Coupland and Caspar lay down on straw mattresses in a perfectly dry accommodation drummed upon by the rain. Before they slept, Coupland spoke in the darkness and though Caspar was more than half tipsy, he remembered his words.

'That', he said, 'was a most competent demonstration of

strength. They have numbers, arms, organisation and the will to drive hard bargains, I think. And, I fear, we have not shown ourselves in a good light. I think you will agree, Jeavons, that our Sir George has not acquitted himself well as our would-be king.'

10

The rain continued heavy all that night and they slept heavy, too. It was not until full eight in the morning that Caspar woke. The low cot beside his was empty and he could hear Coupland talking in the next hut to Sir George, who was complaining of the filthy drink he had been given the night before. Caspar roused himself. A bowl of water had been placed inside the doorway and a piece of cloth intended as a towel. He washed his face vigorously and dried, surprised to find the cloth soft and clean smelling. He needed light and air and made his way through the huts, away from their voices, until he came to the court where they had held their palaver.

The rain had stopped but the sky was grey and full of swagging clouds that looked full of more rain. The wind was very fresh; above the King's house the long red and blue pennants he had hoisted and the Union flag they had given to him stood almost straight in the wind. Caspar retraced his steps and, not finding or hearing Coupland, went on through to the outermost doorway and found him looking out at the tops of the palm trees swaying above the huts.

He was afraid, he said, that Sir George was at the moment

indisposed and had given out his desire to stay there for at least a few hours. Coupland did not think anyway that they should be sailing in this weather in waters they did not know. 'The sea will be very up with this wind,' he said. They would not sail today unless it abated. They must busy themselves organising what supplies of rice and grain, livestock and such like were needed to replenish their stores. He called out to Jackson, who was billeted with the seamen in a hut across from the palace.

Jackson reported that he had been up early and down to the boat to see if everything was safe there. Nothing had been attempted and the guard they had placed had not been bothered in the night. Children from the village had followed him there and back, and behind them had trailed a couple of Tabellun's men, fully armed.

'But nothing untoward?' asked Coupland.

'A peaceful place,' said Jackson.

Coupland smiled at Caspar and then at Jackson. 'Good man,' he said. 'I want you to take two seamen, row out to the cutter and bring the trade goods. You can get a list of what's required from Sir George. When that gentleman is fully awake again. In the meantime please go and find Mr Knox and ask him to come to us so that we can parley with the King.'

'You put a great deal of trust in that man,' Caspar said when Jackson had gone.

'He is a good man and a damned useful one,' said Coupland. 'I think sometimes he is a walking example of what we hope to achieve here. A free, intelligent man, who can help us build our colony. I need to go back to our room – I suppose we can call it that.'

Caspar sat on his cot as Coupland searched amongst some papers in his bag.

'Aren't you afraid of – well, resentment or anger from some of the others. You know what I've heard against him from Meares.'

'Jackson will be fine. As to Meares and his lot – to paraphrase Signor Machiavelli – while I am in command on board I am their prince and they are the servants of a prince and until they get a prince of their own, God help them, they will not touch me.'

'And when we are on the island? The Committee will be in charge then, will it not?'

As if overhearing them, there came through the wall from the next room a sudden shuddering snore.

'Ah, yes – the Committee,' said Coupland.

One of the King's servants, coughing discreetly before shouldering aside the mat over the entrance to their room, brought in a wooden tray on which were arrayed a number of glass tumblers, each one two-thirds filled with rum, from the smell.

'Breakfast, I think,' said Coupland. 'We'd better take one.'

They took two glasses and raised them to their lips and sipped. Satisfied, the servant bowed and went on his way. Coupland put his glass on the floor without taking a drop more. 'A little early for me,' he said.

But the steward hadn't gone far. They heard Sir George's voice, plaintive and reedy asking that his thanks be conveyed to the King. Then silence as he presumably took his draught. Followed by a long grunt of approval and the sound of him settling himself once again on his cot.

Knox came in and said that they must wait on the King's pleasure. They should make a list of what they would like to buy and he would try and negotiate a fair price.

'For gold?' asked Coupland.

'For gold,' said Knox. 'I shouldn't, if I were you, tell too many about your gold. There are very long ears on the coast.'

Coupland compiled the list of provisions needed. Knox perused it, made one or two suggestions and asked what limit they would go to so that he might haggle with the King. Fully prepared for his transactions, he went away.

They could hear the voices of women and the cries of children nearby. 'How's your head?' Coupland asked, holding up a paper to the light and squinting at it.

'Not too bad,' said Caspar, laughing.

'One lesson you learn in the Navy is how to drink.' Coupland lifted another paper to the light and read on.

'I should have brought a book,' said Caspar. 'At least I could have amused myself.'

Coupland continued to read but said rather forcibly that Caspar could have amused all of them by reading a book aloud. But he softened. 'I'm a great reader myself. Plenty of time on board.'

'We all looked up to you at Ratcliffe,' said Caspar. 'We thought you'd be a great man. Well – you are.'

'Good of you to say so, we'll have to wait and see, won't we?'

There was silence for a moment.

'Why did you leave?' asked Caspar, feeling immediately that he should not have.

But Coupland was easy enough with the question. 'Simple. Money. Or lack of. Pelf. I hope you think yourself lucky that we both went to Ratcliffe and you now find yourself here. Didn't remember you much from school – you were one of the little ones – but your estate was only a few miles from my father's old parish. Knew the name – Jeavons. Read your book of verses. That's why I got in touch with you about this expedition. Thought a literary chap would be just the thing to take to an African island.'

Caspar felt a little embarrassed. 'I'm sorry that I don't remember your father. We went to church in the village.'

'I said his old parish. He died when I was young. That's why I left the school. Fell on hard times.'

Coupland seemed in the mood to talk – a rare enough occurrence. His father had left a widow with three children. Coupland was then just fourteen years old.

'Perhaps I should have become a parson too, like father,' he said and laughed. But his widowed mother had taken the advice of her uncle, a retired military man, who recommended either the Army or Navy.

'I chose the Navy.' For no better reason than that there was a broadish stream flowing at the bottom of the rectory garden and he had played endless battles with his brothers in the old falling-apart hulk of a rowing boat moored, or rather half sunk, under the willow.

He had become a rather elderly midshipman in a ship of the line. They usually start at about twelve or thirteen, he said, so he was quite the man amongst them. Within three months he had seen action in the West Indies.

Coupland fell quiet as Knox came back in.

The King would be pleased to deal with them; rice, flour and vegetables would be furnished; he would have gold in a rental for his people who would be their *grumetas*, their word for labourers. An amount would be payable each month for each man. A mixture of goods would suffice for payment of the other goods. They could take with them what they could carry; the rest he would ferry to the island in the next few days. He asked particularly for rum and tobacco. His stock was running low and they had no tobacco plants.

'And by the way,' said Knox, 'the King has asked me to fetch the Reverend Tolchard to him. He is most taken with our priest.'

'Where is Tolchard at present?'

'I understand he is making a tour of the town. No doubt spying out a suitable site to build a church. Or cathedral. I have to go and find him. He shouldn't be difficult to spot.'

II

The Reverend Tolchard had never before travelled out of England. The whole world was a puzzling place but his ignorance of its ways did not bother him in the sense of wanting to learn more about them. It was the sheer perversity of others that bewildered him. The alien world began a score or so miles across the Channel with the French and their papist ways and radiated out in ever more bizarre and unholy practices the further one went from his own small green island where the true Lord was worshipped. And now he was in this outlandish and heathen place.

It had ceased to rain but the ground had turned muddy. Eyes watched him from inside the huts; some men and women about in the lanes between the houses made way for him with an odd sort of amusement – could it be? – on their faces.

He came to the edge of the town where a gate in the bamboo fence was open. He was looking out over a field of planted vegetables of some sort, half grown, their large dark green leaves half beaten to the earth by the late rain. A dog came and stood beside him. The animal was also looking out to the field. The view quickly ceased to interest and it turned and wandered off. The clouds were breaking up, moving fast, with rents and streaks of brilliant blue sky opening between them.

Where were the signs of industry, the unceasing industry that most people in England needed to perform in order to earn the merest pittance? The people here all appeared tall and strong and well dressed – after their barbarous fashion. They were abundantly supplied by the trees, swagged with fruit. The cattle further off beyond the vegetable field, the hens scratching before the huts; all these had been given most bountifully by the Lord. But for what in return? And how could these people render their thanks unto God when they did not know of his existence or, worse, denied him?

He heard voices raised in loud, joshing unintelligible banter that ended in laughter. A language never, he would guess, written down; nothing written except those miserable scraps of paper with the Prophet's words on them. The little sack still dangled from the left sleeve of his cassock. How did they prosper so, without the Lord? He had, of course, created this place – this shore, these woods, these people. They must, even in their ignorance, need the solace and promise of holy salvation. All was for some purpose. And all at once he was overwhelmed by the thought that he had been sent here on a holy mission. To show to these poor savages their true state. To demonstrate why they had been created and to whom they owed their very earthly existence. He, Peter Tolchard, was the chosen instrument of the Lord.

Others, the Portuguese Catholics, had been here, and they had failed in their mission. Truly, the Lord had stayed his hand. After all, the poor Greeks, despite their much vaunted philosophies and assembly of gods and divinities, had had to wait for two thousand years after the Creation until the Son of God, our Lord, walked on the earth and bestowed his love and blessing on all living creatures . . .

He must make a start.

His hands clenched tightly, his head almost swirling, the Reverend Peter Tolchard strode back the way he had come, his heart thumping in intense excitement.

12

Mr Knox stood on the open ground before the King's palace and thought of the commission he would make handling the buying of supplies for this expedition. He had come to the conclusion that Sir George and the old king were both good men to do business with. One of them was a great fool and the other a shrewd leader of men: he could make money from both. The half-smile that often came to definition on Mr Knox's lips when he was on his own and thinking of his fellow men made a brief appearance. It was so very easy for a sharp-witted man to make a good living in these parts. There was always need for a shadow to slip between natives and Arabs and whites, a man who understood lingoes and could make deals so that each party had no complete knowledge of what exactly he had arranged. It was his mastery of the obscurest corners of agreements that had garnered over the years the goods and money that had built him a warehouse down the coast in Sierra Leone and a house amongst the few good whites.

His passage out had been illuminating and profitable. What he was to do with this strange party he did not know. He had never come across such a rabble. There were idealists amongst them, certainly, the ones who wanted to remake man in their own image. But only God could make or change a man. They would come to realise that – or come to grief.

Mr Knox saw the world as a whole and solid construction

that was neither arranged for his convenience nor obstructive to it. He sought out those pieces of the world that were most congenial to him and ignored the rest. The affairs of others were nothing to do with him; they must sink or swim according to their own talents. Such a view did not rule out pity or tenderness on a purely individual level, but he could not feel pity for a mass of generality of slaves, for the idea of the slave. He did not own slaves and could see no circumstances in which he would want to, but he saw, simply as a matter of common sense, that there would be no possible advantage in abandoning such a lucrative trade. The blacks here on the coast – the King and his court and those he traded with – he knew only as free men. The two classes were different: the free man and the slave. Fate had separated the two, what was the point in trying to destroy the difference? It would simply reverse the roles. Mr Knox knew well enough that, without strength or position, any man might become a slave. But not a white man. Such a notion might be held by the Arabs up north, but down here it was unheard of. A white man walking in a line of chained black slaves would be immediately plucked out and saved. By other white men.

Knox sometimes thought he could detect a deeply hidden, almost contemptuous streak in Tabellun's attitude towards the white man. Could it be that the blacks were consummate actors, playing parts for the white man, and being quite other creatures amongst themselves?

The King was a great warrior, in control of this run of the coast for nearly forty years. His subjects were numerous and strong. Apart from a few weeks in each year when they planted their fields, the men were hunters – of beasts or men. Why should they fear this party of people with their unwholesome white skins? Knox had witnessed the revulsion mixed with amusement the natives had shown when he and some Portuguese had bathed naked off a beach. White apes they had been called.

Ah, there was our man of God.

The Reverend Tolchard came from between the huts and stood on the edge of the square. He took off his broad hat and wiped his forehead with a large white handkerchief. But he did not look bothered by the sun or the oppressive atmosphere, rather his face had a look of radiant happiness. The sort of glory that comes on a man who has been drinking.

'Hello, there,' shouted Knox. 'It's getting hot, eh? Time to come inside, my dear sir, I think.'

He was sober, it now appeared to Knox, but wonderfully wound up over something.

'I know why I am here,' Tolchard said with great excitement. 'Mr Knox – I know why I have been brought to this place.'

'Indeed,' said Knox.

'It's important that we begin our work at once. Have you a Bible or a New Testament in Portuguese that I may borrow? I need to teach myself the language and to spread the Word and, as I may say that I know the Gospels tolerably well –'

'I'm afraid not. But come along, old chap.' He took Tolchard's arm. 'You've been summoned. Old Tabellun wants to see you. Your chief heathen, I think.'

'Don't make light, Mr Knox, of my intentions.'

'Even in darkness?' Knox laughed as he guided Tolchard through the dark interiors that led to the King's inner chamber.

13

Tabellun sat in his high-backed chair. On the wall behind him hung a huge mirror in an elaborately gilded frame that had lost here and there a piece of moulded decoration. Before him were two wooden armchairs with white and pink striped silk covering on their padded seats. Some of his women sat on a bench to his right. His priest was on a low stool at his left hand. The King had changed into a pair of trousers of white and black checks and a plum-coloured long coat. At his neck he wore a long scarf of wide stripes of the most extraordinarily vivid colours over a canary yellow shirt. He bowed his head slightly as the two men entered and indicated that they should be seated. He spoke to Knox and Knox turned to Tolchard.

'The King would like to hear about our god or gods. He has a great interest in our beliefs. Be brief and allow me to translate.'

Tolchard stood. Knox saw that he was trembling, but not through fear.

'The King is very kind to wish to hear about our religion,' said Tolchard. His Majesty would, he truly and sincerely hoped and desired, come to see the truth of his message and so be welcomed into the care of our Lord Jesus Christ.

Knox's rapid translation seemed to be a great deal shorter than Tolchard's opening statement.

Who was this Christ? Tabellun asked. And heard, in Knox's

rendering of Tolchard's enthusiastic speech, that Christ was the son of God. That God had sent his only son into the world. That Christ had moved amongst the people and spread the Word of God and had performed miracles . . .

Miracles?

Great magic, Knox told him. Healing the sick. Raising the dead. Converting water into wine.

'He became a great king, then?' asked the King.

Knox repeated this to Tolchard, who said, 'No. Anything but. He went as a poor man amongst the poor. As a teacher amongst the Pharisees.'

'A great warrior?' asked the King.

'No. When struck he turned the other cheek.'

'Did he have no people? No army to fight for him?'

'No,' said Tolchard with an exalted air. 'Our Lord was taken by soldiers and crucified. He went to his death to take on all our sins to himself, to die so that all men might be saved.'

'He was killed without fighting?'

'To save mankind. And after three days he rose again and later ascended to heaven, there to sit at his father's right hand and there to reign in glory for evermore.'

'He is still there?' asked the King.

'He is still there,' said Tolchard triumphantly.

'And what of men? Do they rise again?'

'Yes, at the Day of Judgement. When they die they go to heaven – if they have led virtuous lives. If they have not, they go to hell and there suffer eternal punishment.'

'But they all die?'

'In that sense, yes. But at the last great judgement all will rise from their graves and be judged.'

'Again?'

'No, not again. Not as such,' said Tolchard.

'But if they have died where do they go to await this day?'

'They wait.'

'It seems a shame to wake them,' said the King and rested

back in his chair. 'Let my priest tell you a story about death,' he said.

The old man rose at the King's signal. He began to speak in a high reedy voice, like a door swinging slowly back and forth and creaking in the wind. But his tongue or his way of talking made him completely unintelligible to Mr Knox. The King saw this and let the old man wail on a little longer and then terminated his tale with a clap of his hands and words that Knox did not bother to translate, but that meant obviously: Enough. Enough. I will tell the tale. He signalled for Knox to translate and fixed Tolchard with a fierce glare and asked, 'Your god – you say he made the world?'

'In seven days,' said Tolchard piously.

'Ha. Ours in four.' The King laughed. 'Now the story.

'It is indubitably true that god,' he began 'our god and yours, which assuredly are the same god, there being only one god – created all mankind and all the creatures of the earth. And when he created man and saw that he would grow old and die, he took pity on his creation. He said, "Why should they be born only to suffer and die or to be happy and then die? I say that they shall live and die but then shall rise again."

'He had placed men on earth in a good and fruitful place but knew that he must tell them of their fate so that if they did become old and suffered they should not despair.

'He had two messengers at his side: one was the turtle and the other the mountain hare. And the turtle begged to be allowed to take the good message to man. He had so little to do and so much time to do it in. So god gave him the message to take to man and it was this, in god's words, "As I die and dying live, so you shall also die, and dying live, as do the sun and moon." So the turtle started, slowly, slowly, on his journey. But on his way he was overtaken by the hare, jealous that he had not been chosen, who asked him what errand he was bound on. And the turtle told him the words he was taking to man and the hare said, "Well, let me take the message. I can run so very much faster than you."

'So off the hare ran and the turtle plodded on. When the hare reached the dwellings of man he gathered a crowd and said, "God has sent me to tell you that as I die and shall not live again, so you shall die and live no more. Live for the day, my friends. Eat, drink and love."

'When the poor turtle arrived and gave them the true message he was not believed and was treated as all false prophets are by being overturned, killed and eaten up in a great feast.

'And so man, stupid and wayward as he has been ever since, was condemned by god to grow old and never to rise again.

'The priest', said the King through Knox, 'could have told it better, but no one can understand him any longer.'

'But surely', said the Reverend Tolchard, 'the hare was possessed by the devil and delivered a wholly wrong message to man?'

Knox raised his hand and smiled warmly on Tolchard. 'Allow me, Mr Tolchard.' He proceeded to address the King in a short speech that evidently pleased him mightily. He laughed and moved his head gravely up and down in Tolchard's direction.

'I would be most grateful, Mr Knox, if you would ask His Majesty if he would be kind enough to accept this small gift. A copy of the Gospels. In English alas – but I should be pleased to read and discourse upon any passages . . .'

'Yes, yes.' Knox took the book. 'An object of limited utility here, I am afraid.' He spoke again, pointing back to Tolchard, and then gravely presented the book to the King, who held it between his hands, murmured a few words as he gazed down at it, and then, without opening it, handed it to his priest and addressed Knox.

'He thanks you very much for the gift of this holy book,' said Knox. 'He says he has books. From the fort. The Portuguese left them behind. One of them has a picture of our crucified Lord. He was shown this by one of their priests.'

Tabellun rapped on the floor with his staff. He rose to go,

while his priest stepped forward and started to speak in his high swaying voice.

Knox said in a whisper, 'We are excused. His Majesty has had enough of theological debate. We may go. He will send the books to us.'

'But . . .'

'Come, Mr Tolchard. While the going is good.'

Tolchard followed Knox through the dark huts again. 'What did you tell him? I had no chance to expand on my message from Christ.'

'I told him how enlightened you were by the tale of the hare and the turtle. Strange how these tales have common ancestries with our own legends, eh?'

They came out into the daylight.

'His tale was absurd and irreligious. Blasphemous even.'

'Where do you suppose the others are?' said Knox evenly. 'I think we should find them, don't you?'

14

Tuesday, June 5th

My dear Torrington, we have been here for days in King Tabellun's town and are waiting for the weather to clear. I thought I should go mad, but the Reverend Tolchard kindly allowed me to borrow his pocket notebook and pen and ink so that I may while away the time composing this letter.

A tedious time indeed. Tabellun has evidently concluded that he has done all he should in providing entertainment for his guests. When Sir George – at last risen, his face rubicund and unshaven – today demanded to see the King, one of the chamberlains, or whatever they should be called, sent word through Mr Knox that the King was leaving to go upriver. Mr Knox hurried off on some business before the King should go.

Jackson, meanwhile, has seen very well to the unloading of our goods in payment for the cession and to the stowing of the cutter with the rice and fruit and vegetables the King has sold us. Our labourers must follow. Sir George has paid for three months of their labour, but Coupland was impatient to get back to the ship and to set about our lawful occupation of the island.

Yesterday evening the Reverend Tolchard was very excited when Mr Knox returned carrying a bundle wrapped in sacking. It had been given to him by one of the King's sons who reigns in his absence. When opened, the sacking revealed the books of which the King had spoken. They were mildewed and one fell to pieces as Tolchard handled them, some of the pages falling out, one drifting and settling on the dirt floor to show a most obscene engraving of a priest, who kneeling, observed through a gap in the bed curtains the sexual congress of a girl and a man. Mr Knox laughed and, saying, 'I'll take that,' leaned over and whisked the lewd print into his coat pocket. But Tolchard had his prize – a Bible in Portuguese.

'With this one gift from our Lord I shall be able to learn. And to teach,' he informed us. He began to read from the Holy Book until Mr Knox covered his ears and said, 'Nothing against your orthodoxy, my dear vicar. But your pronunciation leaves more than a little to be desired.'

Coupland counselled we should get well rested as he

had decided to sail this morning if the wind was in the least favourable.

Rest was easier spoken about than achieved. Whatever riots were arranged by the natives for the evening – wrestling matches, dancing, or whatever – all had to be accompanied by the drummers, and the drums continued half the night. Tolchard was particularly bothered by the sound.

'How can they work the next day?' he enquired rattily. Sir George said that he had not observed anyone doing any work as such.

'Oh, they do work,' said Knox. 'When they have to. Their king is a warrior and a trader. You see how well dressed and armed are his people. They grow or pick or hunt what they need to eat. They work to supply a sufficiency, not to warehouse an excess. They don't engage in the slave trade. But when they go to war their prisoners are sold to the traders. They would be fools not to do this. If Tabellun did not procure slaves for the traders and protect his own people by the arms he can buy from his profits, then his own people would fall prey.'

'When they come to work for us as free men they will have no need of that dirty commerce,' said Coupland.

'And they will come to see the evil and errors they have fallen into,' said Tolchard.

'How do you mean – that they have in some way fallen?' said Knox. 'That in some previous century they were members of the Anglican communion and have deserted that faith?'

'Of course not. But once I have mastered their language, or they ours, then they will be converted and believe in our Lord.'

'They need example, not lectures,' said Knox. 'The Christians that they see daily and have seen for many years are traders in human flesh, drunkards, womanisers, common sailors. If you say to Tabellun that he may not have four wives, taken quite legally, or that he must give up drinking rum because these things are sinful he will point out to you the habits of our own countrymen in these parts – who have introduced prostitution, tobacco and rum all along the coast, whereas these are unknown in the back country.'

'The Word of our Lord conquers all.'

'I don't mean to slight or insult you, my dear sir,' said Knox, 'but I had the greatest difficulty in persuading the King that you were not quite mad. The tenets of the faith that you described to him sounded so unnatural and bizarre that it would take a regiment of guards to convert him, because, I can assure you, nothing else will.'

'Perhaps that's what they need,' said Sir George. 'Redcoats would soon point out the error of their ways, what?' And he laughed warmly.

Such argument passed away the evening until we retired. The drums accompanied our conversation and then our attempts at slumber. I went to sleep at last and was woken, I suppose, by unexpected silence, the lack of their sound sometime in the early hours. It was near enough dawn, I reckoned. I could not sleep so got up and went outside. The stars were pricked out brilliantly above me and the half-moon cast my shadow as I walked. I went down towards the sea and came out on the edge of the beach. I walked down. There were figures slumped on the sand: our sailors wrapped in whatever cloths they could get against the cool night. By our boat a figure was seated, looking out to sea. It was Jackson. I had completely forgotten about him.

The weather is clearing now and we hope to sail this afternoon.

15

Coupland sighted the *Pharaoh* a little before sundown. The ship's familiar outline was obscured by walls of canvas and tarpaulin that made a box-like tent on the upper deck. On the shore of the island, several small tents had been erected. Women and children stood around a fire up the beach, near where the woods began. A group of men were disporting themselves naked on the rackety jetty. They were diving in, swimming back and hoisting themselves up again and repeating the dose. He could hear their laughter over the water.

The cutter sailed slowly closer in.

'The damn fools,' said Coupland. 'What do they think they are about?'

Sir George, coming to his side, said, 'Trouble, old man?'

'I gave strict instructions, the Committee signed them, they were posted, that no member of our party was to go ashore until the island was secured. Our treaty, Sir George, if I may remind you, does not come into force until a couple more days from now. That was to give Tabellun time to spread the word amongst his people. Now these silly fools have broken our word for us.'

The thundercloud of Coupland's anger hovered over all of them as they were rowed back to the ship. The sun-like face of Dr Owen appeared over the rail. His welcome to Coupland was ironical: while they had been away certain events had transpired. Sickness. Drunkenness. The two were not intimately related, but had occurred at the same time. There had been a breakdown of order and what might be called general good conduct.

'I left Lieutenant Fortescue in control of the ship,' Coupland said with a cold expression to his tone. 'But Sir George left you and Mr Crabtree in charge of the settlers.'

'Well,' said Dr Owen, 'I cannot answer for Mr Crabtree, but can only say that the colonists, in the person of Mr Meares, informed me that I could put my authority up my arse. I had no real sanction to gainsay this suggestion. Perhaps you will now take personal command.' Here he made a deep, mock-heroic bow to the Captain.

'Where's Crabtree?' Sir George asked.

'Unfortunately,' said Owen, 'Mr Crabtree is not here.'

'Where is he?'

'I have no idea. He went ashore. In an attempt, I believe, to keep some sort of order amongst the colonists. The last I saw of him, he and Mr Meares and a few others disappeared amongst the trees there.' He pointed to the shore.

'How long have they been gone?'

'Since around ten this morning – I don't know what that is in your sea watches, or if our land watches keep the right time here.'

'Well, where have they gone?'

'Hunting, I think. They had a rare old feast last night of venison from a deer they shot. Though I would have let it hang a little longer for good taste. I presume they have caught something this afternoon. I heard gunfire a little earlier.'

'What is everyone else doing?' Sir George asked irritably.

'There are seamen about. There, there, up there, along there. I presume they are not invisible to you?' And indeed there were sailors, lounging about or sitting on coils of rope and steps.

'I mean the people. Our people,' said Sir George. 'Are you intoxicated, sir?'

'Not particularly more nor less,' said the doctor. 'But I am, though, damnably tired. There has not been much rest here while you were away. We have sickness aboard.'

'Sickness? What sickness?'

'A fever. We have a dozen or so down with it and I fear others may follow unless we can extirpate the cause and there seems little chance of that.'

'And where are they?'

'I have confined them to one area below. You needn't fear for yourself.'

Sir George's face reddened. 'Do not be so insolent. You will prepare a report on the medical situation here together with your recommendations.'

'Your servant, sir,' said the doctor, bowing low. Mr Knox smiled behind Sir George's back.

'Present your report tonight, after dinner,' Sir George shouted and hurried off to the ladder down to the stern cabin, his thick body hunched in anger.

Coupland addressed the Lieutenant. 'What of the ship, Mr Fortescue?'

'As far as that goes, Captain Coupland, I think matters are tolerably in hand. I have no power over those . . .' He pointed to the island. The divers had ceased their gambolling and were looking towards the ship, holding their hands over their privates. From a long way off came the crackle of musket fire.

'Mr Meares is hunting,' Coupland observed. 'Make the longboat ready. I'll go ashore with a dozen men. Armed, if you please. Arrange that, will you, Jeavons? Doctor – thank you for your efforts. Is there no one you can put in charge while you rest and prepare your report?'

'My wife and Mrs Hood can be employed as useful nurses. They have proved themselves capable before.'

'Very well. Get some rest. I shall see you again this evening.'

Coupland turned to Caspar, or rather on him, and asked savagely why he had not got about his business in arming the men and why was he standing there grinning like a loon?

16

The first person they saw on landing was Hood, the carpenter. He stood alone on the jetty, the merrymakers having made off further up the beach where they were busy dressing themselves by the fire.

'I'm sorry to greet you in such a ragged manner, Captain,' said Hood. He explained that some of the colonists, led by Meares, had insisted on landing on the island, and had been shooting deer and other game. There had been feasts at night and much drinking, he said. Caspar felt sorry for the slight man standing, cap twisted in his hands, before the righteous and robust Coupland. They had run low of fresh water, said Hood, and the streams on the island were no good for replenishing their supply.

'What do you mean, man?' Coupland demanded. 'That everyone is living on wine? What is that?'

He pointed to the trickling water making its slow way down the beach through a delta of tiny rivulets in the sand. They were not natural streams, Hood repeated: if there were no more rain they would dry out by evening. The colonists had attempted to dig a well on the beach, leaving a mound of spoil like a huge molehill. There was water down there, but brackish. Some had drunk it and some of those were sick now. Dr Owen had given instructions for tarpaulins to be rigged on ship to catch the rainwater.

'We were told', said Coupland, 'that the island had fresh water from its hills. What has become of that?'

'There's none to be seen,' said Hood. 'Mr Crabtree and the doctor have been digging about, but have found no water.'

'A proper search must be instituted,' said Coupland. 'It is absurd. There are animals here and standing water. It cannot rain all the time. The pools must be replenished by underground springs.'

'What about the rice fields?' Caspar asked.

'There's plenty of rain in the rainy season,' said Coupland with great irritation. 'But the ground will be waterlogged and useless for anything else until it dries out. And that fire, Hood. How are they building their fire? Those look good spars they are using to feed it.'

'They build one in the evening so that they can roast whatever the men bring back,' said Hood. 'They say they won't eat on board ship. It stinks and is unhealthy. They're breaking up timbers from the old huts.'

'The fools are consuming the only shelter we have.'

'I am afraid they are of no use for that, sir,' said Hood. 'The Portuguese huts. You can see where the door has fallen off. You go to them and you can put your finger through like paper. I pulled at that door and it fell into dust, just a pile of dust. I don't think there's much we can save there at all. The ants have eaten them away and left only a shell.'

'There must be something we can use. The timbers they are burning look solid enough. Come.'

Coupland began to march up the beach, signalling to Caspar and Hood to follow. The crowd at the fire was composed mostly of women and children but with also a few of the men who had been sporting on the jetty and who would not meet Coupland's eyes.

Coupland squared his shoulders. He halted a few yards off. He hallooed them in an outwardly cheery voice. How, he asked, were they enjoying their new home? Their fire was doing very well. Well enough, he said, for anyone from miles about to see it. Night would be on them soon and suddenly. It was not safe here. Until they had established themselves they must beware of others. He grew sterner. They were behaving as if celebrating some holiday. He was sorry to spoil their feasting. He would leave some of the men here until the hunters came back and let them cook their meat and they would bring it on board to share with all. For theirs was a common enterprise. A commonwealth.

As he spoke the sun dipped down and the sky purpled above. Coupland placed his men and got the beach party of settlers to gather up their belongings and make ready to return to the ship. For return they must assuredly do, he told them. He could not guarantee their safety here at night.

'We weren't doing too bad here the last few nights,' said one of these men in an aggrieved voice.

He might do very badly indeed, said Coupland, unless he and the others returned to the ship before night set in.

'Who's to do badly then?' The voice came out of the trees and was followed by its owner, Meares. He carried a musket. Two men followed him from the wood. Between them a dead deer was hung from its bound feet on a pole bowed by the weight. One more man, carrying three guns, one slung over each shoulder and one in his hands, followed. None of the men looked to have shaved for days. Meares beckoned to his carriers and they coolly dumped their load at the feet of Coupland.

The Captain equally coolly gave them thanks for their hunting trip and was sure that their gift would be greatly appreciated by all on board. Perhaps it should hang a little, but in this warm climate that might not be such a good idea. Then he repeated his commands: they all must return to the ship. He would allow two men to remain, those capable of dressing and roasting the beast. Four men would be left here as guard and they would bring the cooked meat on board when ready.

'Captain Coupland, neither these men nor myself are under your command. We'll do as we wish.'

'No, sir,' said Coupland. 'You are under my command here just as you are on board. I don't think you are in a position to try the matter here and now, are you?'

Meares looked at Coupland's armed sailors, then smiled. 'Not here. Not here, Captain Coupland. Some other time and place, perhaps. But I want it recorded by your little man there', he pointed at Caspar, 'that I shall complain to the Committee at their next meeting. You have force here, Captain, but not I think the right to use it.'

'That would be my decision, Mr Meares,' said Coupland. 'But you are welcome to put your case to the Committee at any time. Now, shall we go?'

So, the colonists were herded down the beach to the jetty and there crammed into the longboat. Coupland said that he would send the boat back for Caspar and Hood, the sentries and, of course, the deer and Meares.

'You're a poet, eh, Mr Jeavons?' Meares said, laughing. 'You should be able to make something out of that rhyme.'

17

In the cramped cabin he shared with his wife, his bottles of spirits and medicines, jars of ointment, packets of powders and his case of instruments, Dr Owen rested on the lower bunk. Phoebe was with Mrs Hood tending to the sick. He reached under the bunk and brought up a bottle of brandy.

He took a swig. 'Fools, fools,' he sighed. His journal, a bundle of sheets of paper folded into half, lay on his chest. Now he would add to the record of the past few days so as to present a full account to the Committee. First, to see what he had got thus far, he began to read, twisting the paper to catch the light from the lantern:

It is plain to me that a ship is a masculine construction, a male creature butting its head through the waters, handled and manoeuvred by physically strong men; the whole a triumph against nature. It is assuredly not a place for women and children, nor indeed any of God's creatures except poor mariners. It is a place in flux and danger afloat on an immeasurably deep and dangerous water that is poisonous to us humans. Above the waterline we are subjected to all the extremes of storm and tempest, the beating sun and soaking rain. The constant motion and rolling of the ship, its ghastly groans and creaks as timbers grind and twist one against the other and the howling, whistling and jangling and flapping of sheet and sail and rope and chain are enough to drive a landsman insane. I suppose it is the continuing variety of these torments and the occasional intermission of them that renders them almost tolerable. At least, one does not know which is coming next. A ship is also a carrier – of its men, but also a butter dish for flies, a breeding ground for rats – and is manned by shaven apes for sailors, officered by young fools and mismanaged by its owners. After weeks of this ill-usage of our innocent passengers, the hardships and privations of the voyage out are at an end. All at an end. Only, not at a complete end, for now I learn that though we are still and have reached our destination, we must all remain on board.

The ship is now anchored in the strait between our island and the mainland of the continent of Africa. We must have fresh water from the island as soon as possible because ours is nearly gone. Perhaps now we will have the opportunity, much needed, to clean the ship. The mass of passengers sleeping on the lower deck, and indeed the close inhabitation of virtually every spare area on board, is not conducive to good health. We piss and shit into buckets, which at least on the open sea can be cast into the vast saline expanse. To heave to here and stay for how long, cooped up on board, does not bear much thinking about, especially now that sickness is amongst us. It is important that we get ashore as soon as possible – but who knows what awaits us there? In this new world of alternating heat and rain, or a mixture of the two in an uncomfortably warm moisture, God knows what invisible poisons lurk?

(On a personal note, the cook tells me that our stores of whisky and gin are almost done, though we have rum and Madeira and some very indifferent French claret remaining. It strikes me now that very soon there will be no further supply of those ardent spirits that my body likes and demands to see me through the day. It is unlikely that the local population have such advanced methods of self-intoxication at their command. Hood seems a capable man – I shall get him to build me a still and the rich ripe fruits of this island shall be scientifically transformed into nectar.)

He laid down the papers and took another swig of his bottle. Then he began to read again:

It seems to my mind, as an old man, an old drunken man, that we on this stalled ship are altogether too sanguine about our prospects for a happy life in this new place. Today we have sat at anchor all day while splendid Sir George, intrepid Captain Coupland, foxy Mr Knox, and the canting vicar have gone on an embassy to the king of these parts. They intend to purchase our freehold to the island and come to amicable agreements with the native population. The sun beat down on us. The women who had been on deck airing their bedding retired to be faint below. The children, who had been running hither and thither in great excitement, dropped away after a while to play or mope with their mothers. Or, if very young, to mewl discontentedly. The men sat about, shifting like cats from shade to shade. There was the sound of hammering and banging as Hood and his assistants began to prepare canvas screens for our shelter in the giant house into which the ship is to be converted. Towards noon, stripes barred the sun, the whole sea became darkened with cloud shadow and oceanic rain was suddenly upon us. It rained very heavily for about half an hour and then more lightly for a further hour. Then the sky cleared and the ship steamed and sweated.

My work has been relatively slight on our voyage out, considering the fact that we are about the size of a village. Perhaps the composition of our crew lends a certain vividness to their complaints not usually met with in the same quantity in an English village. So that I have five gonorrhoeal seamen whom I am treating with nitric acid. Two eye infections of a stubborn kind (the salty sea often clears these, but now we are at rest they will flare up again). These men can perform light duties, but their eyelids gumming together makes difficult any rigging or other work that requires good sight and judgement. One of them is so myopic it is a wonder that he can recognise the farthest limits of the ship or what that great fluid medium is in which we float. The passengers, much more than the crew, being unused to the seafaring diet, suffer from loose motions and dry bellyache – this is distressing for the children who suffer great pain. Other injuries to the crew consist mainly of sprains and broken fingers or cuts. Luckily none of these has resulted in further infection, because in the case of a deep cut or small broken bone it is almost impossible to keep the wound properly bandaged or splinted for the necessary time to heal. It is in the nature of their work for them to be constantly twisting and holding ropes tightly, or swinging from them so that any dressing quickly falls away. I do not know how much they suffer. They either do not notice pain or disguise their feelings. Some of them have chronic internal ulcers, probably (almost certainly) caused by drink. These are somewhat regarded as a badge of honour, as are the various warts and ulcerations of their genitals. The older men are particularly susceptible to chest colds. The venereals are affected by damp still air (some of the older men swear that they are only perfectly healthy when it blows hard). I do not think they will like this anchorage and its climate. But they are all such coarse and stupid men. The way of the sea has brutalised them. Indeed, they say that if a man is not caught as a boy or a very young man he can never thereafter be trained to the hardship of life at sea. And they are indeed hard men, of a different timber to landsmen – seasoned and accustomed to work that would ruin the strongest man's health. They do not live long if they continue at sea. If lucky and disease free, once released back to land they are like to live forever.

But they will sail for home when the ship must return, leaving us to life here. Two of our men are affected by fevers and I have bled them and applied bark. They do not help themselves by continuing to take grog. We have no beer left, and could obtain none in Teneriffe, so that the men have consumed only rum in the past week. A ship is a floating inn. There has been an increase in stomach complaints in both crew and passengers. It may be that these are caused by diet, as I have said above. It is more likely that it is the water. We took some aboard at Teneriffe, but reckoned on replenishing our supplies at our destination.

I inspected the water casks and found that the water taken on at Teneriffe smelt ill and had become discoloured and seems to have been invaded by some foul air. I spoke to Lieutenant Fortescue and told him that it was essential to go over to the island and fetch aboard fresh water. He reluctantly agreed and I (now unwisely, I think) called for volunteers. Amongst whom, first and foremost, were Mr Meares and his cronies. I was just glad at the time that they had seemed to finally become useful members of the party.

We had a devil's own job to find water. There were streams trickling into the sea, but nothing we could easily dip buckets into. I ordered the digging of a well at the top of the beach and we went down about four feet before we found water. We got only three-quarters of a barrel from that in a couple of hours and it seemed to me that it would fill again only very slowly or when it next rained. We walked further into the island and found a pool of water where deer were drinking. At least we could fill our buckets and the water looked tolerably fresh. I ordered a couple of the men to go up into the wooded hills to look for streams or springs.

Dr Owen stopped reading and went a couple of pages on, only quickly glancing through. Then he levered himself upright on the edge of the bunk and dragged the small table with his writing box towards him. He laid out a fresh double spread of blank paper and began:

REPORT TO THE COMMITTEE OF THE ISLAND OF MURANDA

A dozen of the passengers are now ill and I have had to isolate them at one end of the lower deck. How long infection has been latent among them I cannot tell. The damp and warm air may be counted unhealthy ashore, and here on the ship it is little better. I have ordered that our water be inspected for any taint before it is drunk. Surely though, the incubation period of any infection could not be as short as two to three days? I have ordered tarpaulins to be raised to catch rainwater and to store what we can in barrels cleaned with vinegar.

The symptoms are these, as first exhibited by Mr Wilkins. Two nights ago, he suffered an attack of fever. He was sweating profusely, although the night was cool. His wife called me from my bed and took me to him. He complained of a hot pain in the eyes, the lids of which were very red and the eyes themselves pink and watery. He complained also of pains in his upper arms and in the calves of his legs. I made up a concoction of Peruvian bark; this I had brought against attacks of malarial fever, although this case did not present the symptoms of that disease. It seemed that his fever eased and by midday yesterday he pronounced himself feeling much better. But by evening his pulse was greatly raised and his symptoms had returned, redoubled. He was in great pain in his stomach, he said, and I administered opium. He slept fitfully last night and seeing him this morning he was again in pain and I administered two pills of opium but he could not retain them and vomited them up in a violent retching of foul-smelling bile. His wife lies beside him now, also sweating and obviously in the early stages of the same infection. Five others, three women and two men, are in the same way and look rapidly to become worse. They are in pain and restless and I have given them opium at the outset, with bark in a double dose. I shall also dose them with calomel and if there is no improvement will try bleeding and mercury and, to purge the bowels, a solution of salts and tartar emetic.

I must insist that these patients in the close and airless conditions prevailing below deck can only pose a danger to the other passengers, and indeed, to the rest of our company.

That evening he delivered his report to the Committee.

'Do you believe that you have contained this outbreak?' asked Sir George.

'It is not within my power to contain the fever,' said the doctor. 'I can treat the patients and isolate them as best we can – but it is very difficult on board, close and confined as we are. The damp and sultry atmosphere does not help us, and the enclosing of the main deck means that there is lack of movement in the air all over the ship, especially in the heat of the day.'

'But it has given us additional room, and the shelter we need while the ship is at anchor,' said Coupland. 'What do you suggest we do?'

'I would strongly recommend that all of our sick are carried ashore and housed in some sort of hospital. We need to start building one as soon as possible, surely. All other buildings will be empty luxuries if we do not contain this fever.'

'I agree, time is of the essence,' said Coupland. 'But remember that we do need to house all our people securely and quickly. The ship sails back to England in less than three months' time. There's our house gone.'

'As I say, an infirmary is the very first thing we need. Surely we can utilise some of the Portuguese buildings?'

'When Hood inspected them,' said Crabtree, 'He found that all of the wood that had not been tarred had been hollowed out by ants and was completely useless. Their roofs have collapsed. For all practical purposes they are uninhabitable.'

'Yes, yes,' said Coupland. 'He has told me. But we have

men. They can begin building forthwith. We shall begin logging tomorrow. In the meanwhile, Doctor, I think you should go ashore with Mr Hood and ask his advice on erecting a temporary shelter for the sick as soon as possible.'

'Well, gentlemen, our good Captain Coupland seems to have the situation in hand. The houses, sir, the houses are most important when we must leave this wretched ship. Sooner the better, eh?' Sir George leaned back and exhaled a deep sigh. 'Now, I hope Owen's report hasn't put you off your dinners. By Jove, for my part I want to taste that venison. Have we any good wine left, Crabtree?'

18

They ate well that night. Lamps were lit on the main deck and, under the new canopy blotting out the stars, drinking and dancing went on until the small hours. The rains began about three in the morning and drove most down to sleep. Jackson sat beside the bed of Mr Reeves, the unfortunate bookseller. He had orders to dose the man with dissolved bark at two-hourly intervals. It did not appear that the sweating yellow-faced man benefited from this medication. From what he had seen of other cases, Jackson reckoned that Reeves would be dead by morning.

Susannah and Hood, in their wooden nest deep in the ship, held each other and Susannah slept while Hood reviewed the tasks for tomorrow. Along from them, Dr Owen slept, snoring loudly, and Phoebe turned her face away to avoid the sickly haze of brandy fumes that hung about his open mouth. It was her duty to love this man, but perhaps not while he faced her.

Mrs Crabtree, and Mrs Jenkins slept soundly in the stern cabin, separated from their menfolk by thick sailcloth which nothing could penetrate. Mr Tolchard harboured again his dream of a marble cathedral, white within and white without, rising out of the dark green forest with its tall thin needle of a spire. Mr Crabtree counted endless barrels and sacks and crates and could never make his figures tally. Sir George Whitcroft laboured valiantly and vainly over a large naked black woman who disconcertingly and repeatedly changed into Lady Whitcroft, safe in London. Caspar talked of serious matters to Susannah Hood and found himself undressing her.

Coupland lay awake, hearing the raindrops falling without remission on the deck above. He rehearsed in his mind what must be done to secure the future of this settlement. 'Not quite so easy as you thought, old chap, is it?' he murmured softly to himself. Keep to the day. Sufficient unto the day and all that. He composed himself to sleep.

19

The Committee met again.

'I intend to build our stockade after the Roman fashion,' Coupland announced.

'And how is that done?' Dr Owen asked.

'I will come to that. Chart, Jeavons.'

Caspar unrolled the chart of the island on the long table

and they all leaned forward to examine it. The chart was the work of a French captain who had put into the strait a good thirty years before their expedition. It was only part complete, with the coastline of most of the south end of the island left as a blank, and on it Coupland had written many comments and made some small sketches.

'As you can see, gentlemen, the map is patently in error in large parts. De Villiers hardly penetrated beyond the east-facing shore. The additions I have made here on the north-eastern straits side show our present position and our observations of what we must do a little further up the hill. The weather was not kind but I think we managed to establish a few first principles.'

'They are?' asked Sir George.

'We can establish our first camp amongst the Portuguese remains. Unfortunately, as Mr Crabtree has said, little of the Portuguese settlement is usable. The picture we had of a set of buildings that could be rapidly converted to our uses was plainly an utterly false one. The buildings are frauds and ghosts. I'm afraid that we have to prepare ourselves for a much more difficult task than we ever envisaged. There is one substantial building left which is made of stone. At least the ants have not eaten it. It has four large rooms over two floors and was, I imagine, a grain store or some such. The roof needs replacing but we can use the two downstairs rooms. It is out of sight, set back amongst the trees, and, for now, will give our working parties shelter when it rains. The wood is rotten in these build-ings here, but we can use the foundation of this old shed, here, and erect a shelter for our sick. We shall make progress as quickly as we can. While we do so we shall be logging to make our fastness and stores within a stockade.'

'How long is this all going to take?' asked Sir George in a rather alarmed way.

'Several months to complete. But a decent enough dwelling for the sick within perhaps two to three weeks.'

'Meanwhile the rains grow worse,' said Mr Knox.

'Come, Captain Coupland, this is hardly what we were anticipating when we set out on this endeavour,' Sir George said.

'I am afraid I have no idea what you anticipated, Sir George. From my time in the West Indies I anticipated a great deal of hard work. It is bad luck that the existing settlement is in worse condition than we had been led to believe by Mr Crabtree and this chart, which shows a township. We would have had an instant start on our new life if these stores and houses had been habitable. As it is we have to make a new beginning.'

'But where are we to live?' said Sir George. 'This is all very well . . .'

'I should very much hope that your house will be the first to be built,' said Mr Knox, with a neat twist of sarcasm that made Caspar warm to him for the first time.

'The articles of our community', said Sir George, 'preclude my assuming any sort of prior claim to comfort, I assure you, sir. Now, Coupland – this stockade.'

'The principle is simple, Sir George. It is that used by the Romans in building garrisons expeditiously in strange and threatening lands. Their cleverness lay in using as far as possible the surrounding terrain as both protection and as a source of raw materials. The first essential is a supply of fresh water. Mr Crabtree tells me that he could not locate the source of a spring in the hills. The situation is complicated by the fact that with the rains copious amounts of water flow down the cleft between the hills, debouching on to the sandy delta where the Portuguese built. Today we searched again, but could find no natural spring of water. At worst, if there is no spring, we shall have to construct a cistern high in the hills so that we may capture as much fresh rainwater as possible.'

'A cistern – that's a large undertaking, Captain Coupland,' said the doctor. 'We are in need now.'

'Another idea of the Romans?' said Mr Knox.

'And a good one,' said Coupland warmly. 'It is a fair under-taking, I agree. But one that would secure the island as a dwelling place for the future. But, as I say, I still hope to find a spring.'

'The stockade, Captain, return to that if you please,' said Sir George.

'It occurred to me that the ideal place for any fortification would be further up than the Portuguese chose. A ridge joins these two hills. From my observations it is a high and nigh impenetrable natural barrier. Similarly, the two hillsides on this side, that flank my intended site, form a natural hollow or bowl. So that we have natural protection behind and to the side of us. The woods afford mature trees that will supply our timber. We can build almost immediately a protective wall here.' Inking his pen he made a decisive stroke on the chart. 'This would be our inner redoubt. And another wall. Down here.' Another stroke of the pen.

'Why a second wall?' the doctor asked.

'The inner wall, as I have said, is our redoubt, our strong-hold, our place of last resort, as it were. It will house a main Committee chamber and dwelling house, our essential stores and portable weapons and cannon to fire through embrasures that will command the shore. Between this inner wall and the outer you can see is a quite considerable area. Here we will build our storehouses and pens for chickens and hogs. Here also will be built huts for the *grumetas* – that is how they call their native servants – and such workers as we need. The outer wall will have cannon and swivel guns mounted. The timber in front of it will be cleared to allow an avenue to the beach. From the beach, we shall strengthen the jetty. This, in short, will be our redoubt.'

'What about our settlers – the farmers?' said the doctor. 'Surely we are not all to live in this *redoubt*?'

'This accommodation will be necessary until homesteads

can be built on their own plots. For now, the stockade I propose will have to be the administrative centre and trading post and central fortification and shelter for all.'

'We shall need a church for our worshippers,' said the Reverend Tolchard excitedly. 'And a school for our children.'

'Crabtree – have you those paper models we made of principal buildings? We can place them on Captain Coupland's chart,' said Sir George.

'I think that, before you start playing at city builders, our first and overriding necessity is a hospital, Sir George,' said Owen bluntly.

'Of course. Of course, my dear sir. But no point not planning for the future, is there?' said Sir George.

'We are not going to have very much of a future unless we separate the sick from the well as soon as possible.'

'Agreed. Agreed, Doctor. We must set to work with a will, eh, Captain?' Sir George appeared to have recovered his good humour. 'I can see that our crops and timber will be for our own consumption in the first instance, but next year any surplus will be most welcome and we should be in a good way to commence trading.'

'I think you are getting ahead of yourself, Sir George,' said the doctor. 'Let us try to walk before we run; or, at least, toddle.'

'Sir George is quite right,' said Crabtree. The establishment of trade should be one aspect of our plans for the future. We have a jetty. At its extremity the shelf falls to a depth of five fathoms. When it is repaired, ships will be able to put in.'

'Full fathom five thy father lies,' the doctor intoned and he broke into a childishly gleeful smile.

'Dr Owen,' Sir George barked, 'if you cannot take this matter seriously . . . You must have more pressing duties. Perhaps you should see to them.'

'I have indeed, Sir George.' Owen rose from his seat. 'Good afternoon, gentlemen.'

With the doctor gone, Sir George got down to serious business. Crabtree had found the pieces of paper denoting their public buildings and they began to manoeuvre them about Coupland's chart.

20

Hood looked from the shore to the ship. He knew now how ill-prepared they were for the magnitude of the task facing them. If the wretched Portuguese buildings had been of any use at all he could have built on them, repairing and adapting. But they were rotten and the wood only fit for burning. Now they had to cut wood from the living forest.

He had used precious seasoned timber from on board to lay the floor across the foundations of the largest shed. What the Portuguese had built was quickly demolished. They had not time nor materials for proper stone or brick footing. Instead they put down whole trunks of felled trees, tarred and painted against the ants, over which were laid planks taken from the decks of the ship, Captain Coupland saying that they need not worry if it was a little light going back.

The greatest difficulty was in logging. Some of the men were strong and willing; others simply stayed on the ship, idling away time. Sir George came ashore at first to strut up and down and declare his dissatisfaction with the progress of the work, but latterly he had confined himself to the ship or to organising hunting parties in the woods. Out of the men on board, Hood reckoned he could rely on no more than twenty turning to with a will. But then the work was interrupted by rain. They tried to work through but the heaviest storms saw them sheltering under tarpaulin draped over the wall posts of the new hospital.

Coupland had told him that they must proceed faster. Hood countered that he had not enough labour and those hands he did have were inexperienced in this sort of work and that some on board did not want to work at all. Hood looked at the roughly built building they were throwing up and said that it was poor work and that he was sorry it did not go faster and look better. But Coupland had grown tetchy and said that Hood must do the best he could with what he had. He must dispense with all 'fancy' work. Could he not just nail these pieces together – he waved his hand at the lengths of two-inch-square wood that Hood was in the process of notching on his improvised bench under the trees. They did not have time on their side, he said. Hood said that unless the supports were properly jointed they would not bear the weight of a proper roof. With that Coupland had said that he must find a way of speeding the work and had swung off down the beach.

A sort of grotesquely hammered-together construction arose. They used whole trunks, not stripped or planed but with the bark still on them, as corner posts and internal supports for a roof that was composed of roughly laid thinner tree trunks covered with tarpaulin. It took a week to erect this monstrous eyesore. Hood worked eighteen hours a day. He slept one night on board when Coupland ordered him to rest on the ship. He lay beside his wife in the dark bowels of the ship and nothing could keep from his mind the green leaves of the trees, the waves throwing themselves against the silver sand, the blue then grey then black skies, the rain pattering on, then striking down the leaves, the leaning new moon as they worked at night, the hot vertical sun by day, the endless knock of axes on wood, and the endless and ubiquitous giant ants who ran incessantly and uncaringly over the work half-completed, the rich stink of the tar barrel, the rasps of his saws; all were more terribly real than the body of his beloved wife beside him, who now extended timidly a hand to his arm, then to his chest as he lay awake and he knew her eyes were open and that she would not question him, nor dare to call into doubt this whole enterprise because her love and loyalty conquered for now her fear. He fell fast asleep in the middle of his bright vision.

21

'What do you think, boys?' said Meares. 'What do you think of their great new hospital?'

'I'm thinking I'd not like to be resting there,' said Dodds.

'Rest for ever,' said Abercrombie.

'With the rats and the wolves and the mosquitoes eating us up,' said Meares. 'It seems that we have to make some decision, lads. We can't stay here – I've heard the ship goes back soon. We can't go back. Leastways, I can't. Won't go into that. I think, though, that you're in the same boat.'

Dodds sniffed. They all leant on the ship's rail and stared moodily down at the water.

'They're making precious little progress as it is. What happens when the boat goes?'

'Well, as I said – I for one can't go back,' said Meares. 'And I think you men are in the same awkward state. Am I right? Nothing for us back there in England.'

'Precious little here,' said Dodds and spat into the water.

Abercrombie complained, 'Well, I for one can't bear to be under that man Coupland. And we can't wait until this town of theirs is built. That could take months.'

'Now boys – not to despair. As we sailed around this island I saw a row of caves on the north point, close to the mainland. It's only a couple of miles from here. If we take arms and food, we can make our own way over there and have shelter straight off. We can get what we want from the blacks on the coast. I reckon we can hold out there until the time is right.'

'What time?'

'Our time. We can take the whole place for ourselves.'

'Are we taking young Donnelly?'

'Piss on Donnelly,' said Meares. 'He's become quite your little Coupland man. Says the only future we have is to stick together. Stick here, we'll all die, I told him. Write him off. Tell him nothing.'

'What about the Committee? And Captain Coupland?'

'They won't last. We'll go, boys. We'll go.'

22

NOTES OF DR OWEN

We have moved some of the sick to land. There are now ten down with fever. Parrott has died. He was followed closely by Hawtree. Both men exhibited the same pattern of symptoms. Violent headache and dimness of sight, or rather a lack of tolerance to the light and cold shivers. A feeling of great unease that passed rapidly to convulsions and then to a profuse perspiration. Pain in or behind the eyes, lower calf, back. The pulse very quick, the breathing laboured and the breath offensive to a great degree, the skin hot, the pupils dilated. Despite the application of various specifics these were rejected by the stomachs of both men. Then an abatement of the fever and a feeling as Wilkins said 'that the worst had passed'. But then came a further attack of convulsions that, in their terribly weakened conditions, left them prey to a last coma and death.

I had them carried by some of our men – much against their will – to the far end of the beach and buried where the ground was of a clay-like composition rather than the loose damp soil beneath the trees. (Coupland remarked that he would experiment with this white clay to see if it could be easily made into bricks or even a sort of wattle for our buildings.) So the dead yield some good to the living. Mr Knox remarked that it was hardly necessary to bury a man on the island as the ants would strip a body to a skeleton within a day. Reverend Tolchard regarded the suggestion of a lack of Christian burial as indecent. He read the lines over the two fresh graves but had to desist from a further sermon after a tipping down of rain.

I go to inspect my charges now.

Three in the hospital raving in delirium. Their visions are mostly of their homes and children, although they sometimes address myself or Phoebe as if we were friends or acquaintances. One desired to be shrived of the sin of adultery with his neighbour's wife; another was most concerned about his pet cat. I ordered their heads to be shaved – my orderly is one of the seamen who once assisted at Smithfield Market – and blisters to be applied to the skull. This worked well with Mrs Watson on board the *Pharaoh*. The blister drew off her delusions. When she is quieter, this to be followed by a solution of Peruvian bark in wine.

Investigate this regimen: calomel and opium, succeeded by salts and tartar emetic if badly constipated or passing green stools. If the fever returns with delirium, blistering of the skull. It seems to me on short acquaintance with this disease that if the patient can survive the second, the returning of the fever, then he may progress slowly to recovery. A second set of convulsions would appear to be invariably fatal.

We shall see what stronger specifics will succeed. Mercury?

23

Sunday, July 15th

My dear Torrington,
Well, the hospital is completed and is really rather a solid construction. It is to be tarred and plastered in white clay to deter the ants. Coupland is working as fast as he can to erect some shelters for us for when the *Pharaoh* has to sail. Sir George has not stirred from his cabin on the ship.

I do not know whether it is a sore blow or an ill wind that brings us some good but Meares, his half-brother

and four other men have deserted. They lowered one of
the rowing boats last night, saying they had every right to
go ashore to see their loved ones – though they have
none in the hospital. The only watch on deck was the
first mate who could not be less concerned with our
affairs. They were not ship's crew, he said to Coupland,
what right or reason had he to impede their movements?

They have taken, or rather stolen, weapons, provisions
and a good quantity of gold from the quartermaster's
chest. Coupland was at first angry with the mate but, as
Mr Crabtree pointed out, the mate was perfectly right: he
has no jurisdiction over passengers and the ship's crew
want nothing so much as to leave this place and us in it.

During the day, there came a procession over the water
towards us. First came our longboat, with Lieutenant
Fortescue waving to us, followed by a great canoe in the
stern of which sat Tabellun on his state chair. He had
brought us the *grumetas*, he explained through Mr Knox,
when we had hoisted him, chair and all, on board. He
looked keenly about him and to the shore. It was plain
that he was assessing our strength and progress. The King
must congratulate us, Knox translated, it was clear that
we were making enormous strides. Why, he could see the
pattern of our city taking shape before his eyes. He
wished us Godspeed and a long and happy relation
between our two people.

In all of this there was not the slightest hint of sarcasm
or satire in the King's voice or face, although it was true
that as mediated through Mr Knox his comments took
on a certain sardonic edge. Coupland asked the King if
he would like to retire to the stateroom and be in greater
comfort. It might well rain. See, the sky had darkened
over the land. No, no, said the King. He had an
umbrella. He was perfectly comfortable where he was,
and he laughed. Did the King think that we wished to

get him below and do him harm? His canoe was filled with his armed men. Coupland smiled equably and ordered rum to be brought.

Then Coupland told Jackson to fetch Sir George. Jackson turned to go, but as he did, we heard Sir George's voice in a sort of benign bray erupting on to the deck. 'No need, no need,' he cried. 'I'm here.'

The King was delighted to see him and greeted him with, 'Ah, King George. How happy I am that we meet again. Two kings together.'

So then, rum and festivities. Two white cocks Tabellun had brought were roasted. Food and water were sent down to his royal canoe – no rum, he insisted. Sir George declared a public holiday – we had all been working infernally hard – and one of our hogs was slaughtered and roasted all afternoon on the deck.

By the evening, Tabellun was completely intoxicated. At least it seemed he was, but when Coupland suggested through Mr Knox that the King should sleep on board, he appeared to sober up immediately. No, he had business on shore, he insisted. Your men, he remembered – and the twelve native workmen came aboard. The King departed for the far shore, in bright moonlight, his back to us, singing lustily.

For the past few days Coupland and I have been busy on the island. There is no value in being an officer and a gentleman, Coupland said, if we are not willing to show ourselves as ready and able to equal or surpass the efforts of our servants. Coupland and Hood have come rapidly to the view that we must build above the earth and that all our buildings must rest on stone or hardwood piers sunk into the earth. We can then use the wall frames that Hood has prepared separately, the sides panelled with thick canvas, until we should have the leisure to build more lasting and substantial structures. So we have been digging clay and fetching stones and embedding them together in a rough cement. We are dirty and dishevelled after hours of this work. Now that Meares and his lot have cleared off, Coupland has insisted that rosters of all able-bodied men be prepared, including the ship's crew, to work on the island.

My great poem on the subject of our brave colony? Ha, no time for poetry, alas.

24

At the end of work on the last Saturday in July, Coupland was summoned back to the ship for a meeting of the Committee.

'Perhaps', Caspar said as they were rowed out to the *Pharaoh*, 'this means that Sir George is to make a grand announcement that he is at last prepared to lend a hand's turn in the work.'

'That would not be the thing at all,' said Coupland severely. 'Sir George is our commander on this island. It would be unseemly for him to be seen working manually.'

A fair aroma of roast fowl greeted them as they went below. The main cabin was brightly lit by a large number of candles, and everything had been tidied. It appeared most inviting to Caspar after a couple of nights on the island, listening to rain on a tarpaulin roof. The gentlemen of the Committee sat along the table; three of the ladies were seated against the wall sewing, one reading. The table was set for dinner with glasses glinting and a small cluster of wine bottles in the centre. But it was obvious that a meal had already been consumed and a good few of the bottles drained. Plates had been pushed aside to give room to the chart of the island and Sir George's little paper buildings. Sir George's chair was empty. As Coupland and Caspar entered, the Reverend Tolchard cried, 'Gentlemen, oh gentlemen – if we had but known you were coming over.'

'I knew. I knew,' said Sir George, bustling in behind them. 'There is food for the gentlemen. Here, Jackson, fetch your masters their meal from the galley.' He gestured at Jackson, who had hung back at the door. 'Get on, get on,' bellowed Sir George.

'Cut along, Jackson,' said Coupland. When his man had gone, he closed the door of the cabin and sat down at the table. 'I must ask, Sir George, that you do not give my man orders. He is perfectly competent and should be treated as such.'

Sir George had by now taken his place opposite them and seemed reluctant to meet their eyes. 'No time for that. No time for all that,' he said. His blustery but evasive manner was most odd. He fidgeted with his wine glass, took a draught, looked to his left, to his right, addressed a whispered aside to Crabtree, told Tolchard to drink up and then sat a little irresolutely, one forefinger moving his paper buildings on the chart before him a little this way and that. Plates of food were brought in by Jackson and the two men fell to with great appetite. This seemed to cheer Sir George, who leaned back and for the first time looked squarely at them.

'You want my report, Sir George?' Coupland asked between bites.

'When you've done, my good fellow. When you've done.'

When he had eaten, Coupland wiped his hands vigorously on a napkin, and began. He told them that the completion of the hospital and the erection of shelters meant that they might work on land without most of the men returning to the ship each evening. The lower floor of the stone house had been made habitable and he thought that the womenfolk with children could now safely lodge there. As they all knew, the two bamboo fences of the stockade before the blockhouse had been erected. A group had begun to lay the foundations of the blockhouse itself.

'I have a sketch here,' said Coupland and he had begun to draw a paper from his coat's side pocket, when Sir George waved his hand in a rather floppy way as if to say, no, that would not be necessary.

'I have seen your progress from the ship. I must congratulate you on the headway you have made in what must be rather trying conditions.'

'And my men.'

'Indeed – your men. But – we must have a reckoning sometime, my dear Coupland, and this would appear to be that time.'

'A reckoning, Sir George? You are not satisfied?'

'I am not dissatisfied. No, heavens no. You have done as much, more, than any man could have expected you to have done. The question we must pose is this: is it enough? No – hear me out.'

Coupland shifted in his seat, hunching his shoulders forward. His face was tense, Caspar saw, his lips thinly pressing together as if to suppress angry speech.

Sir George spread himself in his chair and began to speak. 'We all know, of course, it was planned that in only a few weeks from now we would lose the ship – it must return to England. I consider that those of the sick who can travel should go with her. But who knows between now and then who will have recovered and who will have perished. We are bound to have sick and whatever ministrations our good doctor may bestow upon his charges it must be that they will receive better and more experienced care in Freetown. From there they can either return to this island or proceed by one of the many ships plying from there back to England. Therefore another question arises. Who shall accompany them? In short, Captain, we are too many. Too many in number. Too many in tenderness of years: the children; or sex: the ladies. While, no doubt, the accommodations you are in the process of building will be quite excellent and comfortable after their fashion, there are not more than three or four as yet habitable. Am I correct?'

'There is the hospital.'

'Serving?'

'There are twelve there at the moment. It could hold another half-dozen.'

'Yet, according to Dr Owen, it might be that in the near future we might well have a larger number, a much larger number, of sick on our hands.'

'There are other shelters. And we do still have the ship.'

'Not for long. Can you guarantee shelter for all our people?'

'No – that is quite impossible. We need to work through the rains. Once they begin to clear we can press ahead with our building work at a much faster rate. If we are given time, yes. If you will only delay the ship for another two months. Delays happen at sea.'

'And on land.'

A high colour mounted on Coupland's cheekbones. 'Work would have gone a damn deal faster if all our people had hauled to and taken a part.'

'I must ask you to mind your tongue in front of the ladies, Captain.'

'I begin to catch your whole drift, Sir George. You intend to send the ship back regardless of our situation here. On board will be our sick, the seamen we need to help with our work, and the women and children?'

Sir George was silent for a moment then said, 'That is the way of it. Some others . . .'

'So – who is to go and who to stay?'

'That is up to every individual. Captain Coupland, I meant, I mean, no criticism of your great efforts. But it is clear that things are not as we thought them to be. We expected some settlement here, some existing buildings that we could repair and adapt rapidly to our needs. That is not the case.'

'We knew surely that there would be difficulties. We are not in Gloucestershire, Sir George.'

'We had not anticipated *such* difficulties. The fact that it seems we now have to make our own houses in the most hostile of conditions.'

'You begin to sound like Meares,' said Coupland.

'Meares? Who is Meares?'

'The leader of the deserters,' said the Reverend Tolchard apologetically.

'I shall ignore your insolence, Coupland, and put the position more plainly.'

Sir George laid out his 'position'. He knew that there were many who were discontented with what they had found on reaching this isle. Meares and his followers were merely the most extreme. If caught they should of course be punished for what amounted to desertion. He thought he was right, was he not, Captain Coupland, that the men were still under naval discipline and law on board ship?

Coupland made no response.

But there were other problems. The sickness, the fever, that Dr Owen, for all his valiant efforts, seemed unable to stem. The rains which were increasing and which were slowing the work on the island. Indeed, the whole prospect of another two months of rain under inadequate shelter, the consequent impossibility of cultivating and tilling the ground – unless they were to be confined to eat rice all their days. The destruction of what livestock they had placed on the island. It had been hoped to fatten up the hogs, but they had been taken at night by some stealth, by wolves of some sort.

'Jackals,' Mr Knox murmured.

There had been miscalculations, serious miscalculations, said Sir George, both in the intelligence they had received as to the nature of this island and the feasibility of establishing any sort of large colony in the time they had to hand.

'What are you going to do?' Coupland asked wearily.

Sir George gathered himself. An extraordinary meeting of the Committee had been summoned and certain decisions taken.

'Why was I not summoned earlier?' said Coupland.

'We were quorate,' said Crabtree.

'Go on, Sir George. Go on,' said Coupland.

'It would have been foolish and perhaps fatal to procrastinate,' said Sir George. 'The Committee has balloted the settlers and servants as to who wishes to remain and who wishes to return when the ship leaves.

'Again, in my absence,' said Coupland.

'We were within our rights,' said Sir George. 'Within our rights.'

'What was the result?'

'Of those on board at the time the poll was conducted, fifty-one have voted to go back.'

'What about those on the island – in working parties and the sick?'

'I – we – had intended to count their votes upon their return and before the next roster.'

'And the subscribers?' asked Coupland.

'The Reverend Tolchard, Mr Crabtree and Dr Owen have voted to stay; the remainder are for return – and soon.' Sir George leaned forward and said earnestly and warmly, 'This by no means indicates that either I or the other subscribers intend to desert the expedition. No, once returned to England we will be able to raise new funds and recruit more colonists, of a rather higher calibre than our present mixed crew. A relief company will return in the dry season.'

'I am much afraid that you will not, Sir George. Once you have tasted the comforts of home, eh?' said Coupland bitterly. 'No, let me speak. What, I ask you, did we come here for? It was to make a new and better world. We were not to be given an old world to refashion. We knew that we should have to work hard, perhaps suffer. When we met in London we were given warnings about illness and mortality in these regions. Mr Knox has told us repeatedly of the dangers. We have had deaths. We shall probably have more deaths. When was a colony settled without these risks. In the Americas? The West Indies? India? What did you expect – a May Day holiday? I shall of course remain. It would be shameful to give up so quickly. When do you leave? The sooner the better for all, I think.'

'I am sorry to hear you take that tone, Captain Coupland,' said Sir George. 'Such a reading of my intentions is erroneous and insulting. We shall sail in three days. We will not wait another month.'

'In three days only? God be with you.' With which Coupland rose, pointed down to the table in front of Sir George, and said, 'Don't forget to take your paper town with you, Sir George. As a keepsake.' He swept away, with Caspar and Jackson scurrying in his furious wake.

The working parties and the walking sick were canvassed the next day and another nine voted to return. The final tally of those remaining came to:

48 men
13 women
12 children

'The tally does not, of course, include Meares and his men still loose somewhere on the island,' said Coupland. 'It does include, somewhat to my surprise, Mr Knox. He says that we have taken his fancy and he intends to see us through. We need an interpreter and someone to look out for our interest.'

Those who were fit enough spent that day and the next carrying ashore all the spare timbers and canvas they could gather and every other supply they would need: water, fowls, flour, all of the stores. They stripped as much of the ship as they could – Sir George remained in his cabin, not wishing to be a witness to their pillaging. The sick who could be moved were ferried to the ship, which left five in the hospital. Sir George grudgingly made over the ownership of the *Sprite* – the cutter – and the longboat to Coupland, who said that these were essential to the colony and that the cost must be borne by the investors in London.

On the following day, stiff farewells were exchanged. Sir George shook hands gravely with Coupland and the other subscribers who wished to remain, wished them God's protection and assured them that he would see them again, and soon. And so the colonists went back in the longboat and from the shore watched the *Pharaoh* unfurl her sails and start to move slowly away, down the strait towards the open sea. She gave a salute of three guns as she neared the point. Coupland ordered just one from the cannons they had brought ashore.

Further along the beach, the *grumetas* lolled under the rough shelters they had erected for themselves. They ignored the proceedings of the colonists, grateful for a rest from their labours.

25

They heard the salute from the cave. As the ship rounded the point on the way out to open sea, Meares and his party watched her go. 'So, they're leaving,' Meares said. 'I wonder how many remain.'

And Lieutenant Fortescue, on the bridge of the *Pharaoh*, saw what he thought was a man moving in the mouth of one of the caves on the headland. 'We are well out of it,' he murmured to himself. Then he turned to the manifold tasks involved in the start of a lengthy sea voyage.

Part Four

I

'And so, to conclude, I would return you to the subject of my sermon, which is the innocence of the young in the sight of God. In a way, all is in a state of innocence here. Of utmost innocence.' The Reverend Tolchard paused and the silent congregation on the beach could hear nothing but the fall of waves upon the shore and the harsh cries of birds from the forest. 'At first we were affrighted. Truly, "the isle is full of noises", as the Bard said. But he also told his auditors "not to be afraid". Vastly more erudite minds than mine have bent themselves to the problem of earth and paradise. We know that the rebellious angels fell into the infernal regions, but to do so they must have first passed through the terrestrial zone of the earth. It appears that in this part of the world the natives have lived in perfect and untutored ignorance since the Creation, with no knowledge of the Lord God's making of the world, nor of our saviour, Jesus Christ. So, are they innocents, or, as we are, in a state of Original Sin? For, surely, when God first created the earth, paradise was not located in a single spot or place; surely his bounty extended to the whole earth? And yet in one place we see poisonous creatures, venomous snakes and wild beasts which would rend us to pieces; and in other places and continents great stretches of desert and frightful bare and snow-covered mountains and deep gorges filled with perpetual darkness where no man can live. Are these the places where nature was corrupted at the Fall by Satan and is it not therefore our duty to attempt to rescue nature from evil and restore it to God?

'That was how Bishop Burnet would have seen the physical and spiritual state of the world some one hundred years ago. I think, though, that his fearful picture of a determinedly unbenign world can be balanced. For here, on this island, we have been sent to perform a task for the Lord and, by his mercy, for our fellow man. I would like to read you another view of the Creation, by Mr Addison in the *Spectator*.'

From a pocket in his cassock the Reverend Tolchard wrestled out a book. He read: "'The Creation is a perpetual Feast to the Mind of a good Man, everything that he sees cheers and delights him: Providence has imprinted so many Smiles on Nature, that it is impossible for a Mind which is not sunk in more gross and sensual Delights to take a Survey of them without several secret Sensations of Pleasure . . ." I omit a little here and take a small liberty with one of Mr Addison's sentences, without, I hope, distorting his sense: "It does not *merely* rest in the Murmur of Brooks and the Melody of Birds, in the Shade of Groves and Woods or in the Embroidery of Fields and Meadows, but considers the several Ends of Providence which are served by them, and the Wonders of Divine Wisdom which appear in them. Such an habitual Disposition of Mind consecrates every Field and Wood, turns an ordinary Walk into a morning or evening Sacrifice, and will improve those transient Gleams of Joy, which naturally brighten up and refresh the Soul on such Occasions, into an inviolable and perpetual state of Bliss and Happiness."'

He closed the book and laid it carefully on the corner of the deal table that served as his altar.

'I think we may well bear those words in mind. We have come as newcomers to a part of the world which has seemingly little in common with our own dear homeland. It is not blasphemous, I think – I should very much hope not – to see ourselves as landed in Paradise in little, and to see ourselves as Adams and, of course –' he raised his hand to his mouth and coughed, 'Eves, in our discoveries. We are surrounded by much that is strange to us, by creatures and plants and trees that are truly nameless. But does not the Book of Genesis say, "The Lord God formed every beast of the field, and every fowl of the air, and brought them unto Adam to see what he would call them; and whatsoever Adam called every living creature, that was the name thereof." Let us not be afraid therefore of what is strange here. God has ordained that we shall name those things which have so far rested in ignorance and use them for our benefit. Therefore, let us pray.

'May God be praised who has surrounded us with such bounty and plenitude, and guide us in the ways that we may rightfully and diligently perform our tasks and build our Holy City in his eyes that he may be pleased with our work. We shall say the Lord's Prayer.'

Their voices murmured together. The women and men and children were all on their knees, but some of the older children looked out across the strait to the dark green forests and rolling hills of the mighty continent.

2

Thursday, August 2nd

My dear Torrington,
Last night, on the cutter, Coupland addressed our new Committee.

199

He was grateful, he would be eternally grateful for our loyalty – Messrs Tolchard, Crabtree, Owen, Jeavons – we who had been sturdy oaks when other trees had bent and broken before the first winds. They had been our friends and colleagues: he hoped that they may prove so in the future, but he rather feared not. One man he had not named, because he was not of our original company. He was a gentleman with whom he had had his disagreements, but this gentleman had loyally thrown in his lot with us.

Coupland raised his glass. 'Mr Knox, I thank you,' he said.

At which Mr Knox rose and gave a droll bow from the waist and said he was much obliged to all present.

For his part, Captain Coupland said that it was likely that Mr Knox would prove invaluable in dealing with the country and its inhabitants across the water. They were in both a worse and better case for the absence of so many, but they were strengthened by the knowledge that those gathered here were sincere in their desire to remain. But they must all of them recognise a need for change in the way they went about building this settlement.

Since coming to this island, much work had been done, but in a haphazard and ill-directed way. Progress had been made but by no means were they as far forward as he had hoped at this stage. He said that he had seen men and women wandering about to no end or purpose. Really no idleness could be permitted and he hoped that Reverend Tolchard would not take it amiss that he now thought it necessary to extend their labours into the seventh day until they had reached some tolerable form of housing and shelter. After all, he said, a ship does not stop sailing on Sunday.

He knew, he went on, that this was intended from the outset to be a democratic commonwealth, but now they were in a battle for their very existence and it was necessary for discipline and order to be imposed. 'We must know what we are doing and what we expect to be done,' he said. We could always relax discipline at a later date, but if it was not imposed now it would become progressively harder to impose as each day passed.

He intended, if he received a general vote of consent from the Committee, to introduce the following regulations, which would be administered under the rules of naval law in case of any breach. I reproduce them here:

1. To divide our men, where sickness permits, into four equal parts.
2. Of these, one quarter of our men shall be on watch, to be divided between the cutter and the beach and stockade.
3. That these be kept and regulated as naval watches and only to be relieved by the express command or consent of an officer.
4. The officers to be Captain Coupland as commanding officer, Mr Jeavons as his adjutant. Second in command, recognising their ability to act in possession of their full abilities and allowing for absence or illness, to be in this order: Mr Crabtree, Dr Owen, the Reverend Tolchard and Mr Jeavons.
5. Each member of a watch to be furnished with a musket and shot and to be given responsibility during the day for superintending working parties, with the knowledge of an officer.
6. Working parties to be equally divided between the remaining men, with lighter or more appropriate duties to be undertaken by women and any minors judged capable of such work.
7. In case of any dispute, naval law as upheld by the Royal Navy to be enforced at all times and such punishments as shall be found necessary to be in accordance with those laws and regulations.

There followed after this any number of stipulations regarding working parties, the actual tasks to be done by men and women and the sturdier children, the division of stores between the colonists, the washing and general upkeep of the cutter and the regular fetching of provisions from across the bay, which he would regularise by sending an embassy to Tabellun.

3

'This is all very well,' said Crabtree. 'We can do all this but we have lost the ship, the rains are worsening and our temporary shelters are inadequate. We have not resolved the question of shelter, particularly for the women and children.'

'The women and children', said Coupland, 'are to go into the lower floor of the stone house, as I have promised. It is the only substantial building. The roof can be patched and I hope that the upper storey can come into commission soon.'

He would, he said, keep his cabin here on the cutter, together with Mr Jeavons. There was room, at a pinch, for another fifteen men. The rest would have to make do with the temporary shelters erected over the old Portuguese ruins. Dr Owen and his wife were to share the cabin erected at the end of the hospital building.

He directed their attention to his original map.

'What about the *grumetas*?' asked the Reverend Tolchard.

'The natives have shown themselves quite adept already at improvising shelter a little way along the wood's edge.'

'You might do well to study their building methods,' said Mr Knox.

'I intend them to become a part – an equal part – of our enterprise,' said Coupland rather stiffly. 'To that end, they will live with us in our compound.'

'When it is completed,' said Knox.

'When it is completed.'

'Until then, Captain,' said Mr Knox, 'if you can bear the thought, might I suggest that you let off a cannon at intervals throughout the night. Just a discharge of powder. Tabellun may be your friend, but he thinks you are rich, that you must be rich, to come to this place. That you have rich clothes and guns and cannon and a ship – however small the cutter may be. He has seen men come and go. He abides for the present, but he may want to test you some day. He will want some knowledge of your power. Give him a gun every hour. He will be listening to see how you go. And keep your bonfires burning on the beach.'

4

'Must we be parted?'

The oak chest that contained all of their goods sat on the sand just below the stone house. A candle guttered in a downstairs window. The sound of a small child crying came out to them from the house and, from lower down the beach, the sounds of other children playing. Inside the lighted window two women moved about, making up cots.

'I'll take the chest in for you,' said Hood.

'There's more room for that than for me,' she said. She stared out to the strait, gleaming in moonlight between the trees.

'Why couldn't we . . .' she began. She gazed into his eyes. 'Why didn't we go with them? When they went back?'

'It's not in me to act the renegade.' His face was angry. 'Nor to resile from my duty.'

'What is your duty?'

'I gave my word. I am helping to build this place. We can have a good life here.'

The huge black sky above was filled with stars.

'I'm sorry,' she said. 'We're here. We must stay here. We have to make our bed here. Though I wish it was with you.'

He longed to embrace her, to whisper softly to her, but there were those women down by the fire and children about. He tilted the chest on its end, knelt down and took it across his back. It was a greater weight than he had expected. He blew out, then inhaled deeply.

'Show me where you want this.'

She put out a hand to steady the chest. He shook his head. 'Go on. Go on,' he commanded, and she went up ahead of him as he struggled manfully behind her until they had cleared the front door of the stone house. He followed her down a narrow corridor to a small room, already full of boxes.

'Here,' she said. She tried, ineffectually, to help with the chest. He let it fall heavily to the floor and straightened up with a groan.

'John.' She came close to him. He could feel her hands trying to hold his in their small warm grasp. He twisted away. She had looked at him with a sort of pity when he had put down the chest so wearily.

'Do kiss me, John.'

He did so, awkwardly: for the first time ashamed to think that he was feigning love.

Somebody was behind him. He turned. Mrs Jenkins was smiling broadly in that eternal female complicity of love and affection and she said that she was most sorry to interrupt and that she could come back.

'No, please, Mrs Jenkins. I'd better go,' he said to Susannah. 'Had you?'

'Where will you sleep?'

'Through there. Don't look. There will be ladies preparing themselves for bed. What's the matter? Have I troubled you?'

'My God, no.' He stared down at her dear face as if seeing it for the very first time in that upturned way. Even with the woman rooting among the boxes behind him, Hood seized Susannah and kissed her truly.

'I'd better be gone,' he whispered.

And the woman behind them said, 'You better had,' and laughed.

Susannah smiled up at him, and he turned away abruptly, saying that he must go now. With that, he stepped back into the corridor and hastened out.

He heard a male voice call out from one of the shelters to the women in the stone house. Something coarse and stupid. Across to his left, the door of the hospital swung open and Dr Owen appeared on the steps.

'Nine o'clock,' he bellowed. 'Captain's orders. And doctor's. Goodnight, gentlemen, sleep tight. No creeping about. Goodnight.' The door rattled shut.

That noise, that whispering chattering noise; simply outlandish, un-English, that incessant susurrus of insects and the wind rustling through the trees, utterly unlike the evening breath of England, came from the dark woods.

He went down the beach towards the waiting longboat. The oars rattled as they were hoisted.

'Mr Hood, Mr Hood – we're going,' a voice called.

'God save us all,' he whispered, and hurried towards the boat.

5

Sunday, August 5th

I continue my record to you, my dear Torrington. Some
of my earlier letters have gone back with the *Pharaoh*.
They will take perhaps a month or so to arrive and a
further few days to reach you in Shropshire, or wherever
you are taking your ease. I must admit that my earlier
enthusiasm is tempered by our life here, but I still would
say that you should come, perhaps when (and if) Sir
George should return here with a second complement of
fresh and rather more selectively picked colonists. It is a
new place and a new endeavour we are making. But the
drawbacks, you ask. What are they?

Fortunately for our working parties, the rains have
held off for the last four days. In the day, that is. For we
have grown used to sleeping through the heavy rain that
beats on the deck timbers above us and are so tired that
only the most terrible crack of thunder awoke me in the
early hours of this morning. The cabin was illuminated
brilliantly by lightning: the low beams, the white shirt of
Coupland hanging from the door, the profile of his face
appearing in that second from the darkness then falling
back into darkness. And then a second succeeding clap
of thunder right overhead. I levered myself up to look
past the sleeping Coupland and through the porthole

saw lightning perhaps three miles off, throwing the western headland into relief.

Our work is severe. Those not resting or sick are put to work cutting down the woods, for trunks to be halved for the walls of the cabins we are building, or clearing the ground higher up around Coupland's blockhouse, work for which is under way.

We have completed the fortification of the lower fence and placed two of the swivel guns on either side of the entrance – which still wants a gate. Truth to tell, this first fortification affords, or is intended to afford, more protection for our beasts as we have them penned behind: three hogs, some laying hens, some chickens for the pot, three bullocks and our two dogs who are put on long leashes every night to help protect our stock. We have already lost a half-dozen of our fowl and a hog to the jackals who infest the woods. Fortunately the jackals are not interested in the abundance of fruit we may pick. Four of the other cannons are dug in on the rising ground and point through embrasures of the upper fence to fire above the lower barrier, or if that should fail, they can be depressed to fire dead ahead.

Our system of collecting water is not working very well. Coupland says that we must dig out a cistern higher up the mountain, but this is quite beyond our inadequate strength. The longboat has been despatched across the strait to fill our kegs from the plentiful supply on the mainland. Mr Knox has gone with it and intends to remain a few days doing some business up the coast, he says. He is a most useful man and in some ways not unlikeable, but the very devil's advocate for that filthy trade that we have abjured and that we swore would never contaminate our colony.

The natives and the traders over there and in the coastal towns must think we are a mad crowd, having to buy our water and treating our black workers as our human equals. We pay them for their work and, I think a little to their astonishment, they find they are not our slaves.

They will be equals, as soon as any of us are. I know it is necessary, but our commonwealth, ever since the defection of Sir George and the others, seems to have become Coupland's personal fiefdom. I cannot but say that I think this is laying up trouble in store for our future. Already many of the men are astonished at the amount of physical work that must be done. Quite a few are clerkly types who have never had to work with their hands, outside of weighing groceries or scribbling at ledgers. It goes hard on them. We cannot work when the sun is at its highest and I have seen some of the older weaker men, men in their thirties or perhaps a little older, sitting after their first stint in the morning, looking quite dazed with their efforts and rising very wearily to continue in the afternoon. Some, the harder men, men who have worked on a farm or as seamen, thrive and have contempt for the weaker ones.

I am fortunate in that I assist Hood and another man in the carpentry and joinery. He takes much quiet amusement I think in having me as an apprentice. Our heaviest task is splitting the rough tree trunks and then securing them crosswise to the posts we have driven vertically into the earth, but we work in the shade of the hills behind us in the afternoon.

The work on the east and north faces of the blockhouse is started, as I say, but it is an enormous enterprise. It is intended, at a pinch or in some extreme adversity, to hold all our people, stores and weapons, and to be capable of withstanding assault and siege. Above a certain height we shall space our timbers a little more and fill in with mortar. Perhaps the work will go faster then. God knows it goes slowly enough.

Our minds were further overcast this morning when we had to bury a one-year-old boy who had died in the night. To see that pitiful bundle wrapped in a white shawl, carried by his mother as for a christening, followed by the grim-faced father was quite terrible. Tolchard, in full robes, read words over the child and he was lowered into a narrow hole dug deep in the clay just beyond the woods, in that patch which serves as our ever expanding churchyard. Such a child should never have been with us.

Hot all today. It is good to come back on the cutter at night. One feels (and unworthily) that one is at least in the way of the fresher breezes and away from the sick.

Sunday, August 12th

Coupland quite unexpectedly declared today as a day of rest – and feasting. 'Well, the Captain is God,' said Dr Owen and he laughed loudly, stuffing his face with beef from a bullock we had killed and roasted. Two of our men, who had gone off to hunt duck in the afternoon, came back with half a dozen. While in the forest they had heard gunshots in the distance. They thought they came from the north-western headland. I told this to Coupland when I was back on board and he said immediately, without looking up from his desk where he was writing in his log, 'Meares.'

I asked where he thought the deserters were hiding. He did not care. We had, he said, more than enough to do without worrying about Mr Meares. But when we were settled and the island was ours, then he would take great pleasure in hunting him down and hanging him.

Sunday, August 19th

A week on – these Sundays are the only time I have now to write in a considered fashion. Mr Knox has returned from a trip down the coast and brings us further news of Meares.

Knox has seen one of the sons of Tabellun. He said that his father thought we might like to know what our comrades are up to. It seems, said Knox, that Meares and his confederates are at present holed up in caves on the north-west headland.

'Those were the muskets our men heard?' said Coupland.

Knox nodded. 'Yes. They have enough food and seem quite content to live a troglodytic existence for the moment. They are at least out of the rain.'

'They are not working,' said Coupland fiercely.

'I am afraid', said Knox, 'that it is not necessary to work to live as long as one has shelter and a sufficiency of food and warmth.'

'Such creatures require little else, I suppose,' said Coupland.

'There'll come a time when they will want more, I fear.'

'Indeed?'

'What are they doing for water?' asked the Reverend Tolchard.

'The same as your people – rainwater. I presume they trade in some way with the mainland. Perhaps they are buying water.'

'My God, if I see their boat, I shall blow it out of the water,' said Coupland. 'Well, have your dinner, Mr Knox, and thank you for your intelligence. Where is the doctor, Jeavons? Hasn't the boat brought him over yet?'

'The boat is back,' I said. 'Jackson says that Dr Owen begs your pardon but he is occupied with his charges. He has two more men sick on the island and says that he must watch them. The first, he says, is critical.'

'More sickness. Who are they?'

'Richard Mason and Joe Jenkins.'

Coupland passed his hand wearily down his face. 'Well, I am sorry for their trouble; they are two of the stronger men and it will slow us even further.'

6

Dr Owen, having watched at the bedsides of the two men, and having besides many other duties tending to the sick, was at last able to retire to the screened-off cabin at the end of the hospital building. He had been so busy that he had not drunk any alcohol all day. He undressed to his shirt. Before he snuffed out the candle, he gazed down on his sleeping wife. For all of her labours in helping him as his nurse, the strain of washing soiled clothes and bedding, preparing foods and medicines, here she lay, her long yellow hair spilled upon the sack that served as their pillow, her face fair and hardly touched by the sun. And young – my God, my God, what was this beautiful girl doing with the old wreck, old soak, old brandy barrel he had become? And not far off what he had been when he first met and courted her. Phoebe, the third daughter of Colonel Wagstaffe at Corley Hall, and Owen, the only doctor for miles about, called in to attend his dying days.

With some gentleness he lifted the two thin cotton blankets and slid into bed beside her, taking infinite and sober care not to wake her. He stretched out slowly, not daring to touch her – and was mounting again the wide wooden staircase from the open hall to the landing, to be conducted to the bedchamber of the Colonel.

Propped on his pillows, the figure of the Colonel had been degraded by his long illness; once plump cheeks had withered away, a once fleshy nose now stood out as a sharp-edged prow, once sharp eyes were a watery blue. There was little that any doctor could do for him. He bore scant resemblance to the proud sabre-flourishing soldier of the equestrian portrait on the stairs: one whose career admittedly had been modest. One of Cumberland's keen accomplices in the slaughter of the Scots after the Jacobite rebellion, he had retired at the age of fifty from otherwise largely inactive service. The interests in the West Indies which had bought Corley Hall had been taken over by his only son, and the Scottish estates and their slow-moving sheep, endlessly munching or gazing short-sightedly into the distance, had long ago been sold. So, when the Colonel came to die, there was found to be no estate left for the younger children.

Well, Owen had attended that last night, and listened to the Colonel's death choke, accompanied by the suitably dramatic rattling of the shutters and of the storm outside. He must stay the night, the Colonel's wife insisted. He stayed for several days, helping to sort out the aftermath of the death.

He found himself in a house of women. The widow had early the next morning sequestered herself in the Colonel's study to examine the account books and other financial papers that had been left unattended for several months. There were also the three daughters. The oldest was Alice at thirty years, not married and unlikely to be, in rehearsal to replace her mother. The second born, Grace, married to a naval captain, arrived a week after the death. And the youngest was Phoebe, small gentle, yellow-haired Phoebe, waiting for her prince. So it was Phoebe he had married. The family was left more or less penniless on the death of the Colonel. Alice obtained a position over some unfortunate children as their governess. The price for

Phoebe as the bride of a country doctor was that her mother came to live with them. When Owen looked back on her seven years with them until her death, Africa seemed sometimes preferable. But Phoebe was worth any price . . .

7

Phoebe had not dared tell Joseph. At first she had blamed her sickness on one of the many fevers, major and minor, that afflicted almost everyone on the island, but now it was impossible to ignore the true nature of her body. There had been only one child born on the island, some time ago to a woman already heavily pregnant on the voyage out. One of the servants' wives: a poor thin whip of a girl. Both had died despite the doctor's best efforts.

Phoebe reckoned that she was over a month gone. The child must have been conceived not long before the *Pharaoh* left. On that one hot stifling afternoon when they had gone down to the cabin that served as an infirmary and as their bedroom. In that stuffy room, whose only light was that filtered through the ports of the gun deck above and down the steps and along the narrow corridor, Joseph had loomed dimly above her, pressing her against the bunk, fumbling with her skirt, his breeches, saying over and over, 'Phoebe. Dear Phoebe. Oh, let us. Let us.' It had been so long, he said. An eternity. Then his perfunctory, jabbing performance, with 'Ah dear Phoebe. Dear Phoebe,' breathed hotly in her ear. Then he had juddered to a stop, pulled away, dried himself with his shirt tail, and tucked himself away.

The result of his passion is my duty, thought Phoebe, folding clean dressings in their room at the hospital, staring out of the window, down the beach and on to the calm blue water of the strait.

8

Sunday, August 26th

Coupland has been ill these past four days. Thank God, it does not appear to be a fever, but some cold or chill taken through exhaustion. He works all day with the rest of us and spends half his nights planning or reading. I think he has slept very little in the past few months, worrying about the direction our expedition has taken.

He was able to get up this morning, though still weak. He said that he was worried about those on shore in these days and nights of heavy rain. The temporary tarpaulin-covered shelters were well enough for light rains but not adequate for the tempestuous downfalls from which we more frequently suffer. He has ordered me to devise a system whereby the working parties rotate so that each man spends every other night under deck on the cutter, while we shall have to rough it for one night on the island.

Coupland insists that from henceforth work must be concentrated on building the blockhouse as fast as possible. At the moment, he said, our efforts were being dissipated through the pursuance of individual projects. We must have a common object and that object must be the blockhouse. That would provide rooms for all and be our secure stronghold until we could cultivate our fields and eventually build our farms. Once everyone knew they were working for one common cause then work would go forward much more quickly.

The problem was that there were men chafing and saying that they should now be allowed to build on their own land, or in the shelter of the woods – if the woods be any shelter. Chaos. Pure chaos. No, he was afraid that our grand scheme for farming and trade must be postponed until we had safe shelter for all. All individual building works must be abandoned. The work on them was unequal; some were further ahead than others, all were more or less inadequate. What was going to be the position but one of strife and jealousy and division if the strong were housed before the weak? No – a common purpose was essential for our salvation.

He had proposed the turn and turn about on beach and cutter to allay suspicions that he and his officers were enjoying better living conditions. He demanded to know what progress had been made during his illness.

We had levelled the ground and laid foundations and part of the north-facing wall, I began.

He interrupted me, pointing from the cutter's rail to the shore. We must concentrate on building the rooms in the blockhouse whose windows would face down to the shore and whose doors would open into what would be the quadrangle. By building there first we would achieve solid dwellings, and a secondary line of defence. A tower would be erected at each end of this north wall, with loopholes for cannon and muskets giving a line of fire down to the shore. The rooms would be of equal size for officers, subscribers (such as we had left) and labourers; a cabin would suffice for a married couple with children; the single men would be bunked four to a cabin. One officer and a small armed crew would remain on the cutter at all times – in case any should hope to steal away with her.

'Meares might well take a fancy to our little ship once the charm of the caves has worn off,' he said.

9

NOTES OF DR OWEN

I can hear that canting fool Tolchard droning outside. He came in earlier and read prayers to, or rather at, my poor patients.

Death comes now with terrible regularity. Some die quickly; others seem to rally and are able to go back to work, only to sicken again and die. I have made up doses of calomel and mercury for those in fever.

The general conditions are not good. The hospital should be rebuilt as soon as possible on piles above ground, so that there is a free circulation of air all around the building. The windows should be enlarged and screened so as to give more air and light but also, if possible, to keep out the mosquitoes. The irritation of their bites aggravates the suffering of those prone in bed, particularly the children. The young know not what is happening to them and the constant itching and inflammation render their lives miserable. I thought when we set out from London first that there were too many children. Time and circumstance with their foul subtraction have changed that. It is the terrible fact though that the families with small children were the most eager to stay and make a new life. They little expected this, I fear.

Mrs Hood, the carpenter's wife, has joined Phoebe in working in the hospital. The load is heavy on these two. The floors need to be washed with vinegar every day. Then there is the constant necessity of laundering clothes and bed linen – a large iron pot is kept boiling outside most of the day. Despite their best efforts the place has a constant stink of faeces and the putrid breath of the fever patients. Those with minor injuries – cuts and bruises from their work – prefer to be bound up in the open air rather than enter here. It is important that any wound be thoroughly cleaned as soon as it is received. Jenkins died of the mortification of his hand that he had cut when fishing.

We have at present eleven men sick, but of these two are in the men's shelters not the hospital. Three women and five of the children.

Deaths this week: two men, who brought consumption with them from England and presumably have had their deaths hastened by the air of the island; and one woman, Mrs Ancorn, who suffered agonies from ulcers (one of nine or ten inches long showed the bone below) upon her legs which no treatment could help and which mortified.

The native labourers seem immune to any of the diseases of this place. Perhaps their goodly consumption of rum cleans out their livers. It would be difficult I think for anyone to work under these conditions without the help of spirits.

10

Hood had to show the men how to chop down trees quickly and effectively, otherwise they would have been hacking at them any which way the whole day long and would not have felled a single one. They had taken down all the useful wood immediately around, leaving only the smaller springier trees which were useless for building purposes. He would have to go farther afield for taller stronger trees.

One morning he knew he was sick and was terrified more by the thoughts of the possible consequences for his work than his discomfort. But that was great. He woke in the small hours and felt a pain in his lower bowel and great pressure downwards so that he had to run to the jakes to relieve himself painfully no less than five times and was ashamed at the stink he caused there. He managed to get back to his bunk and lay there feeling exhausted and low spirited. But he forced himself up at dawn and was for a few moments greatly relieved to find his diarrhoea eased. God knows, he must be empty. But, no, he fled again.

He ate no breakfast. Jackson asked him tenderly if he felt ill, but he gave a wan smile and said he did feel poorly but was sure he would improve during the day. So he rested and, still feeling weak and depleted, he got into the longboat taking the afternoon work party ashore.

Crabtree was in charge that day. He could see that Hood was unwell and asked him if he was truly in a fit condition to work. When the man gallantly said that he was ready for anything, Mr Crabtree took leave to contradict him. If he had dysentery he must rest. Hood said that he would go off his head if he couldn't work.

He knew of one task he could do. They had not enough trunks for the stockade walls. He would go into the woods and select suitable trees and mark them for the gang to fell tomorrow. That would be light work. Crabtree reluctantly agreed. Hood took with him a leather water bottle and a pouch containing blue dye to mark the trunks he would choose. Assuring Crabtree that he would rest if the sickness came over him, he went away along the beach and disappeared into the line of trees.

He worked for a couple of hours, wandering deeper and deeper into the forest, startled now and then by a sudden whistling or the harsh cries and clatter of a flight of parakeets taking off above him. He found trees they could use and marked them for felling. He had to stop and rest often and as he sat on a fallen trunk in a clearing he considered how they could live off the fruits of this forest, house themselves with its wood, trap its animals, derive medicines from its plants. They need not disturb this world, but take from it their due and leave the rest to its magnificent life and slumber. And with these philosophical fancies in his head, in the warmth of the afternoon, he passed into slumber himself.

When he woke he at first had no idea where he was. The sun had declined and the clearing was now in deep shadow. As he struggled upright, he saw between two bushes a jackal, with its hackles raised stiffly like nails. It regarded him with no great liking and growled.

Hood had no weapons. He had no idea what this animal might do. He moved slowly back to the trunk of an oak and, weak as he was, hoisted himself onto a lower branch and then climbed up higher. The animal advanced slowly, nosed about the tree, looked up at him, pissed against the trunk and, after sniffing where Hood had lain, padded off the way it had come.

He waited there for what must have been half an hour. He heard very distantly what sounded like the crack of a musket, but couldn't gauge from whence it came. It did not recur and he may have been mistaken in amongst all the outlandish sounds of the forest. The light would go soon, and he had no idea in which direction the camp lay.

He had had nothing to eat all day because of his condition and was now terribly hungry. He searched about and from a tree took a small yellow plum. He sniffed it and found it smelled exactly as an English plum. And, a pleasant thought: the plums in his garden would be ripening at this time of early September. He bit into the fruit and found it a little acidic but pleasant enough. He picked some and put them into the pockets of his trousers.

Now it got dark very suddenly. For a few minutes the small pink high cloud and dark blue sky directly above, glimpsed through the leaves, lasted, then they too went. He was frightened. The birds had ceased their howls and trumpetings and high whistlings. There was what approached to silence. Then came the noise of frogs from some nearby pool and rustlings in the undergrowth. He had no idea how far he had come. He had no source of light with him to show him his marks on the trees. He had misjudged the time and was lost in the forest.

Which way was the ship or camp? If he went in any direction it was liable to be the wrong one and to plunge him farther into the forest. God knows what wild beasts roved in the darkness. Like the monkeys who lived with their families in small colonies in the trees he must make some sort of home above the ground. So, the carpenter once more ascended the same oak tree and made his nest in the fork of branches. A group of monkeys higher up, peaceable creatures, were at first curious about this large ape, but left him alone and soon they all slept.

II

They saw ships sailing out at sea, some going north, homeward bound, or nearer, passing by down to Sierra Leone. Up on the cliff, looking south, they could see far off the slavers bearing to the West Indies. They argued amongst themselves which would be the better bet: home, the free colony, or the West Indies. Meares swayed them in the end by saying that the slavers were the least tricky. They always wanted crew and they could work their passage and make a new life. But if they went to the colony or Sierra Leone – well, that bastard Coupland would have sent word about them to Freetown and they would hang. The very best would be to take the cutter from them, he mused, but who amongst them could sail or set a course? So they bickered, but in the end agreed with Meares. They would row for the mainland and get the blacks to guide them to a slaver's trading post and get away there. They started another game of cards and exchanged non-existent estates and fortunes and drank some of the brandy they had bought from Tabellun's son.

They would wait it out a bit more.

Somebody, Meares said, should pay the other islanders a visit and see how they were prospering. They had seen the *Pharaoh* sail and knew that a goodly number of the other colonists had wanted to go home. It might be there weren't so many left now.

'Not a visit where we'll be seen and welcomed,' said Meares. 'More of a look-see.'

Saturday, September 1st

On his return to the cutter, Crabtree reported that one of his men, the carpenter Hood, had gone missing. A search party had been sent into the woods but had been withdrawn with the signal of a musket shot when sunset came for fear they would also get lost.

We can ill afford to lose our carpenter. Hood is a good man and a brave one. Coupland ordered a light to be kept in the rigging on the cutter and another on the highest point of the stockade on shore. I am too tired to write any more. I wonder when you will receive my previous communication, Torrington. Letters were sent with the *Pharaoh* and she sailed a month back. Do write back to me, my dear sir – to one crowded shared cabin in a small village in hell, located somewhere off the coast of Africa.

Sunday, September 2nd

Mr Hood is miraculously returned to us. He was sighted stumbling along the shore perhaps a quarter of a mile distant. One of the *grumetas* saw him and waved his arms and shouted, much to the wonderment of Parson Tolchard, who had only just then said a prayer for the poor man's safety. The *grumetas* have joined Tolchard's congregation as a good-humoured nonconformist secession who sit apart and at the back of us, watching the service and now and then commenting in their tongue. Reverend Tolchard has had to remonstrate with them to keep quiet. The man called Franks has been appointed their foreman and speaks their tongue. We are gaining some knowledge of it but still rely on Mr Knox to communicate anything more complicated than 'Cut,' or 'Burn wood,' or 'Split logs,' with accompanying signs, if Franks is not about. But the labourers are good-natured and hard-working and help to keep our spirits up, at least those amongst us who are not sunk in the depression of sickness.

Coupland sent two of our men off to help Hood along. We could now see that he was limping quite badly, stopping every now and then to rest, then hopping gamely on, waving and hallooing. A man was sent to fetch Dr Owen from the hospital.

It transpired that Hood had become lost in the forest, which was of a far greater extent than he had imagined, and he had hidden in a tree from wild beasts. When he lowered himself down at dawn this morning he found he had somehow lost a boot and he cut his right foot coming back through the undergrowth. Knowing that our coast faced north-east he had walked towards the dawn sun and sometimes found trees he had marked. At last he reached the forest edge and saw the ship and the smoke of our shore fire above the trees. He would have made better time, only he had been faced with a deep trench of rough and broken rocks which he had to circle.

Owen bid him sit down. He called for fresh water. Then he gently removed Hood's stocking, occasioning him some pain as the material had become embedded in his cuts. He applied some paste to the foot then bound it up. What of his other trouble – his dysentery? Owen enquired. Why that, said Hood with some surprise in his voice at his own answer, that had quite gone. A miracle, said Owen drily. Did he have food and drink with him? No, said Hood, then he rooted in the pocket of his ragged trousers, he had only these. He showed us a handful of small yellow-brown plums, a little squashed and bruised.

Were there more of these fruits? asked Coupland. Many more, many bushes, said Hood. Coupland turned to the doctor; a search must be made for these plums and a quantity delivered to the hospital.

'As I was about to suggest, Captain,' said Owen sourly. 'You should have been a physician.'

'It can do no harm, man,' Coupland replied. 'Lemons for scurvy and all that. Who knows what the forest might contain for our good.'

I have noticed that the Captain's breezy manner seems to irritate Owen more and more. The good doctor closed his watery blue eyes as if weary, then opened them slowly again.

'And who knows what to our detriment, Captain. We know this is no place for women or children, and it is hardly any better for men.'

'This is no place for this conversation, certainly,' said Coupland, bridling at the doctor's words. He lowered his voice. 'The men are close by. They must not see officers bickering.'

Owen ignored his superior officer. He bent and placed one large red hand on Hood's shoulder and shook him gently. 'Well – are you all right now, my man? You'll live. I shall change your dressing tomorrow. Must away now. Must away.'

His tall portly figure stalked off back up the beach to his hospital.

'Study the mode of that walk well, Jeavons,' said Coupland. 'In military law that is termed "dumb insolence".'

The rest of the day went well. A hog was killed and soon the air was filled with the sweet smell of wood burning and the hot powdery scent of charcoal and the sweeter aroma of fresh meat cooking. That evening Coupland announced a dance and fetched over one of the seamen who had remained with us, bringing him and his fiddle over from the cutter. One of the new barrels of ale that Knox had brought back from down the coast was broached. The fire was fed till roaring high, the fiddle struck up, the ladies came down from the stone house and the fête commenced.

In counterpoint, the *grumetas* down on the beach struck in with their drums, beating constantly as they danced separately to their own design. Our ladies danced as close in position to their husbands as they could but inevitably wandered about in the lines of men. The children squatted beside the fire, their sunburned faces radiant in the flames. We have more men than women and the single men stood at the sides until each of them was drawn into the dancing. Despite our life here, we do have some pretty women and they had got dressed especially in whatever little finery they had. It was not a society ball, more of a village dance in the threshing barn. The fiddle skirled, the fiddler's elbow going like the devil. The drummers gave out their persistent, insistent rhythm. The ale and wine went down, and the *grumetas* and some of our men were sharing rum and I saw some of our men whirling among the native dancers, performing awkward parodies of their athletic grace.

We got into a Scottish reel and the women went twirling about us, their faces flushed and their skirts raised above their ankles, their feet bare. Mrs Owen, the doctor's wife, flared past me like a yellow-haired comet, her eyes intense and burning as if some demon had been released in her. Even Coupland had joined in. 'On, on,' someone shouted and the fiddler increased the speed of his playing so that the notes blurred into one another and the music became a single wild line jigging us about on its end. And all of a sudden it stopped and we half collapsed one against the other – deliberately so, I am ashamed to say, in my case as it enabled me to fall against the soft bosom of Mrs Jenkins, the widow of that fine man, Joe Jenkins. We all then stood upright, panting and laughing. I saw Coupland shaking himself like some proud animal, squaring his shoulders, and smiling down at Mrs Owen, who had finished opposite him, her eyes bright and her lips parted about her pretty small white teeth.

As I stood back, catching my breath, I saw, at the edge of the dancers, out of the ring of fire, flame and shadow alternately at play upon his intense and scowling countenance, Dr Owen watching his wife and Captain Coupland as they exchanged compliments on each other's fine dancing – and God alone knows what else in the doctor's imagination.

13

Jackson was at a loss as to what to make of all this. He had heard tales in London of a town, on the coast of Africa, where freed slaves were treated as equals with whites and owned houses and ships and businesses, where the women were beautiful and the climate always summer. And that was what he had foolishly believed this venture was to be.

But the reality was this set of squalid shelters half built in the ruins of old storerooms and houses and the back-breaking labour involved in the building of the Captain's stockade and blockhouse. The Captain had taken him on a tour of the largely imaginary stockade – because it was still mostly air and dreams. On the chart he had shown him the land that Jackson would possess when they were at last settled. But, Jackson reasoned, with a sense of bitter humour, that all he had for sure so far was the rough bunk he had made in an alcove outside the Captain's cabin on the cutter, and that of the so-called 'servants' he was the one and only personal servant here. Oh, he had one more thing, and that in common with the others: the allocation, when it came his turn, of six feet of earth in the churchyard that was growing apace behind the palm trees up the beach.

He was only a half-man, a man in between. He had been given a little authority and, as long they were in port or on the voyage out, he had the greater authority of the ship's officers behind him. On the island many of the settlers were sullen and did not talk to him unless they had to. He had a lack of duties, except to be perceived as the Captain's man and spy. And one hog of a man had suggested drunkenly one evening that Jackson's place was amongst the labourers, the *grumetas*, not with good white Christian folks.

So, he had spurred himself into the work of felling and hauling and ground clearance and burning, to show himself as tireless and as willing as the next man, be he white or the blue-black of the labourers. But he knew that white men thought of him as a black man, and the *grumetas* saw him as neither white nor black, but an odd sport. There was no reason a man like him couldn't get on, Jackson reasoned to himself. But to get on he would have to get out. Not as Meares and the deserters had. It had to be done honourably. The Captain would have to release him, that was the only condition on his freedom.

He owed this chance of a new life, though it looked to be a grim prospect ahead and not the chance he'd thought to seize, to the Captain. He couldn't rightly skulk off from him like a thief in the night.

But it wasn't comfortable and seemed to be getting more damned uncomfortable by the day. Perhaps Coupland was worth sticking with, if only for the ride to hell. For Coupland didn't seem to see white or black people, or, indeed, people at all. It occurred to Jackson that his master – and that's what he was, no dressing it up – saw the future as a glowing achievable vision that was suspended in time before him and believed that their present wretched position could be driven and coaxed and willed towards that other existence. They might not get there, but Coupland would not relent. And it was not that all men were equal to Coupland; such a notion would not have occurred to him. No, Jackson knew that to the Captain there were simply men who had the spirit and fortitude to help him achieve that vision. Those who could not were unfortunates; either weak-willed or positively idle and maliciously opposed to his purpose.

Yes, yes, Captain, Jackson said to himself, we are all in your chariot and you are driving us to heaven. I'll go along for the ride, because I haven't got anywhere else to go. But if anything happens to you, my good sir, I'll consider myself released from our bargain.

Honour. That was the word of a true man. Honour.

14

I think the man quite mad and a wholesale autocrat, or perhaps I should say a nautocrat. This mad dream of a fort, a castle – nothing less – that he is determined to build with our bones. He seems to think that we are all of his ship's crew and is determined to bring us to port. Well, we are there and a fine place it is too.

We buried two more today: a labourer, Jones, and the poor little four-year-old child Richard Meares whose father deserted us and, far more despicably, his child. The son goes to rest in our only flourishing garden. He was not an attractive child, forever whining and crying, but who can truly blame him. Stripped of our compulsion to conform to a common expectation of 'gentlemanly' conduct to preserve our peculiar *esprit de corps*, is not the temptation to simply sink down and rest in this heat? To sit with one's back to a tree, eyes half closed to the brilliant twinkling water – when it is not dark and turbulent with rain – and simply let the senses wander where they will.

I am writing this in the early morning. One cannot write or read at night or indeed display any light without attracting aggressive insects. The mosquitoes come with or without light. We have experimented with nailing the ladies' fine lace shawls across the window frames, but the devils still get in somehow to torture us. Our bedsteads' legs now stand in pots of water, which seems to be the only thing the ants will not cross or devour.

I saw them. I saw Coupland looking down at my Phoebe as if he were some damned tree leaning over a little stream. Worse, I saw Phoebe *regard*, not *disregard*, the good Captain. I sit here with this sheet of paper laid upon a book and write and it is as if my heart is somewhere on that dancing ground and is being pulled this way and that and torn by jackals and my head turns over and over the possibility, the probability, the real sight of the two of them kissing, embracing, coupling. I know none of this is true – the peculiar circumstances of our being thrown together in this confined community, where we all eat and drink and all but defecate together, render it impossible that my dear one and the robust Captain have ever humped together.

But *do* I know? Oh, dearest Phoebe, I ask forgiveness for doubting your virtue, but my mind cannot rest and wanders and twists in these dark overhung lanes of jealousy. I sit here, at the coolest time of day, before the sun has risen above the forest on the mainland and I dare not look up, down to the cutter. It is quite ridiculous, but I really dare not look down to the cutter. There will be that small circle of glass on the end of his telescope searching the beach, reaching up to me as he regards his domain. Does he search for his love? Is this not a rare dereliction of duty, Captain? To put your own needs and desires before those of the company? And his foul glass scans the hospital to pierce, to penetrate the walls, to reach inside to my fair Phoebe.

Or is it to be foul Phoebe?

Are you foul, Phoebe, my dear? My dear who sleeps, presumably sleeps, now, at this hour. Or when my back was turned at that dancing or at some other time while I slept did you steal away into the forest? When I crossed to the ship, leaving him ashore, did he come to the window of our room in the hospital and whistle softly and did you come from the patients and to our small room, confused with packages and barrels and shelves holding my medicines and our narrow bed, and did you answer him and call him and wait for him to come then bid him wait – while you undressed slowly before him? First the dress, unhooked and peeled down and stepped out of. Then the bodice. Then the white petticoat. Until you stood before him and he was staggered by the whiteness of your body, the roseate tips of breasts, your pretty slightly swelled belly, there, there, down there . . . Does he reach forward and upward as you move to him in that confined space, and does he tenderly lay you down, cover you?

Phoebe. Your name is holy to me and your name revolts me. I venerate you when you come from the poor men and women and children in our charge at night and wash in the bowl by the light of one candle and then lie beside me and say what can we do for these poor folks, what can we do? And then turn and fall almost immediately asleep. I thought you were simply tired. And you were. You must have been. But what about the times I was abroad in the day and Mrs Hood was in the hospital and you rested? Did you rest? Or did you again steal away? Were you swooning and groaning under the good Captain elsewhere? Did you hurry back and put on that virtuous, long-suffering, gallant little face for me when I returned? Did I not see the Captain swinging breezily down the beach from the direction of the hospital as I hauled up medicines and water? Did not his servant, Jackson, assist me? As a sort of

distanced pander, no doubt, for his master. A lookout. A
spy who can blend in the night.

It is early morning, there is a breeze blowing slantways
across the shore. The union flag waves on the cutter,
another behind me, out of my view, on the blockhouse.
The first excited settlers have moved in to their new
rooms in there. I am here with the sick and dying. And
Phoebe. Sweet Phoebe. The gentlest and sweetest of
wives. A panting whore.

15

Sunday, September 16th

My dear Torrington, I continue this journal with not
much hope that it will reach you.

Two more buried in the past week: Mr Wilkins and his
young son, their mother having passed away a few days
before them. We are now down to twenty men and
women capable of work, ten children, only a few of
whom can make themselves useful.

The combination of tornadoes and heavy attendant
rains and strong winds prevents work. When the skies
clear, our workers, only half fit, come out in their ragged
clothes and move slowly about their tasks like ghosts. But
Hood has been very enterprising in continuing to work
on board the cutter, under a tarpaulin, prefabricating
sections of roof. The intention is to roof over some rooms

of the blockhouse so that we can have decent living quarters sooner, rather than wait until the whole edifice is built. Hood's roofs may be carried ashore and each cover two single chambers or a double. They will not yet keep out the most savage weather; for that they must be thickly thatched, we having no means of making usable tiles at the moment. The windows will not have glass in them, but stout shutters.

Saturday, September 29th

I have been ill for the past dozen days and have only now resumed this letter. Thank God I was not confined to Dr Owen's charnel house, but kept on board the cutter.

It was strange that I came down the beach one day feeling perfectly healthy, then, when I got in the boat to come back on board, I felt a great heat in my body. I began to sweat heavily. By the time I came on board I must have been looking queer, for Tolchard asked me in his gentle way if I was quite well. I said no, I didn't think so. I was sent to bed – a real bed, as Tolchard gave up his. There I lay shivering, feeling alternately hot and cold and developing a most vicious ache in my head. I dozed and woke, dozed and woke. I couldn't rise in the morning and all of the joints in my elbows, knees and wrists ached with a dull, enervating pain. Tolchard brought me some cold clear soup of vegetables that he had made specially. I ate it slowly but gratefully, as I had had nothing to eat since the morning before. But almost immediately I vomited it up, in addition to a quantity of green bile which passed hot and so strongly acidic that my throat and mouth burned. I was endlessly restless, trying every position in the narrow bed so that the pains in my head and body might be eased.

Later that day, Owen sent over some pills. I don't know if I kept enough of them down to do me any good. The next day, powdered bark in water. Despite my raging thirst, I could not keep this or even plain water down.

It was about this time, after three days of misery, that I fell into a sort of waking slumber, or so I was told later by Tolchard and Jackson who nursed me throughout. They saw my eyes wide open and wild, my face blotchy red with blood as my wits wandered. I spoke, said Tolchard, of the cool green parkland at the Hall; I called for my mother and wished for Hercules, the pony I had as a child, and made motions as if hectically running. This went on for a day and a night and then I fell into a deep sleep, which enabled them to wash and change what must have become a disgustingly soiled body and its clothing.

When I came to it was to full consciousness and a feeling of almost complete alleviation of my sufferings. True, I was utterly exhausted and had to lie in my bed another day and night. But soon I was well enough to sit out on deck, wrapped in a blanket despite the heat of the day, and begin to take some reasonable sustenance.

16

After another few days Caspar was almost completely recovered. He had gone through what Mr Knox told him was called 'the seasoning' that every traveller to these parts received; a fever from which one either died outright or survived. One was reckoned to be the tougher for it. Caspar could only say that he wished he had been spared the ordeal. He was greeted warmly as a survivor at the next meeting of the Committee on board the cutter.

Dr Owen sent word that he could not be spared from the hospital, so present were Captain Coupland, Mr Crabtree, the Reverend Tolchard and Caspar. Mr Knox had been co-opted for his good advice.

'I would like to suggest, before we start,' said Coupland, 'that we invite Mr Hood, our carpenter, to be present at our deliberations. He is as responsible as any of us, perhaps more than all of us, for the good order of such shelter as we have and I have always found his counsel to be based on sound sense.'

'*Hood?*' said Mr Crabtree in a high and aggrieved voice. 'The *carpenter?* A good, sound man, no doubt, but not a subscriber, not a gentleman.'

'He may not have attended what we call a *good* school,' said Caspar angrily, 'but he is certainly an intelligent, well-read man, and an excellent and diligent worker.'

'Mr Chairman,' said Crabtree, 'surely it is not permitted under our rules of governance for the secretary to the Committee to give vent to personal opinions? Indeed any opinions until asked for them.'

Caspar thought meanly in that same moment how small Mr Crabtree appeared all at once; how yellow and gaunt his face, how sparse his hair had become, how reedy his voice.

Coupland deliberated for a moment. Then he said gravely, 'You are totally in the right, Mr Crabtree. We must keep the form, gentlemen. Finding ourselves in this place and in our situation, I think it is more essential than ever to preserve our standards and proper and lawful customs. Therefore, alas, poor Jeavons, you must remain our recording angel – and as quiet and distant.'

But, Coupland went on, he had in all seriousness considered

electing Hood to the Committee. He was such an excellent man, and there might come a time when – God willing that it might never happen – they had need of him to make up a quorum (which under their Constitution could not be fewer than three). At present, Hood could not be spared from his duties. He was already far exceeding his work times and must be allowed to rest. Coupland said that out of all of them the man Hood was the one closest to being indispensable.

And Caspar thought again, sitting mute in the corner, how scrawny in the neck even the bull-like Coupland had become. His royal-blue coat was soiled, the gold ribbing tainted and dulled, his breeches were creased many times horizontally, his hair betrayed streaks of grey in the thick close-cut brush – he cropped it every week, to allow 'the skull to breathe' as he put it. The Reverend Tolchard looked the best of them, though his face seemed to have lengthened and lost its rosiness. Mr Knox appeared much the same as Mr Knox had always appeared.

'The purpose of this meeting is to outline our progress,' said Coupland. 'Frankly, gentlemen, it is not good. Some days there have not been half a dozen men fit to work.' He had decided reluctantly therefore that they must revise their plans. The stockade must be finished sooner rather than later, in case of attack from any quarter. He had not, he said, forgotten Meares and his men, assuming that they were still alive.

Mr Knox nodded and said, 'They are. They are.'

'Assuming that,' said Coupland, 'it must be advisable to look to our defences.'

He had decided to contract the blockade to a hundred foot square with a courtyard in the middle. This was a considerable diminution from his original ambitious plan, but they must face the fact that they had men – and women and children – to protect, and must settle for what was quickest and safest. They did not know what might happen with the Africans on the mainland. Tabellun might fall from power or die – he was an old man and much accustomed to drunkenness. He might be ousted by his sons and they might well covet this island, seeing what progress the settlers had made. A three-quarter-built fortification would be very attractive perhaps in the wars with their neighbours. The *grumetas* were still healthy and working well, he said. He now intended, but he must have the Committee's approval, to offer land to them, related to the amount of work they completed.

'We have had considerable loss, first from the desertion by Meares and his gang and then by Sir George and most of the settlers, and now by this awful toll of death amongst the settlers who stayed, so we find we have land to spare, to be reallocated amongst all of us.'

'You mean to give Africans our land?' Crabtree's voice rose like a rasp against iron.

'That was our original intention surely in founding this colony. To find, liberate, educate and endow our brothers,' said the Reverend Tolchard in a rare and bold foray.

'But the land is entailed to the original investors in this venture. The land of those who have died must presumably be a part of their estates. You cannot simply bundle it up and reassign it,' Crabtree protested.

'It is our island, purchased by us,' said Coupland.

'For one moment I misheard you. You did say *our* island,' said Crabtree.

'Gentlemen, if I may,' Mr Knox interrupted, 'I don't know your arrangements for land here, but I would certainly wish to join in purchasing any land that is available. It seems to me that there is more than enough land for all – dead and living – and to spare. May I suggest that Mr Crabtree is appointed to produce a chart of the island, showing where each claim to land is situated.'

Coupland welcomed the submission. 'A good point, Mr Knox. I think that, after all your efforts on our behalf – I had considered a gift of land to be suitable. We have little else to give you at the moment.'

'I am a merchant, a trader, Captain, I cannot pretend that an estate on the island would not be very welcome – but I think that, before any gifts or sales of land are made, you need to know the state of the usable land on this island, its extent and where your plots are to be situated.'

'I must admit', said Coupland, 'that our plans were not thought through at the outset in London, particularly in this matter of land and rights. We have come here and experienced difficulties which have put our original purpose from our minds. But what you say must be done, for the future. And, as Mr Crabtree says, the proper legal niceties must be seen to. So, Mr Crabtree will conduct a survey of the island. From his evidence we will subdivide the holdings and the land. As to the native workers, I have apprised them of the purpose of our being here and the establishment of a free colony. I think they have worked hard and deserve a reward. We did not come here to provide investment opportunities for either ourselves or our absent friends such as Sir George.'

'Nonetheless,' said Crabtree with great asperity, it is how the Constitution of the island has been framed. Sir George will expect a return for his money . . .'

'When Sir George returns, then we shall give him that return,' Coupland said. 'Until that day, I suggest that we concentrate our thoughts and efforts on our own situation. Produce your chart, your land assignments, our future plots and plantations. It is a matter of our survival. And part of that depends on our friends – and so they have shown themselves – the Africans.'

Mr Crabtree waved his hands in the air. 'All I was attempting to say is that we have our obligation to the Association we formed and which is enshrined in law in our charter. Sir George or no Sir George, he and the absent investors in London must have their rights protected.'

'Very well,' said Coupland wearily. 'Produce your chart. Tell us where we are all to go and what we are to have. Until then we have only a half-built shelter. My job is to put fresh heart into our colony and to enable our men and women to see what can be achieved. They are the only tools I have to work with. Investors in London might as well be on the moon.'

So, it was decided that Mr Crabtree should produce a chart of the island and show the various land allotments. Meares and his men would be included in allocations, but as soon as possible word should be sent to the Association in London that their desertion meant forfeiture on their part of all claims on the island.

It was asked of Mr Knox that he make another journey to Tabellun's capital and there procure a half-dozen more *grumetas* to hasten the work of building.

17

Mrs Owen, Phoebe, stared at her husband's back. He sat in his shirt, bent over his desk, writing up that day's sick list.

If her father had died and left, instead of nothing, a small competence for his children; if she had not listened with filial piety to her mother; if Joseph had not been the only half-eligible bachelor for miles around; if she had not married him; if she had not . . . My God, what an awful number of ifs had gone into the making of the child she carried.

Joseph Owen bent to his writing.

It was grim news, but there was a certain satisfaction in

confounding Captain Coupland's hopes. His weekly report was much fuller than the usual bald accounting of the numbers of the sick and well; the not very quick and the very dead.

DR OWEN'S REPORT

I cannot keep men and women well in face of the dreadful combination of perilous conditions in which we find ourselves. It is almost as if the island is cursed. Wounds do not heal, but mortify almost at once. The fever takes different forms, so that one remedy, seeming to be beneficial in one case, utterly fails in the next. The extreme fatigue of our men and women, brought about by the intense labours demanded of them, opens them to infections and leaves them less able to fight them off. There is an increase in despondency even among the well. What they have experienced is not what they were led to expect, or what they might have expected after making their investment in this enterprise. We have lost the lazy and unwilling through desertion; those remaining are the hardest working and most enterprising of our people. Now they move like ghosts about their work. I saw one man, Whegall, standing in the heavy rain the other day, simply standing motionless, his face cast down to the beach, while water ran over his rotted shoes. I spoke to him, trying to rouse him, saying, 'Be of good cheer, old man. Soon stops, eh?' But he did not move, hardly lifting his head, when he said, 'Nothing ever ends here, does it?'

He is right. The rain, tornadoes, high winds, more rain, fog drifting from the woods, hot beating sun (the temperature, now averaging the high eighties, seems destined to climb higher daily), the terrible humidity when the great low clouds hang over us, the endless stupefying labour. Nothing ends.

And it seems to me, Captain Coupland, sir, that their

labour is expended in your cause, in the aggrandisement of your power and authority. We put our trust in you, surely, and voted you *de jure* ruler of this place. The upshot is that now our people seem like so many Calibans and you their lordly Prospero, conjuring your own dreams from their labours.

I say plainly, my dear Coupland, that we must have, and as soon as possible, an extraordinary general meeting of all – sick and well alike – to consider our present and future position in this place. There is great dissatisfaction among the colonists who seem to work, as I have said, to this one foolhardy end of the Great Stockade. There is much muttering against your command and I think that those who wish to either leave the colony or to suggest practical alternatives to your authority must be given their opportunity to speak. I wait to hear your early appointment of a date for such a meeting.

I respectfully and sadly append the sick list you asked for:

Men: Twenty-five, of whom twelve are in the hospital, of whom two are likely to die very soon. The rest are the walking sick or wounded in some way. The walking sick are far from well, some are harbouring dysentery that may worsen at any time, others are recovering from fever but slowly and by rights should not be put to work.

Women: Five sick, all in the hospital.

Children: Three sick, at present all are lodged in the stone house.

By my computation that leaves us with the following who are well, or seem so at the moment: five men, three women and four children. In addition you have four seamen on board the cutter and a dozen or so *grumetas*.

In the past week we have buried two men and two male children. At this rate of attrition we shall all in a very few weeks be buried in our churchyard, leaving presumably only yourself to finish burying the last of us and to sail away single-handed.

I remain, etc., etc.

Joseph Owen, physician and surgeon to the Muranda Association.

He sat watching his own words as they dried on the paper. He turned abruptly. Phoebe, who sat sewing, dropped her gaze a little too late, so that it was only too obvious that she did not wish to meet his glare.

He had been cold to her ever since the night of the dance. They had worked ever since in near silence in the hospital. Any questions she asked or statements she made were met with an off-handed economy of words delivered irritably and quickly as if he wanted to be rid of her nuisance. There seemed to be a deep anger in him which she could not understand. If she went to bed first, when he lay down beside her there would be no word and he would turn roughly away from her. She could sense him lying there, his body tense, his foot jerking away if she accidentally met it with hers. If he had retired first and she came in and wearily undressed, she knew that he was feigning sleep, his too regular breathing and the lid-hooded eyes almost daring her to say something or to extend a hand towards him.

But now he gathered himself to speak to her. He said curtly, 'I have seen Hood going up to the women's house. Get you up there and give him this.' He folded the paper into four. 'He is to take it to Coupland on the cutter.' He tossed it so that it fell a little short of her and she had to bend to pick it up. When she straightened he had already turned his back on her and was writing in his log.

She was glad to be out.

Out of the stink of urine and faeces and bad breath and vinegar and the pot of herbs they kept burning in the hospital room to try to purify the air. Out and away from Joseph and his drink. She looked out to the strait. A lantern hung in the rigging of the cutter.

The sky was clear tonight. The stars blazed in constellations, familiar but perversely misplaced. She walked up the newly made road between the beach and the stockade: 'Coupland's triumphal way', her husband had called it. The woods on either side were dark and unquiet. There never truly was silence here. Always the stirring of the palms in the wind and the alien call or cry of some creature, rustling of small animals, croaks of frogs, or sly susurrations of insects. Ahead of her a warm soft light came from a crack in the closed shutters of the stone house.

She knocked loudly and a voice called, 'Oh, do come in.'

The hall was unlit, a figure appeared in the doorway bearing a candle. 'Who is it? Oh, it's you, Mrs Owen.'

This was Mrs Crabtree, the oldest of all the surviving women on the island, somewhere in her middle forties. A woman at heart kind, but with some of the same acerbity that her husband showed. She, like him, was long and thin and her face was now lined and a deep brown from working in the open. In the room behind her, Mr and Mrs Hood and Mrs Waring, whose husband had died of fever two weeks before, sat at table.

Hood rose to his feet and bowed his head politely to Mrs Owen.

'Do have a seat, my dear,' said Mrs Crabtree.

'I won't, thank you,' said Mrs Owen. 'I have only come to bring this for Mr Hood to take to the Captain.' She held out her husband's report and Hood took it from her and stowed it carefully in his coat pocket.

'Nonsense, sit down,' said Mrs Crabtree firmly. 'You may join our little tea party.' Mrs Owen sat down on one of the upturned boxes that served as chairs.

'You're not going back yet?' said Mrs Hood plaintively to her husband.

'I shall soon.' He remained standing.

'You may at least enjoy your tea,' said Mrs Crabtree. She turned to Mrs Owen. 'You see, my dear, how it is. We do try and keep up our evenings amongst ourselves, sadly depleted though our numbers are. Now, may I offer you tea?' She lifted the dainty porcelain pot.

'Thank you,' said Mrs Owen, smiling round at the others.

'Of course, we used up our real tea some time ago, but this is made from some leaves that one of the men first tasted and found pleasant. It makes a passable substitute. The bread is made from the King's flour and baked in the oven that Mr Hood so cleverly made for us. The butter is from the goats. It is the best we can do and generally very excellent it is too.'

Mrs Owen felt how very excellent it was too, to be sitting there with three good women and a good man and to be taking tea and bread and butter, but how unreal it seemed to her after the work that day in the hospital.

'And how', said Mrs Crabtree, 'are our sisters in the hospital? On the mend?'

Mrs Owen lied, both to make her present companions feel better and to distance herself from thoughts of the hospital, 'They are all doing very well. My husband is bending his mind always to find out new alleviations and cures. It is in the nature of the place, he says, that we have so much sickness.'

'The Lord spare us,' said Mrs Waring.

'Amen to that,' said Mrs Hood.

'This house is too big for us now. Absent friends – too many absent friends, I am afraid,' said Mrs Crabtree. 'But – we must not repine.'

There were four rooms, she explained, on the ground floor. This one, in whose cool interior the working men ate in the hot noontime, had three cots propped against the wall until their night-time use. Next was a room that served as a further dormitory for women and small children, and there was another for the older boys. The fourth room served as kitchen and wash house. Because of the dilapidation of the roof, the upstairs rooms were still unusable.

'If we get any fewer, we shall be able to find some space for the men,' said Mrs Hood.

'Ah – no husbands, thank you. No offence intended, Mr Hood. Your dear wife . . .' said Mrs Crabtree.

Here Mrs Waring got up suddenly, holding one sleeve of her dress like a bar across her eyes, and made her way half blinded out of the room.

'Oh dear – we should not have spoken about such matters,' said Mrs Crabtree. 'We try and keep up our spirits, my dear Mrs Owen. But it is too soon for poor Mrs Waring.'

'I will go after her,' said Mrs Hood. 'I'll say goodnight, John.' He stood up awkwardly. She came round the table to him and, reaching up, pecked him affectionately on the cheek. Then she went to comfort Mrs Waring.

So the evening petered out. Mrs Owen explained that she did not like to leave the hospital for too long. Hood said that he had to get back to the ship; the boat was waiting for him, he should not have delayed so long.

Perhaps, Mrs Crabtree enquired, Mr Hood could see Mrs Owen safely back down the road to the hospital.

If he might be permitted . . .?

It was her pleasure.

They walked in silence.

Near to the hospital, she whispered, 'I shall say goodnight here, Mr Hood. My husband has retired, I think, and I don't want to risk waking him.'

The half-dozen or so men who had been working at the stockade had returned to the ship. Jackson and a seaman lounged in the longboat, half asleep, waiting for Hood. Two seamen remained on the shore, taking it in turns to be the night watch. The *grumetas'* camp was quiet; the last gutterings of their fire gleaming against the dark forest.

In the unlighted room, Dr Owen squinnied his eye again to the crack in the shutter and saw his wife bid farewell to a tall gentleman in the starlight.

18

It being a Sunday, and the first fair day for a week, and they being all gathered together for prayers, Coupland announced after the service that he wished everyone to remain for a meeting. 'Dr Owen, I believe, would like to address us all with some concerns he has.'

Dr Owen rose heavily and looked about him. 'I had expected a little more notice, Captain,' he said. 'But, it were well that it has come now than at some later hour.'

His voice gained in confidence.

'I have brought – I have been forced to bring – certain discontents to your notice, Captain.' He turned to his wider audience. 'Now, we all know that the Captain is a good man, a great man in some respects. He has conveyed us here and no doubt done his best to try to counter our disappointment at what we have encountered here.'

He paused for a moment, then boomed on. 'All of us had been led to expect a settled colony, where we could take up our lands and farm and trade or pursue our professions and prosper. Life was not easy back home for many of you. But whatever you have left behind must appear most inviting compared to what you have now.'

The doctor's tone was bitter but so coated in his usual bluff, seemingly good-humoured banter it took a while for his audience to discover what lay behind his remarks.

'It remains the truth', he said, 'that things are not as they should be. Persons have come to me and evinced their doubts about the way the colony is tending. In this supposedly free commonwealth, they have been first deserted by – I hesitate to say the detested word in such a democratic enterprise – their supposed 'betters', then forced to labour on what seems a hopeless and quixotic enterprise.

'It has been hardly possible, given the first circumstances of the lack of dwellings and the perils to health in these parts – the distempers of the air, humidity, storms, tornadoes, rains . . .'

'King Lear,' Mr Knox whispered in Caspar's ear.

'But not only that.' Dr Owen raised his voice, contending against the rising wind and the sound of waves breaking on the shore. 'I must now say that the very original purpose of this colony, that democratic, free-thinking republic of charity and good works, has been reduced to a petty fiefdom. The Captain will forgive me . . .'

Coupland stood as still as he had throughout, his arms folded, his shoulders squared.

'But we can submit no longer to his martial law. The work is unremitting, we all know how excruciatingly little by little the stockade is growing – I have to say that I have more than once heard it referred to as Coupland's Folly, and this vain project proceeds while the well become sick and the sick become dead and fill the graveyard.'

He paused.

'So what, Doctor, is your solution to our quandary?' Coupland's question rang out.

The doctor addressed himself to Coupland. 'The sick – those who can move – must be taken from here, together with the women and children. This is no place for them. And any one else who wishes to depart must be allowed to go now, leaving only those fully in accord with your wishes and desires. Whatever they are.'

Coupland stirred the toe of his boot in the sand before him, then he spoke slowly and deliberately.

'It so happens, and he may be surprised to learn my opinion in this matter, there is much truth in what the doctor says. Believe me, I never meant to impose my law upon you. It was always the King's law and designed to bond us together. We had suffered two sorts of desertion – and I must here say that I shall not and cannot think that anyone now wishing to leave is deserting those who choose to remain. The hardship is severe. It may be that the sick will have a far better chance of healing in Freetown, or, if they can go that far, at home in England. I agree that the women and children should now go. When our colony is fully settled, that will be the time for our family lives to recommence.

'What I promise is this: that I shall remove all of us who lodge on the cutter in the next few days and embark the sick – and any others who now wish to leave. I cannot captain her myself, but Mr Crabtree will be in command and the seamen are perfectly competent. We shall send the cutter down to Freetown and sufficient funds will be provided for a passage to be taken on a boat from there to England. That is the best I can do.

'But – to those who wish to stay, I say this – you can see the immense progress we have made. The side rooms are almost ready in the north-facing wall of the blockhouse. We shall have enough room for all within two weeks when the roofs are fixed. We can proceed to build proper quarters for the native labourers. We shall all then be safely inside the first wall of the stockade and can start on our other great task of exploring and expanding our colony. I know that you all share my hopes for the free and equal land we came here to establish. Now, what do you say – who is to stay and conquer with me? And who is to return – defeated and empty-handed?'

There was silence for a moment, then Caspar shouted, 'Myself, sir. I shall stay.'

'It is the Lord's will,' said the Reverend Tolchard.

Dr Owen broke in.

'This is hardly the way to conduct a poll of such importance, Captain Coupland. Those who want to go may be constrained to say they will stay, through some sense of loyalty to yourself. The ballot must be taken secretly and examined and counted in full view.'

So, paper and pen and ink were brought from the hospital – Mrs Hood alone remaining to see to the sick.

The tally came to this: to leave, six men, all sick and able to move, the four women still sick, and all of the children. To stay: eighteen men, though of these three were too sick to move, and ten more were recovering or still poorly in one way or another. The three wives – Mrs Crabtree, Mrs Hood and Mrs Owen – were also to remain, though Mrs Owen was unwell herself.

Most surprising of all, Dr Owen elected to stay, saying that he was still the appointed surgeon of the Committee and there were sick to be tended.

The cutter would sail, weather and wind permitting, in three days' time, Coupland announced.

19

Abercrombie said bitterly, 'Why did we not bring the women? We have no women. I want a woman.'

Meares said, 'Shut up. We all need a woman. We all need to get off this bloody island. It is not much practical help to sit there on your fat arse and complain of your underused cock, is it?'

They sat about their fire at the entrance to the cave. It shelved back deeply; just where it narrowed too much for a man to go any further there was a steady trickle of cold fresh water through the rocks above them. This was their secret supply. Meares knew that the colonists were shipping in water. If he could barrel water from his spring he would have something they might trade. Especially if the settlers upset the blacks across the strait.

Meares had been looking for a way to strike back at Coupland. He had no real cause to hate the Captain; it was that he loathed Coupland for bringing him here, for it not being as he had thought; the threat of endless labour in some *common* cause was not attractive to a man of his mercantile bent.

One of the sons of King Tabellun had visited them. The savage had the temerity to look amused at finding white men living in a cave, but as he had a dozen or so armed men in his canoe it was not a good thing to argue with him at that moment. The prince had cordially agreed to bring rum and rations from the mainland and also brought across a milking goat. Not that all of this was done out of charity. The prince was willing to accept payment only in gold. And their supply would not last for ever.

There were six of them; two seamen, who had deserted from the *Pharaoh*, Meares and his half-brother Michael, for whom he bore little love, but whose strength and vicious temperament might come in handy, Abercrombie (who had abandoned his wife to the colonists and was unaware that she now lay in the graveyard), and Dodds, a coiner and a man handy with tools and fire.

They kept the fire in at all times. From the mouth of the cave they looked out west to the ocean; mounting the cliff path, they could stand on the top and look north-east to the mainland. To the south-east, across the island, lay the stockade and the colonists, hidden by the forest.

They had been here for three months now; letting each day slip away in idleness until they hardly noticed them go. They had beds of straw stuffed into sailcloth. They were well armed, with muskets and ammunition, and a swivel gun from the ship mounted in the mouth of the cave. Their muskets brought them a ready supply of wildfowl and deer to roast. But they were prisoners of their own liberty; they knew that much. They washed themselves and their clothes occasionally on the rocks below them, but their hair and beards had grown long. They were browned by the sun, but still healthy. They did no work. To amuse themselves they got drunk, and warmed themselves by the fire and with dreams of seizing Coupland's treasure chest – an article they had none of them ever seen, but which was perpetually in their thoughts.

They spied sometimes on the settlers; stealing through the forest and the high grass of the savannah, working their way around over the hills. They could see the work going on in building the stockade and the blockhouse. And they could see the cutter moored a little off the jetty. It would have taken only an hour to row to her and seize her. But she always had a watchman and the longboat went to and fro at all times of the day.

But they had noticed that as time passed there were fewer of the workers, until there appeared to be hardly anybody working and the place looked empty. Then a figure would move amongst the timbers of the half-built blockhouse, or the boat would row across with just one or two men in it.

The time, Meares thought, was getting near when they could take possession of the colony.

Until then, to amuse himself and the others, Meares proposed a little entertainment. An elephant hunt, no less.

20

Wednesday, October 17th

Well, Torrington, the cutter sailed this morning.

We have spent the past two days removing our goods
from it and setting up house as best we can in the
completed rooms of the stockade and the stone house.

There are fewer of us, but we feel more secure now
that we are all gathered into the stockade. We have set
up two of the four-pounder cannons on platforms behind
the outer stockade wall to cover the road from the beach.
Two swivel guns are mounted on the low towers at each
end of the north wall of the stockade in case our
perimeter is breached. We have a good stock of weapons
and powder. In case of a successful breach we would
defend ourselves from the stockade while the women
were sent back to what would be our last redoubt in the
stone house.

Last night we made a final feast of a bullock for all
who were well enough to attend. In the morning,
affectionate farewells were made to the sick and the
others who were leaving. There was no ill will. All
have good reasons for not remaining; the doubt begins
to lie in our reasons for staying, perhaps.

Our total numbers are now these. On the cutter:
Mr Crabtree, three sailors and two *grumetas*, all of whom,

God willing, will return to us. On the island: fourteen men, three women and eighteen *grumetas* – these I should, by rights and by their efforts, have included in our number.

We are all at once feeling spent. Although we are all now presumably like-minded men and women in our endeavour, our colony is pitifully reduced. I must admit that when I saw the cutter round the north point to breast the sea my courage, such as it is, wavered and I wished myself on board and away from this place.

But the weather has been clear for many days now, though infernally hot in the day so that work is done in the early morning or late afternoon. I keep the date, restoring it to my records, after I was ill, from the log of Coupland, a dry and terse description in naval fashion of the weather each day, the number of sick, the progress of building. There are scant descriptions of persons. 'I rely on you for the dramatics,' he said when giving me the date.

It is late autumn in England. The trees will be bare. Grandmama will sit beside her fire reading or, rather, now, looking at the hour, she will be asleep in bed, her thin lips pursed as she watches some dream of the folly of mankind, her stern nose beaking in the steady dim light of her night candle. She would regard our night as one in hell.

Reasons to be thankful? The rains have ceased. We are much reduced, but determined. Our decisions will now only affect those willing to be so affected – the disaffected having gone their several ways.

I hope that when I write further I shall have much better news for you.

21

THE REVEREND TOLCHARD'S PRAYER

Dear Lord, that I should have the temerity to address you
in this manner, not on my knees, but in my bed with
this paper resting on my lap. It is my duty to ask why,
Lord, our people have had to suffer so? I get no answers
from my prayers.

What ideas I had. To take this island, empty except for
the dumb creatures of the wild, and to transform it into a
place of praise unto God. To make a green cathedral of
its forest, to have the calls of birds join with our voices
in the praise of the Lord.

When on the mainland, among the heathen natives of
these parts I was happy. I could see that they must have
some propensity towards belief, even if their beliefs are in
error. And I thought that once a man is inclined to
believe a thing in error, he can be guided from his
wanderings to believe in the one True Faith.

I would have built, after I had helped with the
building of our necessary physical lodgings, a small
church on this island for our settlers, and in the fullness
of time, God granting me the time, a greater church on
the mainland. I saw in my vision churches and schools
and the gratitude of a people, their old sinful habits cast
behind them, finding their life in the example of our

Lord. Huge congregations, their voices soaring above the jabber and horror of the forests, the confusion of fogs, the battering storms and felling heat. I saw the terrors of ignorance and war and slavery consumed in the fire of the angels. I saw the descendants of these savage people troop gently forth from the conflagration, to kneel at the altars of our dear Lord, and to receive his blood and his flesh between their lips in communion. I saw the villages, cleaned and whitened, the drums laid silently aside, the modest women covering their bodies, the barbaric warriors become farmers. I saw their children walk their mild way to the newly built school; the gentle murmuring of lessons.

And all this was vanity.

For in this parish I have no marriages or births to celebrate and consecrate, all I have is death. This month has been a constant, quickening parade of mortality.

On Monday, in the hospital died Mr Kelly. Buried the same day.

On Tuesday, Mr Marston died and was buried.

On Wednesday, Mr Donnelly died and was buried.

Today, young Gerald Thornton is a wasted, yellow, rotting corpse beneath a covering of sand and clay and I can find no reason for it. The Scriptures for the first time sit on my table, not taken up for my evening solace. The prayer book falls open now almost of its own accord at the expected page. I can find no comfort for these souls any more.

I must not say it, but this is to where my mind has come. There is no plan in heaven for our community, our great adventure. A few miles to the south of us the slave traders ply in and out. Men pursue their wickedness, ignorant of my pitiful prayers for them. God brought us here, and has given us what? A nameless place, full of monstrous unnamed creatures, a place that God has not visited since its brute creation; truly godforsaken. There is no plan for us, no divine plan, no intercession, no pardon, nothing. There is only this out of the window at night – a gibbering chaos. Blackness. The madness of the forest. That is all.

22

Sunday, October 28th

Last night, the Reverend Tolchard, who, of all the party, had so far remained free of any illness, went to bed in his room shared with Mr Wharton, was seen to turn over with a sigh, heard to murmur something, and was found dead this morning.

A strange occurrence, as we buried the good man, we heard the distant crack of a gun, probably a small cannon; then again, and again, in ragged, isolated shots; a poor salute to the late pastor. Coupland finished reading the words over the open grave and the *grumetas* began to fill it in, swiftly and expertly.

'You hear that gunfire?' he asked me.

'Do you think it's our friend, Meares?' I said.

'Up to some damn tomfoolery,' he said.

And today, another odd coincidence brought us the Reverend Tolchard's self-declared friend in these parts, King Tabellun, on a visit.

Jackson, acting as lookout, spied the King's war canoe

rounding the north point, with Tabellun on his throne in the middle and perhaps a dozen rowers on each side, coming across the strait. Another canoe was a few lengths behind, with another twenty or so men. When Jackson came up to report, Coupland said to me, 'The King is coming to view our strength. He will know that the cutter has sailed, but he knows we are not all gone because he will have seen our smoke.'

He turned to his man. 'Jackson, take yourself and Waller and load the two forward cannon with grapeshot and have slow matches ready. Jeavons, be a good fellow and see to the swivel guns on the towers.'

It was to be a brave show. Half of the *grumetas* had been issued with muskets, although, on Coupland's instructions, they were not provided with powder and ball. He did not yet fully trust some of the newcomers among them. Jackson and Waller stood to behind their cannons. Similarly the swivel guns were loaded and could be quickly manned if required. More of the *grumetas* worked at squaring roof planks under Mr Hood's supervision. Those of the sick who could walk and make at least a token attempt at work were fetched from the hospital and put to light tasks. It was most important, Coupland insisted, that we appear busy and contented and in control of our island.

The first essential was not to let the King into the inner square, except on his own or with a small retinue. He must not see how our world was only half built. Four fowls were killed and set to roast. A tent was pitched halfway down the beach for the King to be received and a table placed outside it, laden with fruit and two bottles of rum.

The war canoes nearing, Coupland went to his quarters and came out ten minutes later in full naval uniform with cocked hat. Two Portuguese armchairs, riddled with woodworm, but still handsome solid pieces, were brought down from the stone house and covered with red cloth. In one, Captain Coupland arranged himself in a negligent pose, a book in one hand, at his other a steaming cup of our home-made leaf tea. Mr Knox, who was again to act as interpreter, sat on a stool. The other, empty, chair awaited the King.

The *grumetas*, in a medley of European clothing and shouldering their unloaded muskets, were deputed to meet the King, with myself leading this guard of honour. We marched down to the jetty to meet the first canoe as it glided in. A rope was flung up. The King arose and mounted the rickety steps, clutching his gown with one hand and holding the rail with the other. I noticed, looking down on him, that he appeared older and less physically sure of himself than in his own camp.

But when he reached the top, he straightened his bright gown, drew himself up and stared about the beach and further to our wall and the stockade beyond with a shrewd and searching look. He was surprised and pleased when I greeted him with words from his own tongue. (I had learned a sentence or two from Mr Knox.) He looked hard at the *grumetas* in their shirts and pantaloons, and more particularly at their muskets and he rapped out some guttural and harsh-sounding words to them. Then he turned, smiled again and I beckoned politely to him to follow me.

The *grumetas*' honour guard lagged behind us. The King forged ahead with myself and a half-dozen of his own people.

At the red and white sailcloth tent, Coupland and Mr Knox stood up from their seats to greet the King. His eyes were all about the place, spying what we had been doing, looking through the gateway up to the blockhouse (which looked most imposing, though partly a stage setting, with the one finished wall facing us and half a dozen rooms behind, but the rest unfinished).

The King enquired politely after the Captain's health. He had heard a number of our party had not been well. If there was anything he could send over . . .?

No, Coupland replied equably. We were perfectly well suited to look after our sick. We had a sufficiency of bark and calomel, in fact more than we could use, so that if his own people should need any of our medicines . . .?

At this, the King smiled and was silent for a moment, and then asked where our ship was. Our little ship, as he termed it. He had seen it sail away and thought we had quitted the island. But no, said Coupland. We had simply sent the cutter for more supplies to Freetown.

We could have applied to him, said the King, for anything we needed.

We were feeble creatures compared to his people. White men required special drugs to withstand the climate.

The King appeared puzzled. Then he said triumphantly, 'But what about your god. What about your priest's god?' And then, 'Where is your priest? Why is he not here? I thought that gentleman was my friend.'

It was his sad duty, said Coupland, to inform His Majesty that the Reverend Tolchard had died only the day before.

The King frowned. That was indeed a pity. He was a young man. Could not his god save him? How could that be?

'He was a servant of the Lord and the Lord above sets our time here below,' said Coupland.

'A short time for many of you,' said the King. 'Your prayers are misdirected perhaps.'

Just then a procession of Mrs Hood and Mrs Crabtree and Mrs Owen brought down the roast fowls and some trays of cooked sweet potatoes and stewed greens we had gathered up in the hills. Tabellun ate and drank with hasty yet graceful determination, throwing every now and then a piece of food to the men squatting at his side, as if feeding dogs.

Pausing in his feast, he told us the reason for his visit today. It seemed that the occasion of a full moon marked tomorrow as the most propitious day for the hunting of the elephant. This island was the sacred ground for elephants. Only at this time of year was it permitted to kill the bull elephant, the oldest and greatest of which was reserved for the King's hunt.

The King took a draught of rum.

'The finest tusks also,' whispered Mr Knox to me in an aside.

'Tusks,' said the King loudly in English, but almost absent-mindedly, not looking at us. And I knew then that he understand more of what we said than we had thought.

So, he said, once more through Knox, he would be greatly honoured if the good Governor, Captain Coupland, would accompany him on the hunt in the morning.

'Alas,' said Coupland languidly. 'If you had given more notice of your expedition I would indeed have been glad, but matters of state keep me from such enjoyments at the moment.'

This being translated, the old man looked rather out of sorts for a moment. But then he said that he quite understood that kings and other high officers must tend their realms. Whether this was meant satirically, I do not know, but Coupland smiled and said that His Majesty was most gracious. He would not hunt alone. His chief steward, Mr Jeavons, and his chamberlain, Mr Knox, would be most honoured to accompany him.

At the end of the feast, well into the early evening, Coupland invited the King to see the improvements we had made since his last visit. The King was a little tipsy as he rose from the chair. Only he and two attendants walked up the beach with us.

Coupland let him have good sight of the cannons on the palisade, and the swivel guns on the towers of the stockade, and the four-pounders up on the ridge.

I could swear the King said what sounded like 'Well, well,' in English to himself as we went round. By God, we must have seemed a poor lot, but not so that the King was minded then to attack us as we had feared. Coupland audaciously said that he hoped the King would accept his hospitality in the new stockade. He had ordered that Tolchard's room be emptied and the bed made up anew in there. The King's men, Coupland said grandly, might take up the *grumetas'* quarters near the beach. (And he ordered a watch of two armed men to be relieved at regular intervals throughout the night to make sure that none of the visitors roamed forth.) The *grumetas* would take up their new quarters within the stockade's precincts.

These guns of ours, the King enquired, how far could they throw a shot? To demonstrate, Coupland himself went up to one of the four-pounders on the ridge above the stockade, loaded the charge and a ball and turned the gun slightly on its housing. He discharged the cannon and with what must have been a deliberate aim sent the ball so that it took its flight across the beach, over the King's moored canoes and dropped far from the jetty to send up a fountain of water out in the strait. The lesson was obvious and obviously impressed the old king. His face lit up in a great beam of a smile. It was time, Coupland judged, for more rum.

The King retired early – for him – before midnight.

Knox and I are to take the first watch from the palisade on the *grumetas'* quarters. Knox has sworn himself fit for duty and for the hunt in the morning. A little fresh air, he says, will do him good.

I will close now.

23

Meares' men had shot at the beast a few days before, but it had escaped them. Abercrombie said they would have to have a bigger weapon to do it more serious damage next time. Their musket balls only buried themselves in its thick hide. So Meares had thought and hatched a plan for the downfall of the elephant.

They knew that the elephants swam ashore from the mainland at its nearest point into a small bay not far from their caves. The bay had a shelving beach and the elephants came in at high tide because then they had a sure footing. Because, said Meares, when the tide went out what was left was thick mud. If they could drive the beast back at low tide there was a chance they might trap him. He had seen a couple of young elephants stuck there one time, struggling in the mud but having to wait for the sea to come in before they could swim free.

Why didn't they kill those then, said Abercrombie, seeing as how they were a sitting target? Because, muttonhead, Meares rejoined, they weren't there now, were they? If they waited for the coincidence of tide and inexperienced beasts they might wait for ever. What they had to do was make the conditions favourable. To themselves.

'Fire and water,' said Meares. 'Fire and water.' He wanted the big beast. He outlined his plan.

They set out at dawn, armed with muskets, knives, swords and bayonets. They had made torches of tree branches wrapped round with dried grass tied with twine. There were only six of them, but if all played their part they must prevail over a dumb animal.

They mounted the path from the cave to the top of the cliff and entered the woods. They knew that the elephants grazed fruit on the edge of the woods and that they loved to meet the morning sun on the savannah.

The sky was clearest pale blue above. Dawn light flooded the treetops. And there, under the trees, stood the elephants. Their trunks curved up in a slow gracefulness to take down fruit. Mothers and their calves, a couple of young males, but above all, the huge bull. Even at a distance, his size and the latent power of his motionless body were overwhelming. In this primeval light, in this sound of birds and insects, of his females and calves and male underlings breaking fruit from twigs, conveying it by those serpentine trunks to chop and chomp between their teeth, for how many years had he been master here, for how many thousands of years had his ancestors stood here in his prideful place?

Well, he couldn't tell you. That was what Meares would have said if asked that question. A beast could not answer a question. The man looked at the huge and powerful animal and considered how he could destroy it.

Meares was a mean man but with ambition. He never expected to have power over very much. He had it over these five miserable men, waiting beside him in the new light, clutching their weapons, waiting for his word, his commands, his plans. They would *do* this creature, this proud haughty stupid creature with its mass of flesh and the riches in its white curving tusks. They would sell those and buy new weapons from the blacks and perhaps recruit some of the blacks and have them help fight and win the camp of Captain Bloody Coupland.

God, that journey out from England. And then to have to listen to his canting lectures. To have him take over their lives. If it was liberty they had come for, well they would have it. To be king of this place would be a start. Meares would be magnanimous. Put Coupland on trial. His people could have no love for him now. Hang him, then. Dangle him. The colonists could choose their own fate. Those who didn't want to stay could clear off. If there were many left. Who had sailed on the cutter? They'd see soon. Leave them to stew.

'Meares? What do we do?'

'I told you. You two go that way into the wood at their side, we'll go round and come through the grass. When we fire the grass I'll let off a shot and you beat the drum and thrash the trees, whatever to make noise. They won't attack if we don't wound them. They'll want to get away from the fire. We need to drive them down the path there, the path they've made through the wood from the bay. We'll chase them across the fields, behind the fire, making an unholy din. The wind is our way. The tide is out. With any luck they'll rush down to the bay and try to swim across. They'll find only mud and with any luck the buggers will stick. Let's get to it.'

Dodds and Abercrombie went away into the wood. Meares left a man on the south flank of the savannah with instructions to fire the grass if the herd should shift that way. He and Chamberlain made their way under cover of the flanking wood behind the elephants and emerged on the open savannah. Meares carefully, but with a feeling of sudden excitement, unwrapped his flint and tinder.

They laid their fires. The wind was behind them. The grass was dry after a week of hot weather. It went up quicker than they expected. With rushing onward movements as if chasing itself forward, the grass crackled and burned. Meares fired off his musket. The elephants were stirring now, uneasily, and moved about a little this way and that in some panic. Birds startled away from the treetops as the drummers advanced below them.

Meares was proud of his generalship of this small band. The beasts began to move slowly, then more quickly as the fire approached. The infernal din came from the woods at each side, so that they were funnelled to that gap between the cliffs where the ground went down in a smooth incline.

The elephants, in their terror, appeared to be marshalled by the great bull. He hung behind as the young and their mothers disappeared, then he too went between the trees on to the track downwards, and was the last to show, his thick folds of skin flapping like some sort of stage curtains. Then the trees' lower branches and leaves flickered into flame. In the heat, the drum-beating men had to seek higher rocky ground. They could hear the elephants crashing their way through the trees to the bay. Then the men too raced from the rocks, and pursued the elephants down the path. They banged their drums and hallooed even more fiercely and loudly.

The elephants debouched on to the beach and entered mud instead of water. They went out deeper and deeper, to find the sea, but the sea lay many hundreds of yards off. They became stuck, lifting each heavy limb slowly and with great effort from the red mud. They got in worse and worse until their legs were quite under the mud and only the very hugeness of their bodies prevented their sinking any further.

'What sport, eh, boys,' Meares shouted. The men stood at the edge of the mud, discharging their muskets at will at the elephants who threw up their trunks and trumpeted and bleated in anguish as the balls struck home. 'Don't waste your fire on the young 'uns,' Meares cried out. 'Get the big one.'

The big bull raised his trunk and let out such a blast of

rage that for a moment they stopped and were afraid that his mighty stirring would allow him to break free. But, no, he was stuck faster than any of them. They directed their fire now on him. To the head, which twisted this way and that in pain, all the time roaring. One eye burst open and they thought they had him. They must have loosed off fifty shots at the creature and still he would not die.

'This is no good,' said Meares. 'We shall be at this all bloody day. Jack, you and Walter bring round the boat with a dozen shot for the swivel gun. We'll finish him with that.'

It took an age for the two men to get out of the muddy bay and up and across the rocks. By the time they had got the boat launched, and the swivel gun primed and loaded, the tide was not far from the turn.

Meares kept asking where the hell were they? At this rate the beasts would go free. The men were tired. The elephants continued to move and moan and toss their heads. Most were wounded, but none as grievously as the bull, who now and then lifted his trunk and gave out a huge bellow, the fluid and blood from his punctured eye drying on his leathery skin. Every now and then one of the men out of boredom would take a potshot at him but even that had grown wearisome.

'Here they are,' shouted Abercrombie as the boat hove into view at the far entrance of the bay.

'You can't get in any further,' Meares shouted through his cupped hands. 'Bring the gun across the rocks.'

Ten minutes later the two men arrived sweating and cursing and lowered the iron gun to a rocky platform.

'Even you should be able to hit the bugger from here,' said Meares.

It took them three shots to range the bull. The fourth smashed his back leg and he sank slowly, raising his trunk in a moan to say that he was broken. They shifted the gun and the next shot went over his head and crashed and rolled into the rocks across the bay. The sea was ebbing in and some of the elephants were in prospect of floating free soon.

'He's not going nowhere,' said Meares. 'Load carefully, lads.' They depressed the cannon and this time, the bull's head lifting in agony, the shot, at just the right elevation, hit him square in the side of the head.

'Christ,' said Abercrombie.

The shot had smashed the elephant's skull. What great power had kept the animal upright during its long torment was dispersed suddenly and it stood on straining front legs for but a moment, then sank and its head and trunk and the whole front of its body wallowed in the mud, slowly writhing and sinking as if seeking rest.

When perfectly sure of their safety, they waded out. They had with them saws and bayonets and knives and for two hours they worked assiduously at the dead creature. They detached the trunk with relative ease. This, they had been told, by the mainland natives, was a great favourite at feasts. The tusks were more difficult. They gouged up into the cheeks to find the limit of the ivory. The sawing, two-handed on each, was more work than any of them had done for many a day. By now, the sea was coming back in and they had to stop, though they did have both tusks free. 'A great prize, lads,' said Meares.

The other elephants had been freed by the tide, but they did not depart. They swam out a little, but seemed reluctant to go though the men continued to fire sporadically at them with their muskets. The bull was displayed in all his wretchedness on the beach as the tide went out again. The other elephants milled in the water at the entrance of the bay, the water muddied with the blood from their wounds, their trunks upraised and shrilling with pain and dismay.

'Bring up the boat,' Meares commanded. 'We'll load the

tusks and row home round the point. Leave the others. Leave them for another day.'

So they did, though as they rowed past the elephants mourning in the water, the outermost made a lunge towards them as if to capsize their boat. Meares fired at him and cursed while his companions rowed fiercely until they were safely past.

'Like dogs,' said Meares, dropping down. 'Like mad dogs who need a master. A strict master. Not in my yard. Not in my yard.'

He looked back at the dead bulk of the giant elephant. Then he admired the long thick curving bloodied tusks in the bottom of his boat. Here was trade at last.

24

They started out at dawn. The King was in fine fettle, despite his age and the freight of rum he had taken on board the night before. Perhaps he had dismissed the idea of attacking them, as Coupland thought he meant to do, after seeing their cannon and fortifications. Perhaps he felt treated well and honourably, for after breakfast Coupland and he exchanged gifts – Tabellun asking especially if he might have something of their late priest's; he was given a spare black leather Bible. His face was at first disappointed as he handled the book, until Mr Knox assured him that it was the priest's holy text. For his own part he was pleased to bring them some much-needed new stock in the form of six hens in a crate and two goats for their milk.

Caspar walked at the start of the hunt beside Mr Knox and hoped that the man was quite up to the excursion. 'As I said – it will do me good. Fresh air, exercise. Because I tell you, young Mr Jeavons . . .' He glanced quickly at Caspar and then straight ahead as they followed the King, 'that this is not a good place for one's health. No – I don't mean here, with the King. We are in no immediate danger, I assure you. But – it is the island. We were not meant for it. Do you see what I mean. It holds devils in its air and water. Well, let these people entertain them in their bodies. They have grown used to them over the centuries. But we have no business here. Literally, I fear, no business. We should stay off – but, you know, I don't think we shall be able to stay away. It will be America and India again, won't it? Riches, virgin lands. We will come in our thousands, young Mr Jeavons, and conquer and build our homes proudly on the bones of these men.'

'I don't think the King would like to hear you talk of conquest, Mr Knox,' Caspar said jocularly.

'The kings here will have no say in the matter,' he muttered.

But as they walked Caspar thought of what Knox had said, and how wrong he was. Caspar could well envisage in happier days to come the small farms scattered across the land, the spire of poor Tolchard's church rising where their poor colony stood. The healthy and vigorous native labourers – they did not seem to be vitiated by constant fevers and fluxes. If these people could conquer such things, perhaps simply by becoming habituated to them, well, then surely the British could do the same. They could hold on, couldn't they? Their numbers were dwindling, but there must come an end to this constant attrition. Perhaps now the rains had ceased everything would improve.

They had been walking for more than an hour, covering maybe four miles of easy country, when one of the scouts stopped and waved his staff forward. Perhaps another mile ahead, beyond the line of trees, thin twisting columns of smoke rose.

'Burning the forest. Is this the work of your men?' the King demanded angrily of Mr Knox.

'But no,' Knox assured him. 'None of our men are out here. The only white men outside the colony are deserters.'

Then the King's son said something to his father. Tabellun glared at him and shouted an insult at which the son cowered back. He was evidently trying, rather miserably, to explain something to the old man.

They all stopped walking as the King halted to berate his son.

Mr Knox whispered to Caspar: 'The King has learned that his son has been trading with the renegades. He is reminding his son forcibly that he does not think it very sensible to buy from strangers the product of an island he already owns. And no, I do not think it a very opportune moment to remind him that we have title to the island.' He was interrupted by the King strutting on again and furiously waving all of them forward.

The savannah had been scorched down to grey and black wisps of grass and roots. At the edge of the woods the ground still smouldered. The taller trees, though scorched and burned lower down, had escaped complete destruction; either the fire had outrun its energy or the wind had changed, sparing them.

Here the scouts pointed to the indisputable tracks of a herd of elephant and the hunters followed a pathway between the trees. But where the air should have freshened, for they could now catch glimpses of the sea, instead there came a most sickening stench of rottenness and decay.

'Good Christ, what is that?' Caspar said to Knox.

The last of the trees parted and they looked down to the beach. A huge grey mound lay half submerged in the water. The King strode forward and halted at the water's edge. Knox clutched at Caspar's sleeve to prevent him following.

It was the body of an elephant. The top of its head had been caved in as if with a mighty hammer. Its trunk had been hacked off, leaving a stump thick with black flies, as were the cavities from where the flesh had evidently been gouged so that the tusks could be sawn at a maximum length.

The King, greatly angered, turned to them and bellowed at Knox, 'Who has done this? Did your men do this?'

Then he turned to one of his sons and shouted, 'You were to watch these settlers, these thieves.' But his son said, 'No, not these men,' pointing to us, 'but the men in the caves. The men who hid from their fellows.'

'So, I shall deal with *them*.'

'They will see us coming. They keep a good lookout and have a big gun in the cave mouth.'

That was no matter, said the King. A runner was sent off back to the settlement with orders for the King's war canoe to join them at the beach below the caves. The King and the rest of his men would make their way there over the rocks. His son was to go ahead and tell the deserters that the King had come to trade with them. He had heard they had ivory to sell. And the son must tell them to get food and rum ready for a feast to celebrate their great act of yesterday. A day that would go down in legend.

Tabellun pointed to Knox and Caspar, 'You two will come with us and see how justice is meted out to thieves and desecrators. This bull was a king also. He deserved a better death.'

The King's son was to ask permission of the renegades for the King to visit, and to ask if he might fire off a shot to tell the King to come ahead. Tabellun turned again to Knox: the two white men were to lag along out of sight until the business was concluded.

So, the King's son set off and the rest of the hunting party followed at a distance along the beach and over the rocks to halt at the headland cliff.

Perhaps half an hour later, they heard a musket shot and they went down the beach and clambered over more rocks until they came in view of the caves set in the cliffs. A figure appeared in the mouth of one, waving a red cloth.

Caspar and Knox were told to conceal themselves. A signal would be given to bring them forward.

As they went off, the King, a tall and powerful old man, adopted a weak and shambling gait; certainly not that of a warrior bent on revenge.

It took a few minutes for the party to cross the last of the rocks and beach, then the King and his men were swallowed up by the dark entrance.

Caspar waited with Knox. It seemed to him that they waited for a long time. They crept nearer through the rocks. They could see the light of a fire reflected on the inner wall of the cave and caught the thin strain of a fiddle playing. Caspar began to grow bored. Time passed. The fiddle stopped. There came a scream from inside, then another and another.

One of the deserters came out and stood in the entrance. He raised his arm. His left hand was missing and blood pumped from the stump in regular but diminishing spurts. Then his whole body jolted and was flung forward. The echoing sound of a musket shot followed. Then a succession of shots, muffled, the flashes like lightning in the cave. Silence, except for the gulls overhead and the fall of the ocean waves down on the beach. One of the King's men appeared at the mouth of the cave and called, 'Knox. Knox.'

Caspar followed Knox, fearful of what he would see.

A fire burned deep inside the cave, over which a rough spit held what Caspar took to have been the trunk of the dead elephant. Tabellun stood behind the fire, glaring sternly. Only as they advanced towards the fire and their eyes grew used to the firelight after the sun outside did Caspar see the bodies strewn on the floor. And only then did he become aware that there was someone still alive. A piteous muffled moan of 'Dear God, Dear Christ,' then indistinct mumbling came from the creature on his knees at the side of the King. Two hands clutched a face that was a mass of blood.

'Tell your friend, this wretch here, Mr Knox,' said the King, 'that as he cut off the nose of our great elephant, so we have separated him from his own. I have spared his life so that he may serve as an example to others. I understand that he is in dispute with the good Captain Coupland. I give him into your charge. Captain Coupland can have the final say in his fate. White men are most imaginative in their methods of imposing justice. Take him. We shall remove the tusks and wait for our canoe. We have done with the island for today. I shall come hunting some other time, some better day. Take him, if you please.'

Two of his men forced the man to his feet. 'Meares,' the figure snuffled, 'Meares.'

'I would not have known you, sir,' said Knox.

'What about the others?' Caspar whispered.

'The jackals and ants will have them soon enough,' said Knox. 'We had best leave now before the King changes his mind about us.' He turned to the King and delivered what sounded like a most elegant and apologetic farewell speech.

The King continued to frown and waved a hand dismissively and said nothing but one word, in English: 'Go.'

Meares stumbled between them, clutching his shirt to his disfigured face, moaning and burbling unintelligibly.

'Can you walk, Meares?' Knox asked.

A mumble came amid bloody sobbing.

'Well, do so and quickly.'

At last, supporting the wretched man, they reached the turn at the base of the cliffs and clambered over the barrier of rocks to where the stinking elephant's carcass lay, the incoming tide beginning to lap against his bulk.

Meares was in an even worse case than Caspar had first thought. He had other cuts to his body and had lost a great deal of blood. Though Knox had bandaged him as well as he could, Caspar could feel him weakening as they finally got back on the track leading through the wood.

They had almost crossed the savannah and were about to

enter the forest when Meares sank down on his knees and then slumped to the earth.

He could go no further, he said, or throaty bubbling noises approximating to that meaning.

'Well, we can't carry him,' said Knox. 'The poor devil will be dead before we get him back.'

A howl came from Meares. He lay shivering and holding his blood-drenched rag of a shirt across his face.

'You go on, Mr Jeavons,' said Knox in a voice of surprising gentleness. 'I'll catch you up in just a few moments.'

He dropped down on his haunches to Meares and said, 'Just a minute, old man. It will be all right in a minute.' He motioned for Caspar to go on. Caspar turned his back on the two of them with an odd feeling, a mixture of shame and relief. He walked towards the forest and entered the shade of the first line of trees. There came the sound of single pistol shot. A few moments later, as he had promised, Mr Knox joined him under the canopy of the forest.

'A sorry man,' he said briskly. 'Let's get back.'

25

Jackson was on watch at the jetty. There was no light from the mainland across the water. He talked to Franks, the one native labourer who spoke English. Franks was one of those black servants who had accompanied their masters to Nova Scotia after the end of the War of Independence in the new United States. Those whites who had sided with the King, who had tried to preserve the status quo of a colony, had prudently chosen to flee north when the issue was decided.

'Freetown was given to us, ordained to us, by the white folks. It was our reward for remaining loyal to them, as they'd done to the King. Were they the fools!'

'Is it free?' asked Jackson.

'You know – lots of men and women, too, just like you back home. They're from the whites going with the black women. You're not going to get any whiter by wishing.'

'I know that. I know,' said Jackson. 'But none of us are having much of a time here. That's why I asked you – is it free? Is it free for us?'

'There isn't "free" anywhere. Freetown has the blacks and the white whores they gave us, and the whites drinking and whoring and sending their slaves back for their sugar. We are still their boys though. You can make a living if you work hard, but it don't make any difference, Mr Jackson, you've always got a boss above you and what a surprise – he's a white man.'

'Coupland's a white man. He's my master. He's all right. He's all right.'

'That may be. You'd get a better life in Freetown. You got no women here, no health, no good food – you only get a drink when your Captain hands it out.'

'He pays me.'

'He pays me. We work damn hard for him, building his castle here. What good is it going to do him? Tabellun could take the town and all of you tomorrow.'

'I'm paid here – I fight here.'

'This is your land?'

'I've got some land coming.'

'You've got six feet coming. That's all your land you're going to get. Go to Freetown. We want to go. All of us. If we see a chance to go, we will go. Come with us. All these people are crazy. They've no place here. They'll all go away soon and then we'll never see them again.

'I'll stay.'

'You're crazy too, then.'

26

We are in a poor state. It is only through the obstinacy, the obduracy of Captain Coupland that we continue to suffer.

Ever since the massacre of Meares and the other deserters, we have the fresh distress of not knowing our neighbours' intentions towards us and how they may have changed. So that our already diminished strength has to be further weakened by constant watchfulness against the risk of attack by Tabellun. I know not the mental capacity of this king but I think that it cannot be very great if he lusts after our poor fortress. Still, Coupland likes to play soldier and to move about invisible battalions, which in his mind take the place of our bedraggled platoon.

Our strength is now pitiful. We have a *dozen* of the African labourers, whose loyalty cannot be counted upon, four well seamen, myself, Coupland, Jeavons, Knox, Hood and Jackson – a funny hand of knaves, all equal now without distinction of class or colour. Mrs Crabtree died two days ago and her husband of course does not know. God knows how he will take it when he returns in the cutter: to leave a woman so strong and seeming to rise above all of our adversity, a tower of good sense and strength and good example to us all, and not even to find a trace of her on his return. Even her clothing was burned. Only Mrs Hood and my wife remain of all the women.

Of the remaining servants and craftsmen there are only three. One of these is in the hospital. The others seem half well, recovering from minor ailments or shaking off the last of dysentery. A new and unexplainable condition has afflicted at least one man. Yesterday I asked Mason to fetch me fresh water from the barrel at the back of the hospital in a pitcher. I then went to attend to others – Phoebe was asleep in the stone house, to rest for the night when she must take over watch here (I am waiting for her to come down in a few minutes at ten, when I can rest in turn). When I had finished I returned to the table in the doorway, expecting to find the pitcher freshly charged with water. It was not there. I went out and saw Mason pottering about pulling wood across the roadway and letting it drop and then repeating the same desultory work. I shouted to him and he still did not answer, so I went down and asked him what he thought he was doing and where was the water he had been ordered to fetch?

He stared at me and then began idly and stupidly tugging at the length of timber. I asked him again why he had not brought the water and he replied stupidly, 'What water?' I explained carefully and, trying to keep my temper, said that I had asked him to fetch the morning water. He said he had no recollection of that. That he had not spoken to me today. God help us. We are becoming like idiots. I doubted for a moment my own sanity. Had I asked him? Well, of course.

The light is going and I will stop now. There is someone mounting the step outside. Not Phoebe? It is Mrs Hood. I shall end now.

27

Saturday, November 3rd

Thanks be to God that the cutter is returned safely and with another dozen labourers from Freetown. Coupland has been anxious that we must appear weak and winded to the angry Tabellun. He has ordered bonfires on the beach at night and for the first time actively encouraged the *grumetas* to drum and dance as much as they like in the night-time.

Crabtree has brought fresh medicines, for which Dr Owen must be most grateful. But the fact is that the doctor is now ensconced in the stone house where he tends to his sick wife, sitting at her side, half drunk I do believe, and getting drunker as his attempted remedies fail. So Jackson tells me. Dr Owen will not suffer Coupland to come near, but not withstanding, the Captain called at the house two nights ago. I sat outside on the steps and heard them wrangling.

Captain Coupland said he was sorry to hear of the low state of Mrs Owen and hoped she would recover soon. The doctor's voice was raised, saying that he would bet a good sum of money on the fact that the Captain desired the doctor's wife to be better soon. What did he mean by that? Coupland demanded to know. Why, that the Captain desired his wife. He had seen them dancing and embracing. 'I know you, sir,' shouted Dr Owen. 'You are a blackguard and the cause of all the bother here.' Then came the level sound of Coupland's voice saying that he could not be bothered to deal with this type of insanity. It would be best if Mrs Owen was moved to the hospital, if it were possible for her to do so. Mrs Hood and his man Jackson were tending the sick there. They must concentrate their efforts, said Coupland.

'Your efforts be damned,' said Owen. 'They have led us to this sorry pass – your efforts. If it were not for you holding out endless false promises to these poor people we would not have lost so many. It was madness to settle here. To build your "stronghold" here. You will know how much of a stronghold it is when you man it on your own.'

'You intend to leave us?'

'The way the others have, in all probability,' said the doctor. His voice dropped and he said, sounding weary, 'Go now, my dear Captain. Go and rule your kingdom, or principality, or dukedom, or whatever you call it. I must tend to my wife.'

When Coupland came out his face was set. 'Come on,' he said. 'I have been too weak with the man. Nothing to be done for the moment.'

But the moment is surely not far off when something has to be done.

Sunday, November 4th

This morning I woke with the sun hardly up, but with the forest already alive with its early morning chaos of calls and jabbers and gibbers of birds and apes and God

279

knows what else that dwells there. To which frightful cacophony was joined another, much nearer. A drum was beating. A voice shouting out. The *grumetas* were laughing. The voice that shouted was Dr Owen's, but it sounded so queer and strained and high. I scrambled from my pallet and got out on to the verandah.

The *grumetas* were gathered in the open gateway. They gesticulated and pointed wildly to the eastern end of the yard. A couple of our ragged men came out of the side rooms. And here, marching towards the flagpole in the centre of the square, came Dr Owen. He moved with ridiculously exaggerated rigid steps, raising his knees very high in a parody of a military march. On his head was a tall brown felt hat wound round with a bright green watered-silk ribbon. A red handkerchief hung from the band at the back. He wore a black cloth coat with brass buttons that I had last seen on the voyage out. Now it was mildewed and the once bright buttons had tarnished to a muddy green. His usual blue trousers – but his feet bare. One of the native's side drums hung from a halter round his neck and rested on his left hip. He beat this constantly in an arrhythmic way as he marched. He began to shout again as he came to the flagpole and, stopping there and marching on the spot, continued to shout.

'Come join, come join the army of the Lord. The army of Captain Coupland. Coup-a-land. We are the way, we are the way. We are the way for Captain Coupland. Coup-a-land. Through life to death, through life to death, with our good Captain Coup-a-land.'

And with this, he began to drum again and march with those same exaggerated steps round and round the stone-filled circle of dug ground in which the flagpole was rooted. He was perhaps only two feet in the diameter of his mad walk and I thought that he must become dizzy and at last fall away. But no, round and round he went, beating the drum over and over.

'Dr Owen.' Coupland came through the gateway, elbowing aside the onlookers, and bellowing the doctor's name. 'Dr Owen.' He came up to the crazed man. 'What in God's name do you think you are about?' He seized the doctor, halting his circular march, and he struck the drumsticks from his hands so that they fell to the earth. The doctor stood stock-still and stared ahead. The Captain reached forward and gripped his shoulder hard as if to shake him violently. Then he relented and relaxed and he patted the doctor's shoulders gently and said, 'Well, there then. Enough noise, eh?' The doctor's face, expressionless as the moon, stared on. 'No more then?' said the Captain. Then, 'Wharton. Hood.' He signalled to those two men and they came forward slowly. 'Take Dr Owen to the Reverend Tolchard's old quarters and stay with him until I come,' he said.

As they led the doctor across the square, he lolled oddly behind, not resisting, but allowing himself to be pulled along, puzzled as to where he was being taken. Then all at once he did begin to struggle and pull against them mightily and to scream and shout that his wife, his beloved Phoebe was dead and that the Captain was a murderer, a devil, a white devil. The two men pulled him along the verandah and into Tolchard's room and the door shut and the shouting could barely be heard.

28

Coupland had been out early that morning, tending the cabbages and other vegetables of which he was very proud, though they came up at odd seasons. His garden of herbs and vegetables stretched behind the stockade up to the steps leading to the stone house. In the midst of all their travails and anxieties he was gratified to think that he had kept this garden going, either from wild seed on the island or musty seed brought from England. Most of the English seed had not come up, but he was almost childishly pleased when some sweetpeas brought from his father's garden in London did succeed. 'It is important to recreate some of the comforts of home,' he said.

The doctor was still locked for his own safety in one of the completed rooms in the stockade. At night he sang or wept and was drunk. Coupland allowed him a bottle of brandy a day. 'Why not?' as he said. Even the *grumetas* were scared that Tabellun would come and slaughter them all. Wharton and Kirkpatrick were sick. Crabtree was too old, too weak, too enervated by his wife's death to work.

As he hoed, he became aware of Caspar standing on the edge of the vegetable garden. Without raising his eyes, Coupland said, 'You want to see me? I wondered how long it would be before you came.' He straightened and said, 'Let's go inside.'

Jackson was sitting on the bed in the Captain's room, darning his stockings.

'I wonder if we might speak alone,' said Caspar.

'We have no secrets from each other in this room,' said Coupland.

But Jackson got up jauntily and said that he could as well carry on his work outside – the light was better.

'Ah, so you have all got together to discuss it, eh?' Coupland leaned back in his chair and levelled his eyes on Caspar. 'Let's have it out. You see this experiment, this venture, this – oh God, what would you call it? This noble essay at a better world? You see it at an end.'

'Do you, Coupland?'

'No, but I will admit that I am running low on fellow believers. If we can just hang on, Jeavons. Hang on. If Sir George will have the goodness to arrange another ship and fresh colonists, we have a start for them. The hard work is done. Don't you see that?'

'We have heard nothing from Sir George. I think we may have slipped his mind.'

He was silent then, rubbing his hand across his chin.

'Are you afraid?' Coupland said.

'I am sometimes. Sometimes I cannot sleep. The place, the danger of fever, of the mainlanders slaughtering us . . .'

'They won't come here,' he said. 'Not while I am here. Their king thinks that something magical resides in my person – what he sees as my madness, no doubt. He cannot understand that. I have told him of the great power that lies behind us. That if any harm should befall us, those ships that he sees along the coast bearing our ensign will exact a terrible revenge.'

'Does he believe you?'

'How on earth should I know? He is a shrewd and bloody old man. And he has not attacked, has he?'

'Those who are left wish to leave. They are all terrified or sick.'

'I will see them.'

'Let them go.'

'Jackson will stay. Jackson,' he shouted and the man appeared in the doorway. 'Did you hear our conversation?' Coupland demanded.

'I couldn't help but do so, sir.'

'The question is – who is to go and who to stay? Will you stay, Jackson? From this moment I set you free of any obligation you may feel. I'm sorry – not free. Not freed. Released from our contract, let's say.'

'I will stay with you, Captain.'

'Good man. Good man. And you, Jeavons – my right hand, my writing hand. What about you, old fellow?'

'Of course I will, Coupland,' Caspar heard himself saying. There was a pause and then he said, 'But the rest will go.'

'Let them. Let them go. Nothing was ever done without spirit. Will the *grumetas* stay, Jackson?'

'Some will, some won't. If you pay them they'll stay.'

'Should we arm them?'

'They won't fight against their own people. They don't know what you're doing here.'

'My honest Jackson. My pardon, Jackson. I meant no aspersion on your character. You have been a most exemplary servant.'

Jackson studied the floor in front of him. 'I am that,' he said.

'So, it is I, Jeavons and Jackson,' said Coupland. 'A good company, but not, I fear, enough. I'll tell you what we shall do. Sir George has sent no new colonists, nor any word, so I shall send a message to Sir George, to the Committee in England, apprising them of our situation and asking their instructions and saying that unless they are willing to invest further colonists and goods in our enterprise then I must ask to be excused, we must ask to be excused further service.'

Caspar said nothing, but thought that at the quickest it would be at least two months before they heard back from England. Coupland saw what was on his mind, jumping in to say, 'Two months, eh, boys? Just two more months. The rest may go on the cutter back to Freetown and then get a ship home. You will take my letter, Jeavons?'

'I thought I was to remain.'

'Whom else have I to send? The return journey would kill Crabtree. No, you are our ambassador. You know our work. Our achievements. Go and fire them in England. Stir their hearts. But for God's sake bring back a hardier, more honest family of colonists than the ones we have had to suffer.'

29

Monday, November 12th

And that, dear Torrington, is an end of it, for now. We are on the cutter bound for Freetown. The crew is the loyalist labourer Franks, two of his fellow labourers and the two seamen, Wharton and Chapman. There are with us Mr and Mrs Hood, Mr Crabtree, as shrivelled and yellow as a pippin, Mr Knox, as saturnine and smiling foxily as ever, and three sick are below, unattended by Dr Owen, who lies sleeping off his drink, or rather taking an interlude of sleep in his perpetual drunkenness. Hood would have stayed – insisted on staying – but his wife said that she must go, that she must be with the sick, and, besides, that she did not wish him to die in that place 'along with all the others'.

It was touching and almost comic, had it not been so

affecting, to see as our sails went up and caught the wind and we began to swing away to head north up the strait how we all hurrahed as any group of free-born Englishmen might do. And the Captain on the jetty lifted his sword in salute and let it fall smartly and, as he did so, out boomed first one cannon from the east turret of the stockade, then the cannon from the other. We saw Jackson running up the hill and the two guns up there were set off, their white smoke billowing forth and the crack of the explosion following on. We let off two cannon in return and Mrs Hood stood weeping and Mr Knox smiled queerly at me as if even he was moved and there came a confused noise on the companionway from below and Dr Owen emerged, swaying and red-faced, and shouted back at the shore, his face and mouth twisted, 'You devil. You devil. They say their devil is white. And you are their devil.' There he remained, swaying on the deck looking from one to the other of us, his head lowered and his eyes roaming drunkenly. 'You fools. You fools,' he said, but in a now broken voice. He was led below by Mr Knox, who as in all such difficult matters showed an almost feline touch of grace and strength and well-concealed menace.

The guns repeated their salute. We replied in kind. We continued to look back until at last we rounded the north point of the island and they were obscured from sight and we broke into the open ocean.

Epilogue

Hood had a visitor to his cottage. He had opened the door to a soft knock and found a ghost outside. A ghost dressed in a coachman's greatcoat and a fur hat, which he removed to show his woolly hair gone quite grey, his face lined, but breaking into a smile.

'Mr Hood. You didn't expect this?'

'Mr Jackson. I must say I did not think to see you ever again. But do come in. Come in. The weather is freezing.'

'I know that too well,' Jackson said, bending to enter under the low door lintel.

He stood in front of the fire and took off his overcoat slowly and, at Hood's bidding, sat beside the fire.

'Mrs Hood is well, I trust?'

Hood hesitated, and then spoke as if dragging out the words, stuttering slightly. 'She died at Freetown. I regret to tell you. She died of a fever at Freetown.'

'It grieves me to hear you say that, Mr Hood. I am most sorry to hear of your loss.'

Hood was silent.

'She was a good woman,' said Jackson softly.

Then Hood said, staring into the fire: 'She never wanted to go to that place. She never wanted us to go. I made her go. She was my wife. Of course she would go. I did for her there, didn't I?'

'You cannot say that, Mr Hood. You were a good couple, you

could see that. She thought the light shone on you. You could see that.'

'Oh God, don't say it.'

'The place. That was what finished her. It damned near finished the lot of us. It was the place.'

'I don't think she ever knew where she was. She would say the stars were wrong in the sky and I would tell her how many thousands of miles we were from England. She said that every night when she went to sleep she would pretend to herself that it was England and go to sleep and dream of England and wake up and think at first waking that she was back in this cottage because she would hear a bird call that sounded like a blackbird and then she'd realise that she wasn't at home and would have to prepare herself for another day of strangeness. That was what she called it, 'strangeness', and I know that she hoped I'd be cured of that strange place when the first call came, the first chance to come home with Sir George. But I wanted a new life and she sweetly never said anything and she was never anything but loving and wanting to help and in the end she wore herself down.'

Hood raised his right hand and laid its palm flat against the top of a chair and stared into the corner of the room opposite to Jackson as if watching for something there.

'She carried fever away from there, the fever we all had, and she carried on nursing the sick. By the time we reached Freetown she was sickening and she lasted there three days.'

'I'm so sorry, Mr Hood.'

'Mr Jeavons was a great help. With money and arranging a passage back with him. On account of me being a servant to his estate on occasion. He said he would see me here as soon as he came back. They need him at the Hall now the old lady has gone to London. The place is falling to rack and ruin . . .' Hood went on a little more firmly now. 'He was going to see Sir George and come back to you on the island. Did you all travel back together? Captain Coupland, I hope he is well and unharmed. Mr Jeavons could never keep him out of his conversation. To him the Captain was a great man.'

'Indeed, Captain Coupland is a great man. He is well. But Mr Jeavons . . .'

'Nothing wrong with that gentleman, I hope.' Hood's hand rubbed a little side to side on the chair top.

'Mr Jeavons took the Captain's letter to Sir George in London and came back with a reply on, of all things, a slaver. He made his way up from Freetown in a ship to Îles de Los and then in a boat that Mr Knox arranged for him, that gentleman doing business among the islands as usual. All that trouble, all that duty and honour as the Captain calls it, to deliver a letter.'

'What did Sir George say?'

'The Captain read it to us. Just the three of us, sitting out in the stockade square, with a fire built. And in the distance the *grumetas* singing and drumming the way they do – and, you see, the Captain had had no trouble from Tabellun or anyone else. The workers had finished building the blockhouse and stockade – you should see it now, Mr Hood, your wood-working being so good and solid, a fine thing with the union flag flying over, and the Captain tending his vegetables and flowers and the hospital spick and span and clean and setting his sentries and sounding off his evening and midday guns regular as clockwork to warn Tabellun that he had better not try anything with us.'

'The letter from Sir George – what did it say?'

'It said that it greatly appreciated the recently received communication from Captain Coupland and recognised all the fine work he had done in attempting to establish a colony on the island of Muranda in the spirit of that first envisaged by the Committee. But – a fine word to place flaming in the heavens above us – it was regretted that any further expansion of the colony was quite out of the question. The problems of climate and disease and possibly hostile actions by local inhabitants must put off future investment in the colony until sufficient forces could be mustered to build on the work done. And so on, and so on. Regretfully, regretfully, regretfully . . .'

'So, then?'

'So, then I come, in all sorrow, to my mission here. It is to see you and give you this.' Jackson reached over and fetched two letters from his greatcoat. 'I left the Captain in Freetown after we finally quitted the island, he could not come back immediately and so entrusted me with these letters. One is for you, Mr Hood.'

Hood took the envelope but did not open it immediately. 'And the other letter?' he asked.

'For Lady Jeavons at the Hall.'

'She is not there. She has removed to her house in London. The Hall, as I tell you, is shut up. Is it a letter from Mr Jeavons? Is he in Freetown?'

'It is a letter about Mr Jeavons.'

'Where is he then?'

'I have to tell you, Mr Hood, that Mr Jeavons is on the island still. He took ill when he returned and passed. He is the last one, God willing, of our party to be buried there.'

Hood was silent.

Jackson went on. 'It's a sad errand that has a man bringing bad news to a man who has little else. The Captain hoped you would derive some satisfaction from your letter.'

Hood opened the envelope. It contained a money order for one hundred pounds and a letter from the Captain. Hood read it through slowly. Of all the work they had done on the island little would have been possible without Hood's skill and dedication. One day they might return together, the Captain hoped, and complete their brave venture. The money was in compensation for his lost land and was a part of the final dissolution of the funds given to the expedition. The Captain hoped he would be able to pay his thanks in person one day and shake Mr Hood by the hand.

'That's it then. It is most generous. I hope, Mr Jackson, that you . . .'

'I've been well treated.'

Hood called to mind his duties as a host; Jackson must be hungry. The two men ate beef stew that had been cooked the day before in a pot over the fire.

Mr Hood knew that Jackson could not leave this late in the night and hoped that Mr Jackson would not be averse to sharing a bed with him.

Not at all, said Jackson. But now that his duty as a messenger had been discharged he must return to London in the morning. There was a coach from Whitlock at midday. He would get that.

Neither was able to sleep at first, although both pretended to. Jackson stared up at the low, slanted ceiling. The Captain had released him from duty in Freetown a month ago; he was, he said, returning to the Navy if he could obtain a command. Jackson had from the Captain fifty pounds as a gift. There must be many things a man could do in London with fifty pounds. His mind toyed with shops. No more servantry. No carrying a master on his back. Tomorrow night he would see his mother and then go on to see Becky. Sleep now.

Hood's eyes were closed and he lay on his side. He made himself concentrate, as he did so often in order to try and sleep, on the materials and tools and work necessary to construct a piece of furniture. Tonight it was to be a gentleman's travelling case, a microcosm of layers of drawers and sliding compartments to contain pen and ink and paper, medicines, shaving gear, hair brushes, lotions; all the things a gentleman might require in one case. As he worked in his mind, his breathing became regular and he fell asleep.

But his dreams tonight are of dark beams interlocking in roughly hewn joints that pain him by their bad workmanship; of sawing and toppling great trees which when cut open let forth a wave of ants; of the timbers of a ship tearing apart, putting on bark, rounding to tree trunks, putting out limbs, and branches and twigs and leaves and buds that gleam red at their tips and slowly unfurl and form and harden into acorns. Then the sight of a huge and never-ending sea whose waves break and run foaming up a white beach. And of the figure of Susannah, who stands midway between forest and the highest reach of the waves and raises one hand in shy salutation and smiles at him in the brilliant sunlight.

A Note on Sources

~

This is a novel, not a work of historical scholarship. In an attempt to avoid the consolations of hindsight, I have limited my reading as far as possible to material written in or around the period in which the novel is set (the early 1790s).

Many contemporaneous books have extremely long and involved titles and I have taken the liberty of providing a short title for each, together with the date of first publication.

For general sea-going life and the voyage out to and arrival off the coast of West Africa I consulted many works, the principal ones being: *A Voyage to the River Sierra Leone* (1788) by John Matthews; *Narrative of Two Voyages to the River Sierra Leone during the years 1791–1793* (1794) by Anna Maria Falconbridge; and *Shipland Life and Organisation, 1731–1815*, edited by Brian Lavery. For West African life in general an invaluable source is *An Account of the Native Africans in the Neighbourhood of Sierra Leone* (1803) by Thomas Winterbottom.

I read a large number of works by early explorers, but the initial impetus for this book can be found in *African Memoranda* (1805) by Captain Philip Beaver. This details the setting up of a free colony on an island off the coast of West Africa and covers two years of ultimately disastrous efforts to build a permanent settlement. It proved an invaluable guide to the day-to-day life of the colonists; where I have invented freely is in character and event. For the gross liberties I have taken with his account, I apologise to the shade of the gallant captain.